"WHOEVER IS SELLING THESE GUNS IS IN IT FOR THE MONEY."

Hal Brognola pulled the unlit cigar from between his clenched teeth. "None of us are against honest citizens owning weapons and defending themselves, but that's not what's going on here. These guns are going into the hands of criminals and terrorists and are being used for assassinations rather than self-defense.

"Let's get down to business, guys," he went on. "We've got to sniff out a trail that'll lead us to whoever is producing these things."

As the Stony Man teams stood to leave, the fax machine hummed to life.

Price walked to the rear of the War Room and picked up the page. "Denmark, South Korea, Belize..." She stopped reading, looked up and shook her head. "My God, Hal. Whoever is manufacturing the Eliminators has sent them all over the world."

DON PENDLETON'S
MACK BOLAN®
STONY MAN™

PUNITIVE MEASURES

A GOLD EAGLE BOOK FROM
WORLDWIDE®

TORONTO • NEW YORK • LONDON
AMSTERDAM • PARIS • SYDNEY • HAMBURG
STOCKHOLM • ATHENS • TOKYO • MILAN
MADRID • WARSAW • BUDAPEST • AUCKLAND

First edition March 1998

ISBN 0-373-61917-0

Special thanks and acknowledgment to
Jerry VanCook for his contribution to this work.

PUNITIVE MEASURES

PUNITIVE
MEASURES

PROLOGUE

Ulysses Freeman never went by his real name. In fact, very few people knew what it was. To his fellow Crips, and anyone else on the streets, Freeman was "Jimmy Two Blades." He had acquired the appellation due to his habit of carrying a matching set of daggers with eight-inch blades. The knives were looped through his belt and tucked into the back pockets of his faded, ragged blue jeans—one for his right hand, the other for his left. The pockets were always covered, either by a sweatshirt, a jacket or a loose-fitting T-shirt.

This night, Jimmy Two Blades had his two blades, but he also had something else.

Jimmy stepped back a little deeper into the shadows of the doorway. He could still see up and down the street from where he stood, and he watched the few people brave enough to walk along the sidewalk outside Los Angeles's Mc-Caurther Park. A hooker strutted by in high heels, fishnet nylons and a garter belt extending beneath a pair of shorts so minuscule that they revealed a generous portion of her buttocks. A derelict in clothes too tattered to identify followed her ten yards behind, enjoying the view and knowing it was all he could afford.

As Jimmy continued his silent vigil, he saw the hooker suddenly curse, then whirl and draw a small revolver from her purse. She yelled at the man, the gun bobbing up and down as she spoke.

The bum stopped in his tracks, turned and shuffled out of sight in the opposite direction.

Jimmy absentmindedly reached under his T-shirt, his fingers falling over the rough edges of the hard steel stuffed into the front of his belt against the buckle. He had picked up the piece that afternoon from Rags, another Crip. There wasn't much to it; it was some kind of cheap single-shot weapon that looked like somebody with a drill press and a few other tools had stamped it out in a basement workshop. He'd have liked to have used the Smith & Wesson .44 Magnum pistol he'd found during a burglary the week before, but he'd had to ditch it when the cops arrived sooner than he'd expected. He had been lying low ever since, hiding in the attic of his friend, Bagworm, and wondering if the pigs had IDed him as he sprinted away from the scene.

Jimmy didn't think they had made him. If there

was a warrant out for him, word would be on the streets by now. It wasn't.

A blue-suit strolled down the sidewalk carrying a nightstick in his left hand, his right hanging over the holster on his hip and ready to drop over the grips of his gun. Jimmy could tell the policeman had experience. Like any cop who wasn't brain-dead, the yellow light in the man's brain continually flashed while he was working the 'hood.

Jimmy moved farther back into the doorway, pressing his back against the wall to make sure he wasn't seen. He waited until the cop's heavy footsteps faded, then finally disappeared alto-gether, before moving out where he could view the street again.

Jimmy drew the simple gun from his belt and looked at it under what little light filtered into the doorway from the poles along the street. It looked like a plaything, something you'd see wrapped in plastic and hanging from a rack in a toy store. Normally he could have snapped his fingers and had a decent gun in his hands within two hours. But he'd been in isolation for the past week and hadn't been able to get out and do the proper street shopping.

A chill of rage suddenly shot through Jimmy Two Blades's body as that same isolation re-minded him of why he was there. Rags had come back that very morning and told him he'd just seen Too Cute, Jimmy's woman, coming out of Big Willie's upstairs apartment. They'd been kissing and hugging, and grinding their goodbyes while Big Willie's hands roamed all over her body.

The bitch couldn't even wait a week, Jimmy thought as his fingers wrapped around the short grip of the gun. She had to have a man or she wasn't happy. His fingers tightened. He wasn't in love with Too Cute, and he didn't even care if she slept with the other Crips now and then. But Big Willie wasn't a Crip. The fat bastard was a *Blood*. And Jimmy Two Blades couldn't let some fat-ass Blood go dippin' his wick in the Crips' private stock and expect to keep face on the streets.

The angry gangster stuck his wrist into the light far enough to read his watch: 12:25. Big Willie should be coming along any second now, on his way to meet the man he thought was going to be his new big-time crack connection.

Dumb bastard. A phone call was all it had taken.

Footsteps sounded down the block. He jumped back instinctively, farther into the doorway, then leaned cautiously forward, peering around the corner. What he saw made him smile.

Dressed in torn blue jeans, a red-and-black-plaid flannel shirt buttoned at the throat and a red bandanna wrapped around his sweating forehead, Big Willie swaggered his way along the sidewalk like some fat cock in a barnyard. He danced as he walked, his shoulders jerking to the rhythm of whatever rap song it was emanating from his lips.

Jimmy waited until Big Willie was three steps from the doorway before stepping out of the darkness onto the sidewalk, the gun held in front of him, eye level.

"Hey," he said softly.

Big Willie stopped in his tracks like a spotlighted deer. He opened his mouth as if to speak, but no words came out.

"Yo' dick been goin' places it had no business bein'?" Jimmy asked.

Big Willie didn't answer.

"I asked you a question!" Jimmy screamed. "You been havin' fun with my 'ho'?"

"You got it wrong, Jimmy Two Blades," Big Willie said, the sweat around the red headband now streaking down his doughy face. "You got to understand, bro'—"

"I ain't yo' bro', and I don't got to understand nothin'!" Jimmy said. He took a step closer and fired the gun point-blank into Big Willie's face, moving back as the Blood crumpled to a heap on the sidewalk. He dropped the weapon on top of Big Willie, looked down, spit and kicked the corpse twice in the ribs.

Jimmy Two Blades had turned and started down the street when he remembered he had forgotten to wipe the gun clean. He pivoted back around, returned to where Big Willie lay and rubbed the grips of the gun with the tail of his shirt. He had dropped the weapon again when he heard the voice behind him.

"Police! Freeze!"

Jimmy spun on his heel to see the same cop who had passed on the sidewalk a half hour earlier. The man in blue stood less than ten feet behind him, an automatic Sig-Sauer pistol gripped in both hands and aimed at Jimmy's chest.

"Don't move!" the cop ordered. He took a tentative step closer.

Jimmy made his decision more on instinct than on thought. Both of his hands shot behind his back and came out gripping the daggers.

The cop fired twice, both rounds striking Jimmy squarely in the chest. The Crip coughed, seeing blood spurt out of his mouth, then fell on top of the man he had killed less than thirty seconds earlier.

The police officer stepped forward with the gun still aimed at Jimmy. He looked down at the two dead men, then a glimmer of steel on the sidewalk next to the bodies caught his eye. He stared at the cheap, stubby-barreled gun for a moment, then pressed the button on his walkie-talkie. The officer spoke into the tiny microphone clipped to his shirt collar, identifying himself to the dispatcher and telling her what had happened.

Then, his eyes still on the stamped-metal weapon on the concrete, he added, "Tell whatever detectives come out we got another one of the Eliminators."

CHAPTER ONE

Stony Man Farm, Virginia

Hidden more by illusion than concealment, Stony
Man Farm lay in the Shenandoah Valley of the
Blue Ridge Mountains. A casual passerby would
probably give it little more than a quick glance,
as from the outside it looked no different than
any other working farm. The main house was
large—three stories—and it appeared to be owned
by a financially successful agribusinessman. But
so did the other plantations located on the spreads
surrounding it, so the house brought about no undue curiosity.

The tractor barn, sheds and or other outbuild-
ings located near the residence were also typical
of modern farming, as was the landing strip at the
north end of the property.

It wasn't until one entered the buildings that
the secrets of Stony Man Farm were revealed.
Gaining entry to the ground floor required passing

through a coded, heavily reinforced steel door. Once inside, a visitor would have found himself in an entryway with staircases leading both upward and downward directly in front of him, a den to his right and the Farm's security headquarters to the left. Moving past the stairs, he would enter a large dining hall and, continuing left, the kitchen, pantry, house-staff sleeping quarters and a garage-shop. If he turned right rather than left, he would—after tapping in the access code on yet another steel door—find the enormous computer room separated from an office designated the communications room by a ceiling-to-floor glass wall. The ground floor of the main house at Stony Man Farm also featured a porch, elevator, utility room, storage closets, baths and an armory.

The second floor of the house was taken up primarily by the bedrooms and private baths of the personnel who lived on-site.

Had the imaginary visitor taken the stairs downward from the ground floor rather than those leading up, he would have emerged into a level consisting primarily of offices, emergency supply areas, a generator room, and a backup communications center and supplementary armory known simply as the gun room.

But the final room, the largest in the entire house, lay on the east side of the basement level.

It was known to the few who had entered it as the War Room, and it was there that the men and women of Stony Man Farm, specialists in warfare, crime fighting and counterterrorism, planned their missions, missions that began where the efforts of militaries, police departments and other conventional agencies were forced to leave off.

THE ATMOSPHERE in the War Room was somber.

Hal Brognola entered and moved immediately toward the vacant seat at the head of the long conference table. He glanced at the men already seated as he passed. Carl Lyons and the other two men of Able Team sat quietly on one side, while David McCarter and the remaining four Phoenix Force commandos were on the other. Aaron "the Bear" Kurtzman's wheelchair had been rolled up to the right of where Brognola would sit, and Barbara Price, mission controller, sat to his left. John "Cowboy" Kissinger, Stony Man Farm's chief armorer, sat next to Price.

Only one man was missing from the meeting.

"Have you got him on the screen yet?" Brognola asked Kurtzman as he dropped into his seat.

"Hookup's almost complete," the burly computer wizard replied. He lifted the telephone receiver from its cradle in front of him, tapped a button and spoke into a speakerphone. "Akira?"

"I need another minute, boss man."

Moments later the television screen on the wall behind Able Team lit up. The men of Able Team—Lyons, Hermann "Gadgets" Schwarz and Rosario "the Politician" Blancanales swiveled their chairs to face the fuzzy picture.

The interference cleared, and the head and shoulders of a man wearing a navy blue blazer and open-collared white shirt looked out over the people in the War Room. The man's hair was dark, his cheekbones, jawline and other features were hard, as if chiseled out of stone. His expression was just as powerful.

"Good morning, Striker," Hal Brognola said to the screen, using Mack Bolan's mission code name.

"Good *evening,* Hal, Barbara, guys."

Murmurs of greeting came from Price and the others present in the War Room. Bolan had been flown to Australia the week before by Jack Grimaldi, the Farm's number-one pilot. He'd been looking for a member of a Colombian drug cartel who had escaped a DEA hard probe three months earlier and had been spotted in Sydney. Bolan, also known to the world as the Executioner, had been pulled off his chase to join the mission about to be launched from Stony Man Farm.

"Is the room you're in secure?" Brognola asked.

Bolan nodded. "It's soundproof and I've

checked for bugs." He paused, then grinned and added, "The spooks have all gone into the front offices. Seems like a direct call from the President of the United States can produce dramatic results in a short period of time."

Brognola nodded. Stony Man Farm was America's top-secret counterterrorist installation. Few other than the men and women who worked out of the site, and the President of the United States, even knew it existed. That included the Central Intelligence Agency, whose Sydney offices Bolan had temporarily commandeered.

"Let's get down to business," Brognola said. He pulled a well-chewed cigar stub out of the breast pocket of his charcoal gray suit and jammed it between his teeth without lighting it. "Striker, you have the gun used in the robbery there in Sydney?"

On-screen, Bolan held up a steel pistol with an almost nonexistent barrel. "It's just like the others," he said before Brognola could ask. "Another Eliminator."

Brognola nodded, his mind traveling back in time to World War II. The United States Office of Strategic Services—the father of the current CIA—had come up with the Liberator, a unique idea to help resistance groups in Europe. Cheaply made and mass-produced to the specifications of the OSS, the single-shot pistol was packed with ten rounds of .45ACP ammunition, a set of comic-book instructions on its use and dropped in a waterproof bag behind enemy lines. During a three-month period of 1942, one million of the Liberators had been manufactured. That came out to be one every 7.5 seconds, and gave the Liberator the honor of being the only pistol in history that could be manufactured faster than it could be reloaded.

The big Fed stared at the screen. The gun in Bolan's hand wasn't identical to the Liberator, but anyone could tell that the WW II Resistance weapon was where the idea had come from. It was close enough, at least, that the press had picked up on the similarities and dubbed the cheap pistol the Eliminator.

Brognola chomped down harder on his cigar. The reason for the name was simple. *These* guns, mass-manufactured just like their predecessors, weren't being used to help innocent people being repressed by the Nazis. These pistols were being used by street gangs and criminals to assassinate people.

"Then whoever's making these things has connections outside the U.S.," Brognola stated. "Maybe worldwide."

"It would appear that way," Bolan said. "At least in Australia."

The soft whirring of a fax machine drew Price's

attention. She stood without comment and went to retrieve the page coming out. "Looks like worldwide is right. Two more Eliminators have shown up—Spain and Thailand. Wait..." A moment later she shook her head. "This says that the gun recovered in Barcelona wasn't a single-shot. It was a semiauto patterned after the Government Model 1911 but appeared to be stamped out like the Eliminators." She paused and looked up. "And it had no serial numbers or other markings, either."

All heads in the room turned toward Kissinger.

The armorer shrugged. "Once you're tooled up to produce a single-shot," he said, "retooling to make a simple, short-recoil semiauto like the Colt design wouldn't take that much work."

Carl "Ironman" Lyons, the ex–LAPD detective who led Able Team, leaned forward and crossed his arms across the table. "Eliminator Government Models?" he said to no one in particular. "Whoever is behind all this is expanding production."

"Yes, but the question is why?" David McCarter asked. "Does he or she or they have a political agenda? Are they leading toward something, or is this simply a criminal enterprise?"

Price had returned to her seat. She glanced at her notes and said, "The single-shot Eliminators have been found in the hands of Crips and

Bloods,'' she said. ''Fourteen have been traced back to the Ku Klux Klan. This fax says that the gun in Spain was taken away from a Basque, and the Japanese Red Army used a single-shot in Thailand. I'd say that whoever is behind all this is selling to anybody who can pay his price.''

''There's now a political agenda here,'' Brognola said. ''The Eliminators, single-shots and semiautos both, are being made for the oldest purpose known to man.''

Lyons nodded. ''Money.''

No one seemed to argue.

''Okay,'' Brognola said. ''Let's sum things up and get to work. It looks like this organization is expanding. I know that every last one of you in this room is firmly behind the Second Amendment. None of us are against honest citizens owning weapons and defending themselves, but that's not what's going on here. These guns are going into the hands of criminals and terrorists and are being used for assassinations rather than self-defense.''

He turned to face Carl Lyons. ''Ironman,'' he said, ''take your team to Brooklyn. Word has it that one of the street gangs got stopped with a whole trunkful of Eliminators.''

''Where do I start?'' he said.

''Check in with a Sergeant Elmo Waters. NYPD. He trained with us two years ago.'' He knew that Lyons understood what he meant. In addition to carrying out counterterrorist operations the world over, Stony Man conducted training classes for select law-enforcement and military personnel. The candidates were brought to the Farm blindfolded, trained and returned to their respective assignments in the same condition they arrived. They never knew where they had been or who had taught them—just that they had received instruction far superior to any other training to which they'd ever been exposed.

"The NYPD's a big place," Lyons said. "Where do I find this Waters?"

"Eighty-first Precinct," Brognola said, "homicide."

The big Fed then turned to McCarter. "David," he said, "you guys are headed for Ireland. The IRA has some of these weapons and they've been using them around Belfast."

McCarter nodded. "Who's our contact, Hal?"

"An old friend of yours—Felix O'Prunty."

"O'Prunty?" he said. "I haven't heard from him since I left the SAS. He still with MI-6?"

Brognola nodded. "He's stationed in Belfast and he's got a lead." He turned back to the screen. "Speaking of leads, Striker," he said to Bolan, "do you have one on that gun there in Sydney?"

"No, but I'll get one."

"Then let's get down to business, guys," Brognola said. "Eventually we ought to see a trail that leads back to whoever is stamping out these things. Anybody got anything else to say?"

Kissinger looked up at the screen. "Striker?"

"Yeah, Cowboy?"

"The extra equipment you requested is already on its way." Kissinger glanced down at his watch, then went on. "Should arrive there in another couple of hours. Go to the American Express office on Bridge Street and ask for a Mr. Grady."

Bolan nodded.

As the Stony Man Farm team stood to leave, the fax machine hummed again.

Price walked to the machine and picked up the page. "Denmark, South Korea, Belize..." She stopped reading, looked up and shook her head. "My God, Hal, they're everywhere. Whoever is manufacturing the Eliminators has sent them all over the world."

Sydney, Australia

BOLAN HEARD the shots as he opened the door and stepped out of the back room of the Sydney CIA office complex. "What was that?" he asked the men and women scurrying around to drop down behind the desks of the open front-reception area.

"Dingoes, I'd imagine," a man said nonchalantly. He crawled on all fours to the front door, threw the dead bolt in place, then crawled back behind a gray steel desk.

The Executioner knew the man didn't mean the wild dogs of Australia, at least not in the usual sense. The Dingoes could be called wild dogs all right—the word was also the name of one of Australia's most powerful and violent street gangs. They ruled the night in Sydney, Melbourne, Perth and other cities with an iron hand.

But the Dingoes' number-one rivals, the Down Unders, were hardly better. And recently they had been making headway into the Dingoes' drug-trafficking, prostitution, protection and gambling businesses, generating violent encounters between the two gangs.

Bolan didn't really care if the Dingoes and Down Unders killed each other. But with no regard for human lives other than their own, they had a way of catching innocent bystanders with stray bullets.

And the Executioner couldn't allow that to take place. Not when he had a chance to stop it.

Bolan drew his .44 Magnum Desert Eagle from under his navy blue blazer and started toward the door.

"What the hell is that?" the man on the floor asked.

"A pistol," the Executioner answered simply. "Anybody coming with me?"

Everyone but the man of the floor turned away from him. "I don't know who you are," the CIA agent said. "All I know is that the President called, ordered us to let you use the satellite hookup and told us not to eavesdrop on what you said. Those are orders and I'll follow them. But if you think I'm sending any of my people out there to get blown away by a bunch of street punks, you're crazy." He paused. "Besides," the man said, lifting a white business card with green letters from a holder on one of the desks, "we've got a cover to maintain."

Bolan glanced at the card, hearing another round of gunshots outside the door as he read the words Sydney Savings And Loan Company. The CIA used the finance business as a front, even handing out money to those who applied and qualified.

The Executioner moved toward the door without a backward glance, threw back the lock, swung open the door and dived onto the sidewalk.

Muzzle-flashes and the roar of more shots came from behind a car parked along the street directly in front of him as he hit the pavement. With the big .44 gripped in his right hand, he used his left to break his fall and looked up to see a man wearing a black silk jacket firing what looked like a

Colt 1911 Government Model over the hood of the vehicle. The word Dingoes was arched over the back of the jacket in bright crimson letters that dripped blood. The snarling face of one of the wild dogs appeared below the arch of letters, more blood and foam dripping from his fangs.

Bolan fired as soon as he'd steadied himself on the ground, pumping two fast Magnum rounds into the gunner's chest. The big .44-caliber hollowpoint bullets drilled through to the spinal cord of the man wearing it.

Return fire from across the street blew over the Executioner's head, but he was covered by the car. He glanced down the sidewalk to see three more Dingoes using parked vehicles for cover. All wore the black silk jackets sporting the crazed wild dog, and all fired across the street at men behind other cars.

So far, the other Dingoes hadn't differentiated the Executioner's shots from their own. Bolan knew that wouldn't last long and rolled to his side, lining the front sights of the Desert Eagle on the nearest man in a silk jacket. Another big hollowpoint round burst from the Eagle's barrel, entering the Dingo's rib cage before exploding the man's heart.

The three remaining Dingoes finally realized that someone was behind them.

And killing them.

A young man next to the downed gunner was the first to turn and see the Executioner. He tried to bring a sawed-off Winchester 1895 lever-action rifle into play, his lips quivering in surprise and fear as his shaking hands gripped the gun.

His terror didn't last long.

Bolan squeezed the trigger, and the Desert Eagle's fourth round struck the man squarely between the eyes, just above the bridge of the nose. The gunner's head fairly exploded.

The Executioner rolled to his other side, seeing movement in his peripheral vision. As he twisted on the ground to turn the Desert Eagle, he heard a roar as a round struck the sidewalk just ahead of his face. Concrete chips and dust blew up from the ground, miraculously missing his eyes as they stung his face. Bolan dropped the sights of the Desert Eagle on a man with a wispy blond beard and fired again.

The .44 Magnum bullet drilled into the gang member's chest. Bright red blood gushed from the massive wound. The gunner opened his mouth, and more blood shot from his lips before he fell to his face on the sidewalk.

The surviving Dingo cut loose at Bolan with a Colt Single Action Army .45 pistol. Bolan took him out of the play with a head shot.

The Executioner rose to his feet, staying low as he moved up to the car directly in front of him.

The Down Unders across the street continued to fire, not knowing yet that their rivals had been eliminated. Dropping the Desert Eagle's near-empty magazine, the Executioner rammed a fresh stick up the grip of the pistol and peered over the hood of the vehicle in front of him.

A pair of rounds flew his way from different directions. Bolan dropped lower behind the car, letting the bullets strike the engine block. For a few seconds, the gunfire died down, then several more rounds struck the vehicle, reverberating through the steel to shimmy the body.

The Executioner stayed below cover. The Dingoes had been easy to take out, catching them from behind and by surprise. The Down Unders across the street were another story. They wouldn't be taken off guard—they knew they were in a firefight with men outside the Sydney Savings And Loan Company, and the fact that the enemy wasn't who they thought it was made no difference.

Bolan considered his options as the gunfire momentarily quieted again. He could stay where he was and try to pick off the Down Unders one at a time. That would take a long time, and there was always a chance that a lucky round might find him. He could return to the CIA offices, take the back exit he had seen and try to circle. But when the Down Unders received no attack during the time that would take, they might well assume that they'd eliminated the enemy and disperse.

Then the Executioner realized there was another answer to the situation. It was risky, but it might just work.

He would surrender.

Bolan rose slightly so his voice could be heard. Then, effecting his best Australian accent, he shouted, "Don't shoot! Everybody but me is dead! I give up!"

After a moment's silence, a voice from across the street yelled, "Throw out your gun!"

The Executioner placed the Desert Eagle on the hood of the car in front of him and slid it forward. The big .44 Magnum pistol dropped off the other side and onto the street with a metallic clank as it hit the pavement.

"Put your hands up and stand up!" the gang member commanded.

Bolan did as he'd been ordered, ready to drop back down behind the engine block if they had played him for a sucker and more fire came his way. For almost a minute, all he could hear were confused and whispering voices coming from the other side of the street.

"You a cop?" a voice called out.

"No," Bolan said, his hands still in the air. "Just a guy caught in the wrong place at the wrong time."

"What you doin' with a gun, then?"

"Are you guys cops?" the Executioner asked. "What are *you* doing with guns?"

"Funny," the same voice said. "Now walk forward into the middle of the street."

The Executioner moved around the front bumper, his hands still in the air. He stopped on one of the short white lane divider lines.

Slowly, one at a time, three heads rose above the vehicles parked on the other side of the street. The men, all aiming weapons at him, moved cautiously forward. The man in the lead was big, almost as tall as the Executioner. He had blond hair and a reddish blond beard and wore a bright red silk jacket with It's What's Down Under That Counts emblazoned across the chest. He eyed Bolan's navy blue blazer as he walked forward, and the other two fell into line behind him.

The Down Under leader stopped a foot from Bolan and jammed the long slide of a Glock 17L under the Executioner's chin. "Who the fuck are you?" he demanded. "You sure you aren't some pig?"

"Look at the way he's dressed." The weasel-faced man to the leader's right side held a Browning Hi-Power pistol in his right hand. "Of course he's a pig."

"Oink, oink," said the man to the leader's left.

He gripped a sawed-off double-barreled shotgun with both fists.

Bolan took note that only the Glock was pointed at him. With the 17L's barrel about to crush his windpipe, the other two Down Unders had gotten lazy and let their weapons dangle to their sides. It wasn't much of an advantage, but it was all he had.

And it would have to be enough.

"How about it?" the man with the reddish beard demanded. "A pig, are you?"

"Not exactly," Bolan said, and caught a quick look of bewilderment in the Down Under leader's eyes as he moved.

Twisting to the side so that the Glock's extended barrel shot past him, the Executioner reached up with his right hand and grabbed the barrel. At the same time his left hand shot under his jacket, curling under his armpit and reverse-drawing his Beretta 9 mm 93-R pistol. A round of fire shot through the barrel of the Glock, warming the Executioner's hand but flying harmlessly past him. As he twisted the weapon back toward him, Bolan brought up the Beretta and pointed it at Weasel Face.

The Down Under leader's trigger finger broke with a snap inside the Glock's trigger guard a split second before Bolan fired the Beretta. The man opened his mouth, but the Beretta's 3-round burst drowned out the scream. The trio of sound-suppressed 9 mm slugs stitched Weasel Face from sternum to throat as the Executioner ripped the Glock out of the leader's grip.

Still moving, Bolan twirled the subgun in his right hand as the man with the sawed-off shotgun tried to bring his weapon into play. Finding the pistol grip, the Executioner's finger snaked into the trigger guard and fired. The first burst of rounds struck the shotgun, sending the weapon flying from the gang member's hands and causing the man to cry out in pain. Bolan let up on the trigger, then pulled it again and sent a second burst into the man's chest.

Only the leader remained alive. The man's mouth was still open as he clutched his broken trigger finger with the opposite hand. Then, recovering from the shock and pain, he lunged at the Executioner.

Bolan raised the Beretta and pumped a 3-round burst into the angry face. Silence fell over the Sydney street as the body collapsed to the ground.

Quickly the Executioner patted down the gang members, taking their billfolds and coming up with a single-shot Eliminator stuck into the boot top of Weasel Face. He turned back to where the Dingoes lay and heard the door of the loan company open as he bent to scoop up the Desert Eagle from where it had fallen. He cursed under his breath when he saw that the big .44 Magnum pistol had landed on the manual safety. The piece had broken off, and when the Executioner tried to work the slide it was jammed.

Shoving the broken gun back into his hip holster, Bolan moved between two cars to the first man he had shot.

"You ever seen anything like *that* before?" a voice just inside the CIA door whispered.

"I never even *heard* of anything like that before," another quiet voice answered.

Bolan dropped to one knee next to the corpse and picked up the pistol that had looked like a 1911 Government Model. It wasn't. It was one of the newer stamped-out semiautos that Price had mentioned. Like the single-shot he'd found a few seconds earlier, and like all of the Eliminators, it bore no serial number or any other identification marks.

Shoving the gun into his belt, Bolan rose and started down the street.

Brooklyn, New York

THERE HAD obviously been another incident involving the Eliminators. The men of Able Team would normally have been able to walk right into the Eighty-first Precinct house.

As it was, they had to elbow their way through a horde of yelling reporters and photographers.

A long line of blue-suited patrolmen stood at the top of the cracked concrete steps, complete with riot helmets and batons. They gripped their sticks with both hands, one at either end, using them to hold back the mass of newsmen and -women.

"Do you have any idea who's behind the manufacture of the Eliminators?" a woman from CBS shouted as Lyons maneuvered up the steps.

"Is it true that the CIA suspects Castro is behind all this?" demanded a man wearing a jacket with NBC News emblazoned across the back.

Lyons led his men to the top of the steps. Reaching into the side pocket of his sport coat, he produced a set of U.S. Justice Department credentials like those issued to all Stony Man Farm operatives. They IDed him as Special Agent Ray Ryan, and he showed them to the nearest uniformed officer.

"Ryan, Justice," Lyons shouted over the turmoil. He hooked a thumb over his shoulder. "Special Agents Smith and Rodriguez are with me."

The man in the riot helmet looked briefly at the credentials, then nodded and stepped to the side.

Lyons led the way into the ancient stone building and up to the front desk, flashing the ID case once more. "Ryan," he said again. "This is Smith and Rodriguez. We need to see a Sergeant Elmo Waters."

The desk sergeant glanced at the picture on Lyons's card, then picked up the phone. "Yeah, give me Waters." There was a brief pause, then he said, "Yeah, Elmo. Feds out here to see you."

He hung up the phone and looked at Lyons. "Follow the red arrows through that door."

The three men of Able Team walked to the closed door. A buzzer sounded just as Lyons reached it, and he grasped the knob and pushed it open.

The inner sanctum of the NYPD precinct house looked just like every other one Lyons had ever been in—cold, drab, dreary.

As he followed the red arrows on the floor, Lyons passed signs that identified the various offices as Vice and Traffic Control. Finally he saw a sign marked Homicide and turned in.

The Able Team leader heard both Schwarz and Blancanales halt behind him. A tall, lanky man wearing half glasses looked up from a report he was typing.

Lyons recognized Elmo Waters immediately from an advanced-rappeling section he and his teammates had taught at Stony Man Farm. But he could see Waters didn't remember them.

"I'm Waters," the sergeant said in the harsh,

clipped syllables of the native Brooklynite. "What can I do for you?"

Lyons walked to his desk and sat in the single chair in front of it. He didn't speak.

"Can I help you?" Waters asked.

Again there was no answer.

The sergeant looked over the half glasses at Lyons. "Have we met before?" he asked this time. Then a sudden look of recognition passed over his face, and he answered his own question. "Yes, we have, haven't we?" Waters glanced quickly around the room to see if anyone was paying attention. All of the other people in the room seemed absorbed in other pursuits. But just to be sure, he said, "Let's go back in the conference room." He stood.

Lyons, Schwarz and Blancanales followed the sergeant through a door in the far wall and down a short hall past the iron bars of several holding cells. Waters stopped at a solid steel door. Large windows had been set to either side of the door, and through one of the windows Lyons could see a simple wooden table painted an ugly brown. Several chairs—the same shade of brown—stood around the table, and the walls of the room were covered with dirty yellow carpet.

Soundproofing, Lyons thought as Waters unlocked the door and ushered them into the room.

This had to be the conference room where attorneys spoke with their clients.

As soon as Able Team was inside, Waters stepped in and closed the door behind him. "I remember you guys now. Last time I saw you I was wearing a blacksuit."

Waters was referring to the one-piece, close-fitting black jumpsuits that Stony Man personnel wore during operations, and that apprentices trained in. The battle attire had given rise to the nickname for the military and law-enforcement officers who trained at the Farm: blacksuits.

"And you were rappeling out of a helicopter," Lyons added.

"That's right. You ever going to tell me who you really are and where we were?"

"Nope."

Waters shrugged, smiled and snorted. "Fair enough. Just wondering." He paused, then turned serious. "So, what *can* I do for you? You didn't just come here to talk about that guy whose toupee blew off as he jumped out of the chopper."

"No, we didn't," Lyons said. "We came to talk about the Eliminators."

Waters nodded. "What do you want to know?" he asked.

"Everything," Lyons said.

The sergeant leaned forward and whispered. "There's a gag on this one," he said, "all the way down from the commissioner. We've been ordered to keep quiet, even to the Feds.''

"We aren't really Feds," Lyons argued.

"Okay, but if this gets out, I'll be working security at a hospital or standing in the lobby of a bank for the rest of my career." He paused, then added, "That's if I'm lucky. If not, I'll be saying things like, 'You want fries with that?' In other words, you didn't get it from me. All right?"

"All right," Lyons agreed.

"Of course not," Blancanales told him. "We don't even know you."

Waters took a deep breath. "You ever heard of the Falcons?"

This time Schwarz answered. "Street gang here in town. Rough bunch. Into drugs, protection, murder for hire—the usual stuff but with more gusto than most.''

Waters nodded. "Right. There have been two murders in the past couple of days. We've found single-shot Eliminators at both scenes. We're sure it's the Falcons, and more than likely their numero uno greaser, Eddie Caveretti. You know what a greaser is?''

"Gang slang for a hit man," Lyons said. "A cleaner. So then why isn't this Caveretti in jail?"

Waters's face turned hard. "Same tired old sad song. We know it was Caveretti who greased these guys, but we got no evidence. At least not enough to get a warrant, and certainly nothing that would stand up in court."

"You got a file on Caveretti?" Lyons asked. "A recent address?"

The sergeant looked around the room as if the carpeted walls might have ears. "Okay, look. I'll go pull the file. But we're going to have to get it back into the cabinet as quick as we can. There's a copy machine just down the hall from homicide. Take it in there, copy everything and get it back to me. Stick your credentials out where they can be seen, and if we're lucky no one will notice and I won't end up sacking groceries. Okay?"

"Fair enough," Lyons said.

The four men stood and returned to the homicide office. They stood around Waters's desk while the sergeant moved nonchalantly to a row of filing cabinets along the wall, dropped to one knee and slid open a drawer.

None of the other men and women busy at their desks paid any attention.

Waters stood back up, holding several files. He nodded toward the hall again, then led the way out. Ducking into a small office that contained nothing but a copying machine, he set the files on the tray, then left the room without saying a word.

Lyons moved to the machine and looked down at the files. The tab on the first read Caveretti, Alphonse. Lyons turned it upside down and set it to the side. The next folder was that of Eddie Caveretti, and the manila file on the bottom was empty. The Able Team leader began feeding the various reports and other items pertaining to Eddie Caveretti through the machine.

"Come here," he said to Schwarz and Blancanales when he came to several sets of mug shots of the man. "Take a good look. The copy isn't likely to come out well."

Lyons was right. It didn't.

As soon as the file had been copied, the Able Team leader stuck the pages inside the empty manila folder and stuffed them into the back of his slacks, covering the file with his sport coat. He stuck the other files under his arm, then led his men back into the homicide office. Without a word, Lyons dropped the folders on Waters's desk, nodded his thanks and left the office again.

A few minutes later, Able Team was cruising through the streets of Brooklyn on the way to meet a Falcon hit man named Eddie Caveretti.

CHAPTER TWO

Belfast, Northern Ireland

In the days before London ruled Ireland, Belfast had been a fort on a ford of the River Lagan. Known as Beal Feirste, meaning "Mouth of the Sandy Ford," a small village had sprouted up around the stronghold. During the seventeenth century, Protestant immigrants from Scotland and England arrived, and by order of the English rulers the natives were driven out.

Which was when all the trouble began.

Belfast grew at a constant pace, primarily due to the linen industry that developed. In 1791 the United Irish Society was founded by Wolfe Tone in an effort to unite Protestants and Catholics who were already beginning to rebel under the crushing English penal laws. By 1798 the UIS had stirred up enough emotion to spawn a small uprising, one that was quickly subdued by the English overlords.

But the outbreak of violence had begun. And neither Ireland nor England would ever again be the same.

David McCarter opened his eyes in the passenger seat of the Learjet and glanced to the man behind the wheel, Charlie Mott, Stony Man Farm's number-two pilot. Like the other men of Phoenix Force, McCarter had slept most of the way during the four-hour flight from Stony Man, knowing that once the mission got under way it might be quite some time before he could rest his eyes again. Now, as he yawned and came awake, he looked out through the windshield and saw that Mott was dropping the jet through the sky toward the Belfast airport. The busy industrial city appeared below, and as they drew closer to the ground the Phoenix Force leader could even make out Donegall Square. Around the metropolis, particularly to the north, he could see the peaceful hills and glens of Northern Ireland.

Was it possible, McCarter thought as the plane continued to drop toward the airport, that this was one of the most violent areas on Earth, rivaling Lebanon, Rwanda, Somalia and even Israel? Could these tranquil green valleys and vales even now be hiding terrorists from the Provisional Irish Republican Army, its breakaway organization, the Irish National Liberation Army, or the Protestant terrorist group known as the Ulster Defence Association? It didn't seem possible.

But McCarter knew it was more than possible. It was an irrevocable fact.

The wheels of the jet hit the tarmac. Moments later, Mott taxied to a halt at the end of the runway. Behind him McCarter could hear his teammates awakening.

"Customs taken care of?" McCarter asked Mott.

The pilot turned to face him and nodded. "President called the prime minister. Barb notified me on the radio while you guys were asleep." He paused, then grinned. "All you got to do is show them your passports and Justice IDs, G-men."

McCarter chuckled softly at Mott's tongue-in-cheek slam as a very proper-looking man in a British customs uniform came strolling across the tarmac carrying a clipboard. McCarter grabbed his jacket from the seat behind him, lifted the door up and stepped down.

"So," the uniformed man said, "you chappies would be the Yanks we were notified would be coming."

McCarter glanced at the man's name tag as he shrugged into his jacket and the other men of Phoenix Force deplaned and began hauling out their luggage. The tag read Captain Allistair Hall.

"We would be, Captain Hall," he said. He searched the pockets of the coat until he found the Justice Department credentials and passport, then held them up for the man to read.

The captain made a note on his clipboard, then turned to the other men. He made the rounds quickly, looking at the credentials that Gary Manning, T. J. Hawkins, Rafael Encizo and Calvin James held up. "Thank you, gentlemen," he finally said. "Have a nice stay in Ireland and, of course, be careful. If there is anything else in which we can be of service, do not hesitate to come calling. Now, if you will please follow me, I will walk you through the passport stamping. There is a gentleman waiting for you there."

Hall turned on his heel and marched back in the direction from which he'd come. McCarter and the rest of Phoenix Force lifted their bags and followed him through a glass door to a private room, where another customs man was waiting with a stamp. A moment later the passports had been cleared and Hall was leading them into another small room.

McCarter recognized Felix O'Prunty immediately. The Irishman had grown more round and more bald since the Phoenix Force leader had last seen him, and he sported deeper lines in his forehead and around the mouth. But O'Prunty still had that wry smile on his face, a face that looked permanently sunburned from a "wee bit too much of the holy water," as he himself put it.

O'Prunty leaped to his feet from the only chair in the room and stuck out his hand.

McCarter had little patience with most of the Irish, regardless of their religion or politics. He knew this was his own shortcoming—a gross generalization that those of the Emerald Isle were all drunks and troublemakers, and he had consciously worked on this prejudice over the years. Felix O'Prunty, regardless of the fact that he didn't know it, had helped the Phoenix Force leader.

When McCarter had been with the British Special Air Service, he had worked many missions in conjunction with MI-6 and gotten to know O'Prunty well. The Irishman had proved to be an intelligent, competent and fearless operative who might *like* whiskey but kept it well under control.

At least when he needed to.

"You're looking good, Mick," McCarter said, grinning ear to ear.

"Like hell, Limey," O'Prunty grunted, the droll smile never leaving his eyes. "Put on two stone and lost me hair since last you laid eyes on me." He looked McCarter up and down. "But you're looking fit. For an Englishman, anyway."

"I try," McCarter replied. He turned to his men, introducing James, Manning, Encizo and Hawkins.

O'Prunty shook hands with each man, then said, "Shall we move out? Got a wee bit of motoring ahead of us, we do." He led the way out of the airport to a minivan parked in a no-parking zone, opened the sliding rear door and helped Phoenix Force throw its gear into the luggage area at the rear. A few minutes later they had boarded the vehicle and were driving away from the airport.

"All right," O'Prunty said from behind the wheel as they neared the northern edge of Belfast, "here's the skinny—isn't that what you Yanks call it, the skinny?" He glanced over his shoulder with amusement at the men behind him.

"Sometimes," Hawkins said. In the passenger seat, McCarter could see that Phoenix Force's newest, and youngest, member hadn't quite made up his mind as to what he thought of the bold Irishman.

"Anyway," O'Prunty went on, "we've a gent undercover in the IRA, don't you know. Tells me that the Eliminator single-shot the police here in Belfast picked up recently was used by one Bobby McHiggins, of County Antrim."

"Who'd he kill?" Gary Manning, the big Canadian demolitions expert, asked.

"Bloke named Freddy Stone," O'Prunty answered. "Midlevel management in the Ulster Defense Association. The story on the street is that it was payback for a flaming molly tossed into a church in Derry two years ago."

McCarter had to work to keep the smile off his face that O'Prunty's words almost conjured up. He had heard the term "flaming molly" used for Molotov cocktails all his life—that wasn't what was funny. What had caused the Phoenix Force leader's amusement was the city to which O'Prunty had just referred.

The city was Londonderry on the maps, and to most Protestants. But the Catholics and other hard-core Gaelics refused to use the British appellation, continuing to refer to it simply as Derry, the name the city had gone by before the English came to town.

"So," the Phoenix Force leader said, "where are we headed?"

"To find this Mr. Bobby McHiggins and talk to him." The Irishman glanced at his watch. "If we hurry, we can pick him up right after work."

McCarter, Manning, Encizo, Hawkins and James settled in for the ride, watching the beautiful emerald scenery pass by on one side, and the sea on the other, as they bounced up the drifting slopes, then descended into the long, spacious valleys. Forty-five minutes later they turned off the coast road at a sign that announced the Old Bushmills Distillery.

They exited the vehicle, and O'Prunty led the

way into the back door. McCarter saw a peat fire just to the left of the entrance. Several men and women, of various ages and nationalities, sat around the fire sipping whiskey from glasses. He turned to O'Prunty. "Mick," he said, "you sure you didn't bring us here for a bit o' the holy water?"

O'Prunty grunted again. "Would that it were so, laddie," he said. "Would that it were so." He took them into the distillery and pulled out a roll of bills, paying twelve pounds for admission charges, then asking the woman at the counter when the next tour would be.

"Five minutes," the faceless voice behind the window said.

O'Prunty turned to McCarter. "McHiggins is a tour guide here," he said. "I have it for a fact that he's working today."

Five minutes later a tall, reed-thin man sporting jet black hair appeared and announced that the tour was beginning.

McCarter glanced at O'Prunty out of the corner of his eye. The Irishman nodded.

McHiggins gave a short speech about Sir Thomas Phillips, who was granted the first distillery license by James I of England in 1608, then briefly explained how Old Bushmills was triple distilled in the fermented wash using copper-pot stills. He then led them through the building, pointing out various items of interest.

Finally the tour wound down and they were led into a room for samples. Phoenix Force took seats around a large table with O'Prunty and were served shots of whiskey by a charming hostess in ancient Gaelic dress. McHiggins made the rounds, making sure everyone in the room was satisfied. When he came to McCarter's table, the Phoenix Force leader lifted his shot glass and said, "To you, Mr. McHiggins, a fine tour guide if ever there was one." He watched McHiggins smile as he threw back the whiskey, then gradually the man's face turned to one of puzzlement.

"But...how did you know my name?" McHiggins asked.

McCarter rose from the table and walked to where the IRA gunman stood. Moving in close enough that his actions couldn't be observed, he drew the Browning Hi-Power .40-caliber pistol from the belt beneath his jacket and shoved it into the tour guide's belly. "We know more about you than you'd guess, my friend. Now, if you'll come with me and make no fuss, you might just get out of all this alive."

The Caribbean

COLONEL HAROLD J. MADDOX, retired from the U.S. Army, swiveled in his padded desk chair to look out the window of his office. To one side he could see the harbor. On the other the gentle Caribbean waves lapped up onto the sandy beach to tempt him to take the rest of the day off. Catching a little sun might help to ease the arthritis in his hands and back.

As quickly as the idea had come to his mind, it flickered away. No, Maddox thought. No time. At least not right now. There'd be plenty of time for that later.

Swiveling back to his desk, Maddox tapped the button on his intercom and spoke into the speaker. "Gladwyn, my boys arrived yet?"

"They have just arrived, Colonel," Maddox's secretary replied. "Shall I send them in?"

"That's affirmative." Maddox tapped the button again and killed the intercom.

The three men came in single file. The first to enter was Randolph Staggs, a former Green Beret sergeant who had served under Maddox during the colonel's assignment with Army Special Forces. Staggs had a thing about his name, and all of his personal weapons shouted it out. The nickel-plated Colt Gold Cup .45 in the high-rise holster on his belt carried a set of stag grips, as did the big S&W Model 629 that he wore under his arm in a Bianchi shoulder rig. Opposite the .44 Magnum pistol, Maddox saw Staggs's custom-made fighting knife hanging under the man's other arm. It, too, had a stag handle.

Maddox repressed a smile at the childishness of it all. In a way it was like men who seemed to need their initials monogrammed onto everything they owned. What kind of insecurity did it represent, he wondered, having to continually scream your name to the world?

Staggs dropped into one of the three chairs facing Maddox's desk.

Wesley Donalds came next. The big Briton had close-cropped hair and a short, carefully manicured beard that was just beginning to show traces of white and gray. He had been a fine soldier in Her Majesty's army but had washed out of SAS training when he proved short on endurance during long-distance runs. A shame, Maddox thought as Donalds took the middle chair; the man was one hell of a fighter both with and without weapons.

The last man through the door was the one Maddox had always found to be the most mysterious, and therefore the most interesting. William "Shawnee" Morrison was an American Indian who had been a paratrooper in the U.S. Army's Eighty-second Airborne Division. As he dropped into the final chair, Maddox glanced at the medicine bag tied around his neck by a leather thong. He knew that many Indians carried t' medicine—usually good-luck charms of one kind or another—in such bags, and wondered exactly what articles Morrison's might contain.

Maddox pushed the curiosity from his mind. He had business to attend to. "Gentlemen," he said, "how good of you to come."

The polite chuckles from Staggs and Donalds told him they knew damn good and well that it would have been their asses if they hadn't come when he called. These three men were his best, but he had close to a hundred other mercenaries—all former soldiers—working the security detail on his private island. And any of them would take care of Staggs, Donalds or Morrison in a heartbeat if it meant getting their jobs.

As always, Morrison kept silent, his face deadpan, and Maddox wondered just what was actually going on behind that blank expression.

"We have some things to discuss," Maddox said, "and I have assignments for all of you." He stood up behind his desk. "But it's time for a surprise inspection of the grounds. Let's walk while we talk, shall we?" He walked around the desk as the other men stood up and led the way out of the office.

The dazzling Caribbean sunshine hit Maddox in the face as he stepped out of Gladwyn's office onto the sidewalk. It made him smile as he looked out over the sky blue water into the fading horizon. As he turned toward the large metal Quonset hut that housed his farm-implement-manufacturing business, Maddox was a satisfied man. Out of the corner of his eye he could see the jet boats and other craft docked in the small harbor, and straight ahead, on the other side of the island, lay the landing strip. By sea and air he could get anything he needed from Georgetown or Kingston, and he had the privacy he had always wanted.

Maddox led the way up the walk to the hut, listening to the sounds of metal being hammered and other noises as he walked. He had dreamed of owning his own island since he was a child, the son of a poor gunsmith who barely made ends meet with his craft. He had joined the Army right after high school, completing college and entering OCS as soon as possible to qualify for a commission. His nickname, "Mad Dog," had been bestowed in Normandy, when as a young captain he had led his men fearlessly onto the beach himself, then fought with a fury he hadn't known resided inside him. He had fought again as a colonel in Korea, during such famous battles as Pork Chop Hill.

Then, when the Korean War ended, Maddox had rechanneled the energy he had learned to call up for battle into business. Wise investments on the side had meant his portfolio had grown slowly as he completed his twenty years in uniform, th his wealth had multiplied by leaps and bounds when retirement meant he could devote himself full-time to it. Real-estate swindles, junk bonds and a piece of the infamous savings-and-loan scandal had made Maddox rich enough to see his dream of buying an island come true. He had been smart enough to avoid detection on every shady deal, sometimes escaping by the skin of his teeth, but leaving no criminal record in his wake.

Maddox grinned, acknowledging a driving-while-impaired charge in Walla Walla, Washington, the night his third wife left him. Not a bad trade-off for the money that had allowed him to start his own business of manufacturing farm equipment for export to the U.S. and other nations. It was even making a little money. Maybe not as much money as the other business they covered did, but enough to make things look legitimate.

Maddox entered the hut, where he spoke briefly with the foreman. The man, a Cuban exile who had escaped Castro's regime less than a year earlier, had been one of the Cuban dictator's foremost mechanical engineers. Juan was more than just competent—he was good enough that Maddox paid him well and gave him free rein, ignoring all but the most vital aspects of Mad Dog Farm Implements Company.

Along with teaching his son the gunsmithing

trade, Harold Maddox Sr. had instilled in Maddox the belief that the greatest profits came when a man worked in an area in which he was both familiar and interested. Well, Juan was interested and familiar with the farm-machinery trade. That was good. It left Maddox free to concentrate on the *other* production that took place on Mad Dog Island, production in which *he* was interested and familiar.

Satisfied that things in the hut were running smoothly, with no more than the usual petty headaches, Maddox turned and exited the building the same way he had come in. Staggs, Donalds and Morrison followed, and they started along another sidewalk that led to the other side of the island.

"You said you wanted to speak to us?" Staggs said in a questioning tone of voice.

"Yes. I have assignments for each of you—a special detail for someone. But the particulars can wait." He smiled to himself, knowing they all understood what he meant by "special detail," and that they would all be hoping to have it given to them, since "special details" always carried with them a large cash bonus.

The Quonset hut on the other side of the island was larger than the one that housed the farm implements. Maddox opened the door and again ushered his men inside. He followed, and as it always did, what he saw as he stepped inside the building made him swell with pride.

Against one wall of the huge hut, men were busy stamping out the simple parts for the weapons the press had begun calling the Eliminators. On the other side, the same was being done with the simple copies of the Colt Government Model. Against a third wall, workers were setting up machinery in preparation for another manufacturing project. Dust and the sound of metal cutting metal filled the air, and Maddox pulled a pair of goggles and a hard hat off the rack on the wall and slipped them on.

The retired colonel led the other men around the room, briefly inspecting each laborer's work without speaking. As soon as he was satisfied that the individual's operation was progressing well, he moved on to the next station. He spent a little extra time with a middle-aged black man who was drilling holes for the screws that would finally bind the Eliminator parts together. He asked a few simple questions and got a few logical answers.

When the inspection had been completed, Maddox hung his hat and goggles back on the rack, waited for Staggs, Donalds and Morrison to do the same, then led them outside again. He followed the same sidewalk another hundred yards to where a construction crew was raising the steel sides of yet another Quonset hut, this the biggest of all three. He spoke briefly to the foreman of the crew, then turned and began walking toward the workers' barracks on the other side of his office building.

Maddox let Staggs open the door for him this time, then took the steps to the second floor of open bunks. Like the military, each bunk had a foot locker in front of it for the extra clothing and personal items of the man occupying the bed. The foot lockers were secured with simple combination padlocks.

The colonel walked halfway down the long row, stopping at one of the OD boxes. Pulling a list from his pocket, he knelt and flipped the lock over to read the serial number, then consulted the list. A moment later he was twirling the dial of the lock, and a second after that he flipped open the lid.

Maddox dug through the pile of clothes and other items until he came to what appeared to be a wooden puzzle. A steel ball bearing had been taped to the side, and the surface of the puzzle contained a maze of tiny walls through which the ball could be guided when tilted in different directions. Rising to his feet, Maddox chuckled at the puzzled expressions on the faces of Staggs and Donalds, and took note of the ever present deadpan on the face of Morrison.

Pushing on the side of the box with his thumbs, Maddox slid out the false bottom. He reached inside and pulled out a small laminated card. The words Bureau Of Alcohol, Tobacco And Firearms were printed across the top. At the bottom, the name Robert M. Denard had been signed on a line, under which were the words Special Agent.

Maddox held up the card for the others to see. Staggs's and Donalds's eyes grew wider. Morrison's face remained impassive.

"I found this last night during a routine inspection when the men were in the mess hall." Maddox looked at each of the three men in turn, then made his decision. "Morrison, please be so kind as to take our friend Bob with the phony accent on a little cruise this evening. The sharks are hungry. Make sure you're far enough away that nothing floats back to the island."

Morrison's nod was barely perceptible.

Maddox returned the card to the puzzle, stuck it back at the bottom of the foot locker and relocked the box.

"Staggs," he said, "I still need to speak to you and Donalds. But let's return to the office, shall we?"

Without another word Maddox led the way back down the steps of the barracks.

Sydney, Australia

BOLAN HAD CHECKED five of the addresses listed on the Dingoes' driver's licenses and other ID before he found their headquarters.

Pulling the rented Jeep Sierra Wrangler to the curb, Bolan stared at the house. Just off Port Jackson on the bay, he could see the Pacific to the northeast from where he sat, the Tasman sea to the southeast. The house itself looked to have once been grand but now as much of its red tile roof lay on the grass around the dwelling as did on top. The outer walls were in dire need of a coat of paint, and several windows had been broken out and replaced with either cardboard or plywood. Others stood bare and open.

Two vehicles—a one-ton crew cab and a Chevy Suburban—sat in the driveway. Lights were on in the house. Periodically a shadow moved across the illuminated kitchen, opening the refrigerator and pulling out a can Bolan assumed to be beer. Then the shadow would disappear once more into another part of the house.

As he reconned the site, the Executioner saw a bright red Lumina APV pull into the driveway. Two men—both wearing the distinctive Dingo jackets—got out of the cab and opened a rear door. Huffing and puffing, they unloaded a large crate and began to carry it up the crumbling concrete steps to the porch.

The Executioner reached into the back of the Jeep, unzipped a soft-sided leather bag and pulled out a device known as the Action Ear Sport. Unfolding it from its flat packing configuration, he slipped the earpieces over his head and adjusted the collar-level tension band. Pointing the wind-resistant stereo microphones toward the front door, he settled back to listen as the door opened.

"Took you bloody long enough, maties," the man who opened the door said as he stepped back to let the gang members carrying the crate inside.

"Don't be fuckin' us about, Sammy boy," a huffing voice complained. "We're here now, aren't we?"

More idle chatter met the Executioner's ears as the door closed. He tilted the microphones slightly, angling them at a broken window to the side of the door. He heard the sounds of the crate being pried open, then a few chuckles from the unseen men around the room.

"All *right!*" a new voice said. "We'll be kil-lin' a few of the Down Unders now."

"Fuckin' aye," someone else added. "Won't be needing the stupid single-shots now."

"Don't bad-mouth the single-shots, Ricky. It was them let us enlarge our operation so we could buy these."

There were several more comments, and the Executioner estimated by the number of previ-ously unheard voices that there had to be at least six men in the house. Then the distinctive sound of steel sliding along steel—the sound of a gun bolt of some kind being drawn back and allowed to fall forward—met his ears.

"Let's get these loaded and go kick some Down Under ass."

The comment was followed by laughter and words of agreement around the room.

Bolan unwrapped the listening device from his head and dropped it back into the bag behind him. Drawing the Desert Eagle from his hip holster, he twisted and set it on top of the earpieces. He had inspected it earlier and seen that he wouldn't be able to fix it with the tools he had available, which meant he would have to rely solely on the Beretta 93-R for the time being.

He could do far worse in a weapon.

Quietly opening the Wrangler's door, Bolan dropped to the ground and drew the Beretta from shoulder leather. He thumbed the selector to 3-round burst as he hurried across the street to the porch. He wanted to get inside and do his business before the new weapons—whatever they were— were loaded.

The Executioner took the steps in one jump, lowered his shoulder and drove it through the splintering wooden door.

The door burst from its frame, and Bolan stepped in the living room of the run-down house.

Six men sat around the open crate, in the process of loading bullets into long, single-stack magazines. Beer cans and wine bottles littered the floor, and the strong odor of marijuana hung thick in the air.

A blond-haired man with a long knife scar running down his cheek was the first to recover from the shock of the Executioner's entrance.

He was also the first to die.

Bolan turned the Beretta on him as the man tried to draw one of the Eliminator Government Models from his belt. A sound-suppressed 3-round burst shot from the 93-R, taking the man in the face at close range. Bone, flesh and blood exploded into the air as the man's face all but disintegrated.

The big American swung the Beretta toward a man with a dark black goatee. The Dingo had already drawn what looked like a stainless-steel Rossi .44 Special and was trying to line up the sights on the Executioner.

Bolan tapped the trigger again, this time catching the Dingo in the chest and throat. The gangster fell onto his side, just as dead as his friend if not quite as disfigured.

A short burst of fire whizzed past the Executioner, who dived to the floor as he heard the metallic sound of a striker hitting an empty chamber. He looked up to see a red-haired Dingo aiming what looked like an old U.S. M-3 "grease gun" at him, a puzzled look on the young man's face.

Bolan wasn't as bewildered—what had happened was clear to him. The man had gotten the weapon's magazine only partially loaded when the Executioner burst through the door. He had run out of ammo.

And now, his slowness would mean death.

Another trio of 9 mm hollowpoint rounds stitched the perplexed Dingo from belly to sternum. He fell next to his comrades as the Executioner shifted the hot-barreled Beretta slightly to the side. A fat gang member, his jacket stretched at the snaps where it was too small for his belly, tried to jam the magazine he'd been loading into his own grease gun.

Bolan cut him down, and he crashed to the floor in a heap.

Only two men remained when the Executioner swung the 93-R toward a Dingo sporting a black eye patch over his acne-scarred face. He dropped the grease gun in his hands and clawed frantically for the Eliminator Government Model in his belt. His efforts were fruitless. Bolan cut him down like the rest.

Suddenly the Beretta locked open, empty. From both instinct and habit, the Executioner's right hand let the weapon fall.

The surviving gunner saw the empty hip holster

and smiled. He rammed the magazine he'd been loading into the grease gun and prepared to take aim.

He never got the chance.

Without so much as a pause, the Executioner unleathered the Applegate-Fairbairn fighting knife in the Kydex holster inside his slacks. The blade came out clutched in a saber grip, and Bolan dived forward over the wooden crate to sink the hard steel into his adversary's chest.

For a brief second the man was frozen. His eyes widened and his lips fell open.

Bolan hit the floor, rolled to his feet and ripped a fresh magazine from the leather caddie under his right arm. Dropping the empty box from the Beretta, he jammed the new clip home and hit the slide release. A 360-degree spin showed no threat coming out of the other rooms of the house, but he moved through the crumbling shack to make sure. The rest of the house was empty, save for more empty alcohol containers, fast-food boxes and wrappers, and other debris.

The Executioner hurried back into the living room. Lifting one of the weapons still in the crate, he unwrapped the oil paper encircling it. At first glance, it *did* look like one of the World War II–era M-3 submachine guns. Commonly referred to as grease guns due to their cylindrical shape and narrow protruding barrel, they had been an adequate, if not remarkable, U.S. service arm all the way up until 1960. Some were still in use at National Guard armories and other installations around the country.

As he studied the weapon closer, Bolan began to see the differences. The folding stock was slightly different, and the barrel was shorter than the standard eight inches. Like the M-3—and the Eliminator single-shots and Government Models, for that matter—the majority of the weapon had been made with stampings and pressings with only a few machining operations required in its assembly. As he expected, he found no serial number or other indication of who had manufactured the weapon.

As Bolan dropped the weapon back into the crate, a small dark spot of ink near the bottom of the rough wood caught his eye. He leaned over, studying it closely, and frowned. It was either a Japanese, Chinese or Korean character. He neither spoke nor read any of the languages.

Pulling a pen and notepad from his pocket, he copied the character as best he could, then walked swiftly to the telephone on a table against the wall and dialed the police. He gave the address, told the voice on the other end that there had been a shooting and illegal weapons were at the site, and that the front door would be open so they could look inside for "probable cause." He hung up when the voice asked for his name.

The Executioner left the house, descended the steps and started toward the Jeep. There was a weird World War II connection here somewhere—all of the unmarked guns were patterned after weapons of that era. He didn't know what the connection was, but he intended to find out.

CHAPTER THREE

Brooklyn, New York

Jed's Old-Time Diner featured an atmosphere and decor from the fifties. Thin metal Coca-Cola signs and antique bottles from all over the world, as well as other Coke memorabilia, covered the walls. The booths and tables were artificially scarred to look old, and the number-one menu item was the Happy Days Double-Burger Basket with a choice of french fries or onion rings.

Waters had suggested that Able Team try the diner if Caveretti wasn't at the home address listed in his file. He wasn't—in fact the house the Falcon hit man had listed had been torn down. Lyons, Schwarz and Blancanales had changed out of their sport coats and slacks during the drive to the diner. They now wore soiled khaki work pants and shirts with name tags on the upper right chest, heavy work boots and plastic hard hats. Lyons wore a faded blue denim three-quarter-length coat over his weapons. His teammates had chosen light poplin jackets with the name of the factory just down the street lettered on the back.

They didn't look much like the Falcons at the booth in the corner, all of whom wore flashy green jackets with a bird swooping out of the sky on the back. But neither did the men of Able Team look out of place in Jed's Old-Time Diner. There were other hard hats scattered throughout the booths and tables, other name tags sewn onto work shirts.

Lyons sat facing the Falcons, watching them surreptitiously. Several of the men—all looking to be in their early twenties—had come and gone while he and the other members of Able Team ate dinner. But none of them had been Eddie Caveretti.

Gadgets Schwarz took a bite of his burger, swallowed it, then looked up at Lyons. "How long are we going to wait here for him?" he asked.

"Till he comes," Lyons said with a shrug. "We don't have any other leads."

Blancanales pulled the straw from his milk shake out of his mouth. "What if he doesn't come in tonight?"

Lyons frowned. His teammates were being subtle, but they had a point. They couldn't afford to waste too much time here in Jed's, particularly when there were only four of the Falcons here now. Waters had told them that the NYPD gang intelligence squad estimated the Falcons' membership at close to fifty, not counting the girls known as "debs." That meant that forty-six of the gangsters were off doing other things.

Caveretti might not show up at all.

"We'll give it another hour," Lyons said. "If he hasn't shown up by then, we grab the next kid in a green jacket who leaves the place. We'll see if he knows where the illustrious Mr. Caveretti might be."

The men of Able Team finished their hamburgers and ordered coffee.

The hour was almost up when a tall, muscular man walked in. Unlike the other Falcons, he carried his bright green jacket rather than wore it. A black T-shirt stretched across his bulging pectoral muscles, and mammoth biceps and triceps threatened to rip the rolled-up sleeves. Blue jeans and black engineer boots with buckles completed his "tough guy" costume as he swaggered into Jed's and walked to the booth in the corner.

All of the seats were taken as Eddie Caveretti stopped at the table. One of the smaller Falcons immediately stood and gave Caveretti his place.

Lyons watched the smaller man stand nervously at the end of the table. Caveretti obviously commanded respect within the ranks of the Falcons.

The gang members leaned over the table, talking in hushed tones as Lyons continued to watch. Fifteen minutes later the Able Team leader saw a slight movement underneath their table.

One of the other men was handing something to Caveretti.

The muscle boy pulled up the leg of his jeans and stuck whatever it was in his boot. The group seemed to relax. They leaned back in their seats and began talking in louder voices, though still too low for Lyons to make out their words. Five minutes later Caveretti stood to leave.

Lyons, Schwarz and Blancanales rose to their feet. The big ex–LAPD detective took the check, dropped it on the counter next to the cash register with some money, then led the way out of the diner to the parking lot.

Able Team hurried to the Chevy van they had rented. Schwarz jumped behind the wheel while Blancanales slid open the side door and stepped up into the vehicle. He left the door open. Lyons stayed outside the van, talking to Schwarz through the open window as if he might be saying goodbye before leaving in another car.

Caveretti appeared a moment later and strutted toward a midnight blue 1965 Corvette convertible. Lyons gave him time to get to the sports car and reach into his pocket for the key, then walked swiftly up to him. "Can I speak to you for a minute?" he asked politely.

The Falcon turned to look at Lyons, a sneer on his face. "You know who I am?" he asked.

"Yeah," Lyons said as he reached under the denim jacket and produced his .357 Magnum Colt Python. "Dead meat, if you don't walk over and get into that van." He nodded toward the Chevy.

Caveretti didn't scare easily. The sneer turned to a scowl, and he said, "You have fucked up royally, my friend." He stayed where he was.

"Walk," Lyons ordered.

"Fuck you."

Lyons saw what Caveretti was about to do in the young man's eyes. As the Falcon cleaner reached for the Python, the Able Team leader jerked it back and rapped the barrel against the muscle man's head.

Caveretti slumped to the ground as Schwarz brought the van to a halt next to Lyons. "Some people just have to do things the hard way," he commented.

Lyons holstered his revolver, grabbed the man at his feet under the arms and lifted him into the van. He glanced around the parking lot as the van drove away.

No one had seen a thing.

The Caribbean

COLONEL MADDOX LED Staggs and Donalds back into the office building. Gladwyn had left for the day, returning to the little one-room shack Maddox had ordered built for her as the only woman on the island. He thought of her now, probably undressing and preparing to take her late-afternoon bath. He would visit her later, as her job description detailed far more than just typing.

Maddox took a seat behind his desk and reached for the large burr elm box on the edge of his desk. The Zino Davidoff humidor had arrived only yesterday, but already he was noticing the effect it had on his cigars. He opened the lid, surveyed the top rows of midsize Cuban panatelas, then pulled out the lift-up tray and reached for one of the larger "Churchills" in the lower compartment.

Staggs and Donalds dropped back into the chairs in front of the desk, waiting patiently as the colonel struck a wooden match and rolled the cigar around the flame. When the fire had burned too close to his fingers, he dropped it into the marble ashtray and struck another. After the third match, he looked at the end of the cigar, grunted in satisfaction and stuck it between his teeth. "You've been reading the American newspapers?" he asked Staggs and Donalds.

Staggs grinned as he nodded. "You're getting famous. They've started calling your guns the Eliminators."

Donalds chuckled politely next to him. "Yes, and one of the London tabloids has even started calling you—the mysterious force behind the guns—the Eliminator."

"I suppose so," Maddox agreed, taking in a mouthful of smoke and letting it roll over his tongue. "In any case, it's damn good for business. Orders have gone up five hundred percent since the papers picked it up."

He leaned back against the desk chair, then changed the subject. "Gentlemen, I am faced with a dilemma."

Both Staggs and Donalds waited as he puffed again on the cigar.

"While the publicity increases sales," Maddox went on, "I must constantly weigh it against the pressure it will be putting on law-enforcement officials to track down the source. As you just saw, we already had a BATF man in our midst. That means somebody suspected us, and that scares me."

Staggs leaned forward in his chair, frowning. "I don't see how that guy could have picked up the trail. The workers don't have access to a phone, and we screened all their mail. The only people who've been off the island have been you, me, Donalds here and Morrison.''

"Yes," Maddox said, his eyes growing cold. "That is true. And that is *exactly* what worries me." He shifted his glance to Donalds. "Wes, I am sorry to have to ask you this. But I would like you to step outside. One of you, either you or Staggs, is guilty of treason. I want to speak with both of you individually.''

Donalds's face drained of color. "But, Colonel, surely you don't think—''

Maddox held up a hand. "Wes, please. I will speak with you after I have talked with Randy.''

Donalds rose unsteadily to his feet. He glanced at Staggs, then left the room.

Staggs leaned even farther forward. "I hate to sound like a broken record of Donalds, but surely you don't think I'd snitch you off?''

Maddox shook his head. "Of course not." He glanced toward the door where Donalds had left. "It's the limey.''

Staggs sat back and crossed his left cowboy boot over his right knee. "Are you sure, Colonel?'' he asked. "I just can't believe it.''

"Well, Randy," Maddox said, taking another puff of the cigar, "I did a little checking. Donalds got his undergraduate degree at Harvard before returning to the U.K. to study at Oxford. Did you know that?''

Staggs squinted his eyes in concentration. "Yes, sir, I guess so. I mean, I think he's mentioned it."

Maddox took the cigar from his mouth and nodded. "And do you know who else was there at the same time?"

Staggs shrugged his shoulders.

"Robert Denard."

"The BATF guy?" Staggs said, his tone incredulous. "The guy out in the shop right now?"

"That's correct."

Now it was Staggs who glanced at the door. "Harvard's a big place, Colonel. It could be a coincidence."

Maddox stuck the cigar back between his teeth and smiled as the smoke rose to his face. "Do you know who was a fraternity brother of Donalds's?" he asked.

"Denard?" Staggs questioned.

"Very good," Maddox said in the tone of voice used to congratulate a child who had finally learned to recite the alphabet. "And do you know who Donalds's roommate at the frat house was his sophomore year?"

Staggs just stared at him. "I can't believe it. Are you sure there's a connection?"

Maddox was a man of discipline and usually one hundred percent in control of his emotions. But now, in a rare display of anger and frustration, he slammed the cigar into the ashtray. "Are you stupid?" he demanded, his face turning to a mask of fury. "What are you, Staggs, some idiot savant who can kill well but can't even tie his own shoes? You think all this is happenstance?"

Staggs dropped his gaze to the floor without answering.

Maddox composed himself and reached for his cigar. It had broken almost in two, and he opened his desk drawer, produced a knife and cut it the rest of the way. Sticking the stub into his mouth, he said, "All right, Randy. I suppose you know what to do."

Staggs raised his eyes and stood. He nodded.

"Do it tonight," Maddox said. "Make sure the workers don't see it, and be certain the body can't be found."

Staggs walked out of the room, and Donalds walked in.

"Take a seat, Wes," Maddox said.

The Briton obeyed.

"Did you know Robert Denard?" the colonel asked bluntly.

"The man whose BATF ID you found?" Donalds asked. "Of course. He came to work here a few months after we opened shop."

"No, I mean before he came to work here."

For the second time in ten minutes, Maddox

watched the blood drain from Donalds's face. "Of course not. How would I?"

Maddox chuckled. "Oh, I don't know, Wes. I guess I just figured that if you woke up in the same room as a man for your entire sophomore year of college, sooner or later one of you would introduce yourselves to the other."

Donalds's eyes took on the look of a cornered rat's. "Colonel, I had no idea he was coming here. I didn't even know he'd become a BATF agent. He transferred somewhere our junior year and I haven't spoken to him since." He paused. "I swear to God in heaven, Colonel."

"Really?" Maddox clasped both hands behind his head. "You wouldn't be lying to me now, would you, Wes?"

"No, sir."

"You wouldn't just be telling me that now to try to save your life?"

"No, sir."

"You mean if you actually were in cahoots with Denard, you wouldn't tell me you weren't so I wouldn't kill you?"

"Well, sir...I suppose if I was I would. But I'm not. I *swear* to you, Colonel."

"But if you were, you would?"

"Well, probably... I mean, what man wouldn't try to save his own bloody skin?"

Maddox felt the anger rise in his chest again.

Disloyalty was the one thing he had never tolerated and never would. He thought about Staggs, waiting outside even now to take Donalds somewhere and kill him. No, he thought as the frenzy inspired by the cowardly traitor continued to grow in his heart and soul, he would do it himself.

"Wes, if you tell me that this is just a coincidence, I will try to believe you," Maddox said. He opened the drawer that had held the knife and rummaged around until he felt the Smith & Wesson Model 645 under a stack of papers. Drawing it from the drawer, he lifted the weapon and aimed it at Donalds's head. "But even though I may believe you," he said as the Briton looked at him in horror, "I can't afford to take chances at this stage of the game."

The roar of the .45-caliber cartridge exploding racked the walls of the small office.

The door opened and Staggs came sprinting in, his big .44 Magnum revolver clenched in both hands. "What the—" he said, then stopped just behind Donalds's corpse. He looked down at the man still seated in the chair, then up to Maddox.

"I changed my mind and decided to do it myself," Maddox said. He lowered the hammer on the .45 and returned it to his desk. "Get rid of the body as soon as it gets dark, Randy." He glanced at the floor and walls. "And clean up this mess. You'll get the same special-detail bonus as if you'd killed him yourself.''

Stony Man Farm

AARON KURTZMAN WHEELED his chair a little closer to the computer monitor in front of him and set the brake. He punched a button to clear the screen. Picking up his coffee mug, he took a swig of the room-temperature brew and went to work.

With the finesse of a concert pianist, Kurtzman's skilled fingers flew across the keyboard, programming the computers at Stony Man Farm for what lay ahead. He code-named the mission Operation Eliminator and began accessing several programs of his own design, among them a probability program that would kick out "most likelies" as soon as he began to feed it information.

The program set up, and the intel on hand so far entered, Kurtzman sat back as he waited for his magic machines to digest all of the information. While he waited, he turned to one side and looked down the ramp at the other members of his cybernetics team.

Akira Tokaido's head bobbed in time to whatever music was being fed into his ears by his portable CD player. He typed away at his own computer terminal with almost the same finesse as Kurtzman. The big man shook his head, smiling as he remembered his own father not understanding why he kept his transistor radio pressed against one ear when he was Tokaido's age.

People didn't ever really change, Kurtzman thought—only technology. What went around came around. He realized suddenly that he was now walking in his father's shoes where Akira was concerned. There was a difference, though.

Kurtzman might not like the alternative music the young man listened to, but the pandemonium didn't seem to have an adverse effect on Tokaido's production; in fact the young computer genius seemed to do better work when he had the headset plastered to his head. So, unlike his own father, Kurtzman wouldn't complain or condemn Tokaido's music.

Which, he realized as he turned his attention to the second member of his computer team, was the bottom line at Stony Man Farm. If "it" worked, you used it. If whatever "it" was didn't work, you cast it out like spoiled hamburger and found something that did.

Results, not the method by which they had been obtained, were what mattered at the Farm.

Kurtzman studied the ebullient redhead next to Tokaido, Carmen Delahunt. An old-line FBI computer whiz, Delahunt was hardly the stereotypical nerd one imagined spending her life in front of a hard drive. She was a divorced mother of three, and her youngest was still in college, attending classes and making the dean's honor roll each semester at Maryland State. She was waiting patiently for hard copies pertaining to her current project.

Kurtzman looked at the final member of his team, Huntington Wethers. The tall, well-built black man exuded a dignified aura even when he sat and typed. Graying around the temples of his short-cut hair, ''Hunt'' had been a professor of cybernetics at Berkeley before Kurtzman had discovered his talents. Bored to death with the life of a college instructor, Wethers was easily convinced that his destiny lay at Stony Man Farm, saving the world every once in a while, rather than trying to put logical ideas into young heads that had chosen Berkeley because it was a place where liberals could hang out with their weird ideas and ignore reality.

He turned back to his computer screen as the hard drive beeped and told him the programming for the mission was complete. It wasn't yet time to pull the other members of his team off what they were currently working on and order them to focus on various aspects of Operation Eliminator, but he had a gut feeling that the time was coming.

Soon.

The computer wizard of Stony Man Farm turned his attention back to the screen, secure in the knowledge that the people he had working for him were the best in the world at what they did.

Kurtzman sat back in his wheelchair, glowering slightly as he let his brain go to work before he began to attack the keyboard. He knew that any investigation that utilized cybernetics was worthless without human brain power as a catalyst. His magic machines weren't really magic. They couldn't "think" on their own, as the uninformed sometimes believed. The thinking had to initially be performed by people skilled in their use, people with the knowledge of exactly what a computer could do and what it couldn't.

Pulling open a drawer beneath the console in front of him, Kurtzman removed a yellow legal pad and a ballpoint pen. He felt a wry smile creep across his face as he pulled off the pen's cap and began to write. *This* technology—paper and pen—had been around for a while. And it was still not only efficient but vital.

Kurtzman looked at the blank yellow page before him, then scribbled several circles at the top to get the ink flowing in the pen. Operation Eliminator, like all Stony Man Farm operations, was going to be a worldwide undertaking. But like any investigation, whether it be earth-threatening or the mere nighttime vandalism of a soda machine by some teenager looking for pocket change, the basics where the same. They were also the same as those used in journalism.

"Who? What? Where? When? How?" Kurtzman wrote on the page, skipping several lines between each word.

The computer whiz stared at the "Who" at the top of the page. That was the ultimate goal—determining *who,* and then stopping whoever was behind the mass production of weapons that seemed to be showing up all over the world. Realizing he had just answered the next question, he skipped down to "What" and wrote in "Cheaply made yet effective firearms." Glancing briefly at the "Where?," Kurtzman went on. When he learned who, he would learn where, or vice versa. After the word "When," the computer man wrote "Current: First Eliminator discovered six weeks ago." And in the space following "How," Kurtzman entered, "Cheap pressing and stamping utilizing simple patterns of World War II–era weaponry. Distributed underground—probably through an intricate network of front men and/or front companies."

He set the pen down on top of the legal pad and looked up at the screen. He had the what, when and how. What they needed now was the who and where.

Without further hesitation, Kurtzman began typing once more.

CHAPTER FOUR

Brooklyn, New York

The hotel six blocks from Jed's Old-Time Diner was perfect. Maybe not perfect for sleeping—the racket from the other rooms would have wakened the dead. And the room assigned by the desk manager to Able Team certainly wasn't perfect from a hygienic standpoint—the rats, cockroaches, centipedes and other creatures that had previously occupied the place had left trails of spittle and feces that would make anyone trying to lead a reasonably clean life-style feel like taking a shower as soon as he stepped inside.

But the shower would have done little good. It was even more squalid than the rest of the room.

Lyons led the way into the shabby room with a still-unconscious Eddie Caveretti draped over his shoulder. The Falcon hit man had awakened once during the ride to the hotel, and Gadgets Schwarz had returned him to the Land of Nod with a short but well-placed left jab. Now Lyons dropped him down into a seated position in one of the splintering chairs that circled an equally decayed table, and pulled a length of cord from the pocket of his jacket. A moment later Caveretti was tied hand and foot.

The movement had to have brought him awake because no sooner had the Able Team leader cinched the last knot than the Falcon opened his eyes. For a moment they appeared not to focus. Then, as they cleared, an expression much different than the insolent look Lyons had seen on Caveretti's face in the parking lot covered the man's face.

But clinging to the quickly draining courage was a last stab at false bravado. "You bastards are gonna pay for this shit," Caveretti said, his voice suddenly cracking into a falsetto. He sounded more like a pubescent teenage boy than a killer, and the shriek mocked all semblance of the tough-guy effect he'd been trying to achieve.

"We want you to do something for us," Lyons said. *"Capisce?"*

Caveretti's head shot up suddenly, and the Able Team leader realized that the Italian word he had chosen rather arbitrarily had produced an unforseen impact on the Falcon.

The Falcon hit man studied him closely. Then, in a voice completely devoid of both the true bravery he had exhibited in the diner's parking lot and the forced courage he had tried just a moment before, he whispered, "Are you guys, I mean you gentlemen, Family?"

Schwarz glowered at him, then leaned in until his face was less than an inch from the Falcon's. "You expect us to tell some half-assed little street punk like you about Family business?" he said. He dug under his jacket and came out with a Benchmade ATS-34 folding knife and snapped it open with the thumb hole. "This clown ain't gonna be any good to us, Ironman," he said. "What do you say I just stick him now and get him out of our way?"

"No! Wait!" Caveretti shouted, staring at the partially serrated blade. "You haven't even told me what you want yet! How do you know I won't help you?"

Lyons and Schwarz continued to stare.

"Look, I'll help you. What's this all about?"

The Mafia angle was having great effect on the young man, and Lyons decided to play it for all it was worth. "You *know* what it's about," he growled, hoping that Caveretti would take the bait and divulge enough new information to help him keep going.

"Look," the Falcon said, "if it's about the smack on Gates and Throop Streets—"

Lyons leaned in and slapped the man across the

face. "You want to quit playing games with us? You want to get straight before my friend here carves you up like Grandma's Christmas goose. You *know* that's what it's about."

"Okay, look," Caveretti said. "The Falcons that were dealing there the other night, they got mixed up. They knew that was your territory. They just made a mistake. They were doing this deal with this dude, right? He parked on Gates, just a block outside our turf. He forgot his billfold so they followed him to get it. They didn't mean no disrespect, sir. We won't never—"

Lyons slapped him across the face again, then turned to Schwarz. "Go ahead and cut his throat," he said. He glanced around the room. "They'll never even notice the blood in the rest of this filth. Then we'll drag his ass out to the van and toss him out somewhere in Bed-Stuy—let all his friends see what happens if they get over into Family territory."

"Gladly." Schwarz stepped in with the knife and pressed it against Caveretti's throat.

"No!" Caveretti pleaded. "You said there was something you wanted me to do! I'll do it!"

Lyons frowned as if trying to think. He let the Falcon stew in his own terror for a minute, then said, "I want to know about the gun you used the other night."

"What gun?" Caveretti said. Then, in an attempt to regain some of his lost respect, he said, "I cool a lot of punks. I use a lot of guns."

Lyons slapped him hard.

"Do I need to repeat the question?" Lyons asked.

"You mean the Eliminator?" he asked.

"Give the man the Big Brain Award," Blancanales said. "Where'd it come from?"

"I got it from Bobby. Bobby the Deuce—you know him, don't you?"

"No, you'll have to forgive us if we don't keep up with all of you big-time gangsters," Schwarz said sarcastically. "But we'll try harder from now on."

"Where is this Bobby the Deuce?" Lyons asked.

Caveretti shrugged. "Right now? I don't know."

"But you know where he lives?"

Caveretti hesitated, and Schwarz moved in with the knife without having to be told.

"Yeah, er, yes sirs, I know where he lives."

"Then take us to him." Lyons nodded to Schwarz as his friend used his knife to cut the cord binding the Falcon to the chair. "Do a good job and don't screw us around, and you might not end up floating in the bay in the morning."

Northern Ireland

ROUGHLY TWO MILES NORTH of the Old Bushmills
Distillery, just east of Portrush and situated on
one of the steep cliffs along Ireland's northern
coast, stood what remained of Dunluce Castle. In
past centuries it had been a grand place that
served both as a fortified dwelling and an obser-
vatory point for marauding Vikings who came to
the island to murder and plunder. One of the leg-
ends claimed the name meant "mermaid's fort."
There was a strong possibility that this was true,
as a deep cave penetrated the rock on which the
castle had been built.

Now Dunluce Castle lay in shambles. The roof
had fallen, and most of the walls were gone.
Much of the gray stone that had once protected
Dunluce's occupants had fallen over the cliff and
could be seen in the breakers that pounded the
shore far below. Serving only as an unguided
tourist attraction, the castle could be explored between April and September from 10:00 a.m. to
7:00 p.m. Monday through Saturday, and from
2:00 p.m. to 7:00 p.m. on Sundays. During the
rest of the year, the official closing time was
4:00 p.m. and all day Monday.

These hours meant little to the men of Phoenix
Force.

Darkness had fallen over the northern coast
when Felix O'Prunty guided the minivan off the
highway and onto a dirt road. The road led to

Dunluce's deserted ruins, where the MI-6 man killed the engine and stomped the emergency brake.

"We're here, lads," O'Prunty said as he opened his door and got out.

McCarter got out of the passenger side as Calvin James slid the side door open and leaped to the ground. The black Phoenix Force warrior turned, reached behind his neck and drew a modified COMTECH Crossada knife from beneath his jean jacket. Phoenix Force's resident blade expert had been so impressed by the Crossada Bolan had carried recently that he had appealed to Cowboy Kissinger to procure one for him. Wanting a more easily concealed carry, however, James had asked Kissinger to grind the twelve-inch blade down to ten inches, take another half inch off the grip and design an across-the-back scabbard. The fighting knife was still huge, deadly and wicked looking, but it now completely disappeared from view under even a lightweight cover garment.

Gary Manning, the team's barrel-chested Canadian explosives expert, pushed Bobby McHiggins out in front of him. The IRA gunner hit the ground on his face.

James leaned over, grabbed the back of the man's scraggly hair and jerked him to his feet. Twisting the hair, he twirled the man to face away from him and pressed the knife's spear point into McHiggins's back.

O'Prunty led the way over the broken rocks into what remained of the castle. James pushed his charge forward with the huge knife, with McCarter, Manning, Encizo and Hawkins right behind. O'Prunty moved in and out of what remained of the walls, finally stopping in the far northeast corner of the ruins and turning. "This'd be a fine spot to conduct our little interview with this bastard, I suppose."

James looked out through what remained of the wall in front of him to see the edge of the cliff less than ten feet away. Below, he could hear the mighty waves buffeting the bottom of the precipice. A soft wind blew in from the Atlantic, whistling through the collapsed stones and giving the ruins a ghostly aura.

Still holding McHiggins's hair, James lifted a foot and placed it against the back of the IRA man's knee. Jerking McHiggins's head back as he kicked forward, he dropped the gaunt man to the ground.

McHiggins hit on his back, groaned softly and looked up at the stars.

"Sit up," David McCarter ordered, stepping forward.

McHiggins did as he'd been told.

The Briton squatted next to the IRA man,

grabbed his throat and twisted his head to face him. With the other hand, he hooked a thumb toward James. "This man is going to ask you a few questions. You're going to answer them. You're going to answer them truthfully and quickly, the first time he asks them." He paused to give McHiggins a moment to think about it. "If you don't, well, it's really better that you don't bloody well know what he'll do to you if you don't."

James looked down at the man on the ground. McHiggins was a terrorist, nothing more, nothing less. James could sympathize with the IRA's desire for independence from England; after all, that was how his *own* country had originated. But he couldn't remember ever reading about America's Founding Fathers arbitrarily blowing up babies and other innocents in order to establish the United States of America. So while he might empathize with McHiggins's political agenda, he had no patience whatsoever with the means the IRA was using to achieve it.

McHiggins looked up at James, his face expressionless. James held up the knife, letting the moonlight reflect off the blade. The carbon-steel blade wasn't as shiny as stainless steel would have been, but somehow the soft gray glow under the stars looked even more deadly.

The gulp that went down Bobby McHiggins's

throat looked like a python swallowing a small dog. He looked back down at the ground.

James studied the man for a moment, trying to get a read on what would work best with him. His position as Phoenix Force's unofficial chief interrogator had grown out of the efficiency with knives that he had learned growing up on the mean streets of Chicago's South Side, then perfected as a U.S. Navy SEAL. Many men had a fear of cold steel that far surpassed that of bullets. Their assumption, however erroneous it was, seemed to be that death from gunshot came quick and painlessly while the blade was always slow and torturous.

The Phoenix Force Warrior knew that this could be, but didn't have to be, the case.

James knew that some people held a basic fear of black people. It was a learned prejudice that he knew came from viewing all black men as being capable of great violence. Such bigots conveniently forgot the names of men like George Washington Carver, Martin Luther King and Colin Powell, preferring to concentrate on the stereotypical street gangsters, drug dealers and pimps they saw in movies.

He didn't like that image of his race, and his whole life had been spent trying to destroy it. But since it was there, at least for the time being, he intended to use it to his advantage whenever possible.

And right now the Phoenix Force warrior could see in Bobby McHiggins's eyes that it was possible. With a wild war whoop James stepped in and stuck the point of the Crossada knife under his victim's chin. The IRA man jerked back convulsively but McCarter had moved behind him and stopped him with a foot. Pulling up lightly on the knife, James lifted McHiggins's face so that their eyes met once more. The razor-honed edge of the blade barely penetrated the skin beneath the terrorist's chin. A light trickle of blood began to drip onto the steel.

"You killed a man the other night," James growled. "You used a single-shot pistol with no markings. They're being called Eliminators by the newspapers."

McHiggins stared up at him but didn't speak.

"The man you killed was named Freddy Stone. Am I right?" James asked.

McHiggins remained silent.

"Oh, Bobby, Bobby, Bobby," James said, letting the words come out wearily between clenched teeth. "Do we have to do things the hard way?"

Once again his question was met with silence.

James stepped back and withdrew the knife from beneath McHiggins's chin. He looked over the top of the seated man's head at McCarter, and nodded.

The Briton shoved forward with the foot he already had in McHiggins's back. The IRA man's head snapped forward, his long black hair shooting over his scalp and flying up.

James took a half step in and brought the knife around through the air in an arc. The heavy steel blade made a whooshing sound as it sliced through the air. By the time it came to a halt just above and beyond James's left shoulder, the top of McHiggins's hair had hit the ground.

James looked into the shocked eyes, then up to the top of the IRA man's head. Long strands still fell over McHiggins's ears, but the top-center area looked as if it had been shaved with an electric barber's clipper.

"I think that hairstyle is *you*, Bobby," O'Prunty said. "My guess is you'll start a new rage all over London."

Out of the corner of his eye, James saw Manning nod. "I like the look," he said. "Just right for the shape of your face. Who was the Stooge—not Moe or Curly, the other one?"

"Larry," Hawkins said in his southern drawl. "Yeah, he does look a lot like Larry."

James held a hand up to show that he wanted silence once more. "I'll repeat the question. Was it Freddy Stone you killed the other night with the Eliminator?''

This time he got a fast answer. "Aye," Mc-Higgins said, nodding vigorously. "But it was because Stone—"

"I don't care why you did it," James interrupted. "I'm more concerned with how." He paused. "Where'd you get the Eliminator, Bobby?"

McHiggins opened his mouth to speak, then thought better of it. His jaw clamped tight for a moment, then he said, "I can't tell you. Can't rat out me own mates!"

James stepped in again and raised the knife above his head. Slicing down at a slight angle, he severed the strands of hair that hung over Mc-Higgins's left ear.

The Ira gunner screamed, and James saw another trickle of blood appear where he had nicked the man's ear.

"Hey," Encizo said, "I remember that style from a few years ago. Kids all over were letting one side of their hair grow real long and shaving the other. Remember that, T.J.?"

Before Hawkins could reply, James held up his hand again. "Okay, second question, second time. Where did the Eliminator come from?"

"They'll kill me if I tell you!" McHiggins sobbed.

James brought the knife down again, and all of the hair on the right side of IRA man's head fell to the ground with the rest.

"Now he looks like Curly," Manning said.

McHiggins was openly crying now. "I got it from Damon O'Keefe. He's the one who gets all our weapons."

"That's much better, Bobby," James said. "Now, just one more thing and you can go."

McHiggins looked up, his eyes filled with surprise, his face a mask of new hope.

"I want you to take us to meet this Damon O'Keefe," James said.

"My God!" McHiggins cried. "They'd kill me sure!"

"And I'll slit your throat if you don't."

Stony Man Farm

AT THE BOTTOM of the ramp that led to Aaron Kurtzman's computer terminal, Tokaido, Delahunt and Wethers went about their various tasks. At the top, Kurtzman typed furiously, as well. He had been joined by John Kissinger, who had rolled another chair up the ramp and now sat next to the computer wizard. A leather briefcase lay open at his feet.

Two pistols rested in Kissinger's lap, a Colt Government Model 1911 .45, and one of the

Eliminator semiautos. "One of the main differences, Bear," Kissinger said as Kurtzman stopped typing and allowed his machine to digest the information he had just fed it, "is the steel itself. Look at this." He handed over the Colt.

Kissinger continued to talk as Kurtzman took the pistol. "Like most quality firearms, unless they're stainless steel, this Colt is made out of chrome-moly 4140 carbon steel." He waited as the computer man examined the weapon, then lifted the other semiauto from his thigh. "Now, look at this piece of crap. You can see the obvious difference on the surface—the components have been stamped out instead of machined. But there's more. Feel the slide. It's zinc. The other pieces are made out of sheet steel. Now…"

The armorer took the Colt back, disassembled it as easily and quickly as most men opened a beer can, then did the same to the unmarked model. He handed Kurtzman the slides from both weapons. "Have a feel."

Kurtzman frowned as he hefted the Colt in his right hand, the Eliminator in his left. "The Eliminator's slide feels twice as heavy," he commented.

"Well, not quite twice. But it's appreciably heavier. It has to be. The Eliminator has no lockup—it's a straight blowback design." He watched Kurtzman's brain work behind his eye-

brows. The man in the wheelchair wasn't a firearms expert, but he had one hell of an analytic
mind. He understood immediately what Kissinger
was talking about.

"Straight blowbacks are usually used on
smaller calibers, aren't they, such as .22s, .380s
and the like?"

"Right."

"So something in a big caliber like the .45
would blow the slide right off if it wasn't this
heavy?"

Kissinger smiled. "Right again, O Great Cy-
bernetic Sahib."

The whimsical title brought a smile to Kurtzman's face. "I assume that's one of the reasons
these are faster and cheaper to produce," he said,
looking down at the Eliminator. "But I'd also
have to deduct that they wouldn't be as accurate
or controllable or reliable."

"Right on all counts. But these Eliminators
aren't all that inaccurate, uncontrollable or unre-
liable," he added. "It'll still get the job done.
Take a 230-grain full-metal-jacket hardball slug
in the heart, or brain stem, from this rattle-trap
Eliminator and you'll be just as dead as if it came
from a Colt."

"So, from my point of view," Kurtzman said,
thinking ahead several steps as he handed both
slides back to Kissinger, "I need a breakdown on

the makeup of these particular steel composites. If I get that, I may be able to trace the specific batch the steel in these guns came from.''

''What do you mean 'if'?'' Kissinger grinned as he pulled a sheaf of papers from his briefcase. ''You got.'' He handed them to Kurtzman. ''This breaks down, into the most-simple components, each example of the Eliminator single-shots and semiautos I've gotten in to examine. Looks to me like they're all made out of steel from the same place.'' He paused. ''The compounds differ a trivial amount from one another, but that's to be expected. My hunch is our buddy the Eliminator is buying his steel from just one source.''

''Any guesses on who that might be?'' Kurtzman asked, his gaze glued to the pages in his lap.

Kissinger shrugged. ''This stuff is simple to make. It's produced all over the world. It could be Pittsburgh or Tokyo or Barcelona or Moscow. But we're starting to get out of my field now. I know steel from the point of view of an armorer, Bear. I know how to build guns, make them shoot and fix them when they've quit shooting. I know how to make knives and swords and what the best steels are that go into them. And I was able to run the tests on these steel compounds.'' He looked down at the pages still in Kurtzman's lap, then back up to meet the computer wizard's eyes. ''But for what you're trying to do now, my friend, you need a metallurgist." He paused again. "And last time I checked the roster around here, we didn't have one on staff. Happen to know a good one?"

"Not off the top of my head," Kurtzman said, turning toward the phone. "But I *do* know a guy who knows at least one of everything."

Kissenger nodded. "Leo," he said.

A moment later Kissinger had Leo Turrin on the intercom line. He punched the speakerphone button so Kissinger could listen, and said, "Leo, we've got a problem."

Turrin listened as Kurtzman explained the situation. In addition to being Stony Man Farm's undercover specialist, Turrin was a Washington lobbyist, and had contacts in every corner and crevice on the planet.

"Glenn Barrister's the guy you need," Turrin said. "Ever heard of him?"

Kurtzman glanced at Kissinger, who shrugged. "Uh-uh," Kurtzman said.

"Ph.D. and full professor at the University of Pittsburgh," Turrin said. "He's been in research for thirty years and knows more about the business than anybody alive."

The words had no more than left Turrin's mouth than one of the other lights along the row at the bottom of Kurtzman's phone lit up. "Hold on a second, Leo," the computer man said. "I've got another call coming in.'' He punched Turrin onto Hold and tapped the button above the flashing red light. "Kurtzman.''

"I've got Striker on the line,'' Barbara Price said into his ear. "Want me to patch him through?''

"Sure.''

A moment later Mack Bolan said, "Hello, Bear.''

"What can I do for you, big guy?''

"I've got some new intel. Our buddy the Eliminator is stepping up operations and getting into the big leagues.'' He had begun to explain about the new Eliminator M-3 grease guns and the strange Oriental character on the wooden crate when Kurtzman stopped him.

"Hang on a second, Striker. I've got Leo on the other line. It might be helpful if he hears all this.'' He tapped more buttons and connected both Bolan and Turrin to the speakerphone. Turning to his side, he caught Akira Tokaido's attention and waved the young Japanese to the top of the wheelchair ramp.

The Executioner started over with the new intel. He finished by describing as best he could the Japanese, Chinese or Korean character he'd found on the crate.

"You recognize it?'' Kurtzman asked Tokaido. Tokaido shook his head. "No, Striker,'' he said. "I'm sorry. From your description it sounds like Japanese *kanji,* but many other symbols in the three languages are similar. Do you have a fax machine available?"

"Grimaldi has a portable on board the plane."

"Good," Tokaido said. "Please fax me your drawing as soon as possible. In the meantime my guess—perhaps an educated guess but a guess nonetheless—is that it's Japanese."

"That's educated enough for me to head toward Tokyo," Bolan said.

"Okay, gentlemen," Kurtzman said. "Let's sum the situation up so far. We've got guns that appear to have been made from steel that came from the same place." He glanced toward Kissinger.

"Right."

"And we've got an Oriental letter that we're guessing is Japanese."

This time it was Tokaido who spoke. "Affirmative, boss man."

"So Striker is going to get Grimaldi into the air, head toward Japan and fax us his drawing on the way."

"You got it, Bear," Bolan said.

"As soon as I get the fax, I'll enter it, and all the information about the specific steel, into the program, then start tapping into the computer files of the biggest Tokyo steel manufacturers. If the character turns out to be Korean or Chinese, we'll alter the plan accordingly. And Striker, of course, will head toward whichever country is relevant." Kurtzman paused to take a breath. "Leo, I'll need you to arrange for a team of blacksuits to grab this Barrister fellow and bring him here. Can you handle that?"

"The man's as good as blindfolded now."

Kurtzman ran a hand through his hair. "Any questions, guys?" he asked.

"No," Bolan said. "Let's move."

CHAPTER FIVE

Brooklyn, New York

Rosario Blancanales leaned on the cane in his left hand, limping up the four flights of stairs to where Eddie Caveretti had told the men of Able Team "Bobby" lived. Lyons and Schwarz had stayed with Caveretti in the car, sending Blancanales to recon the building alone. There was a good chance violence would erupt, and they wanted to know everything there was to know about the place in order to minimize the chances that innocents in other apartments suddenly found bullets flying through their already crumbling walls.

When he reached the fourth floor, the Able Team warrior limped down the hall. He could tell which apartment the Falcons were in long before he saw the number 411 on the door. Loud rock music blasted into the hallway, shaking the walls with the heavy beat of bass. He stopped halfway to the apartment, ducking quickly into the open door to the common bathroom.

Blancanales locked the door behind him and walked swiftly to the mirror over the sink. He had messed up his slightly over-the-ear hair and wore a ragged brown cardigan sweater over a white ribbed undershirt. In one of the sweater's front pockets a half-full pouch of chewing tobacco threatened to fall out each time he took a step. Soiled khaki work pants and rope-soled slip-on sneakers completed his "old man" outfit.

Satisfied with his appearance, Blancanales left the bathroom and walked along the creaking wooden hall floor to apartment 411. He took a deep breath, then knocked.

The knock went unnoticed under the music.

Blancanales knocked again, louder this time. A moment later the door swung open. The music blew out of the apartment along with a substantial dose of marijuana smoke. The Able Team warrior found himself facing a man in his early twenties who wore a green T-shirt with the now familiar swooping bird on the chest.

"Yeah?" he said. "What do you want, old man?" The cigarette dangling from the corner of his mouth moved up and down with the words.

Blancanales let a nervous smile creep across his face. "Can you tell me which apartment the Choate family is in?" he said in a slightly trembling voice. He had seen the name on a second-floor mailbox on the way up.

The punk with the cigarette grinned evilly. Like all predators, whether two-legged or four, he could smell fear. And he dearly loved to take advantage of anyone weaker than himself. "No, I don't know any fuckin' Choate family," he said around the cigarette. "Who are you? Their great-grandpa?" Behind him several voices laughed above the blasting music.

As they talked, Blancanales had been studying the area behind the young man in his peripheral vision: a living room, looked like a kitchen area just to the side, one bedroom—he could see the piles of dirty clothes on the bare striped mattress beyond where another Falcon reclined on a threadbare couch. The apartment was in the corner of the building, meaning wild shots or over-penetrating bullets to two of the four sides would probably be stopped by the brownstone on the outer walls. But that still left the two other directions—walls that looked like a slow-pitched softball would drill through them, let alone 9 mm bullets traveling at 1400-plus feet per second.

Two more members of the street gang joined the man with the cigarette. "What the hell's this old fart want, Deuce?" a short, powerfully built man asked.

"Wants some Choates. Ain't that some kind a baby pig or somethin'?"

A taller man, looking to be close to thirty, and far cleaner than the other two, stepped in on Bobby the Deuce's other side. "That's a *shoat*, you stupid asshole," he said. "You ain't never been on a farm and seen a pig?"

"Ain't too many pig farms where I grew up. As for pigs, I ain't never met one. But I've woke up with a bunch of 'em."

The Falcons all laughed as if it were the first time they'd heard the joke.

"Okay," Bobby the Deuce said, turning his attention back to Blancanales. "Choate, shoat, don't make no difference. We ain't got none of either, you old peckerhead."

Blancanales had seen what he'd come to see. He had the layout of the apartment and could tell there were at least six Falcons inside. He hadn't seen any weapons. But he knew they'd be there. "Thank you," he said. "Sorry to have bothered you." He had turned to limp away when he suddenly felt his feet fly out from under him.

The Able Team warrior's first instinct was to catch his balance. And his hand almost shot toward the Beretta 92 stuffed into the back of his pants beneath the sweater. But Rosario Blancanales had worked undercover in role camouflage far too long to make rookie mistakes like that. He let himself fall to the floor like a man thirty years his senior might do. The cane flew from his hand and went skipping along the dirty wooden floor. He landed facedown amid a loud chorus of laughter behind him. He rolled over to his side, grimacing as if in great pain, and looked up into the face of the man who had tripped him.

The cigarette was bobbing up and down again, smoke curling from the end up over his face, as Bobby the Deuce cackled uncontrollably at his own joke.

Rising slowly to his hands and knees, Blancanales crawled toward where his cane had come to rest against the wall. He had reached out to pick up it up when a foot flew into his vision and kicked the stick away again. More laughter followed as the Deuce repeated the performance two more times before finally allowing the "old man" to grasp the staff and pull himself to his feet.

"Get the fuck out of here, you old fart," Bobby said.

Then to his friends he added, "Come on. I need some more weed."

Blancanales limped slowly toward the stairs, keeping it up even after he'd heard the door to apartment 411 slam shut. To anyone watching, he appeared to be just another old man who'd been humiliated by street punks and was impotent to do anything about it.

Unless you saw his face.

Blancanales smiled as he started down the stairs. "Bobby the Deuce," he said, chuckling lowly, "you and your friends are about to get a *big* surprise."

In the Air above Sydney, Australia

JACK GRIMALDI HAD barely gotten the PacAero Learstar—a high-speed, long-range, custom-equipped executive version of the Lockheed Model 18-56 Lodestar—off the runway by the time Bolan had set up the portable fax machine and plugged it into the control panel. Pulling the scrap of paper from his pocket, he pressed it onto the screen, then lowered the cover.

A moment later the fax was on its way to America.

The Learstar picked up speed as it burst into the clouds, then rose above the billowy ivory vapors. Grimaldi whistled softly, stopping now and then to make radio contact with the air-traffic controllers.

Bolan glanced at his old friend, the ghost of a smile tugging at his lips. The two men had fought the good fight together more times over the years than he could remember. Grimaldi had been an ace fighter pilot in Vietnam, then after the war, during a weak and financially strapped moment, he'd become a pilot for the Mob. Bolan had met him during that time, recognized the basic good in the man and gotten Grimaldi out of the mess he'd gotten himself into.

From then on loyal beyond what most men would consider good reason to the Executioner, Grimaldi was now a permanent fixture at Stony Man Farm. He flew for all of the teams but was always there for Bolan first.

Bolan reached behind him and pulled the box he had picked up at the Sydney American Express office into the front seat. Setting it in his lap, he used the Applegate-Fairbairn fighting knife to slice open the tape. Inside he found the items he'd requested from Cowboy Kissinger.

The Glock 21 was in its original plastic box. It had been fitted with an Aro-Tek Model 2010 laser sight. The state-of-the-art sighting system utilized a red-orange dot that was projected onto its target and showed up as a one-quarter-inch spot at fifteen yards. Nevertheless the 2010 had an optimum range of five hundred yards at night, and ten yards in sunlight. More important than that, perhaps, it utilized a red "splash" light around the dot; when aimed and activated at the upper chest of a man, it would illuminate his face and enable the shooter to identify his target without the need for a flashlight.

The Executioner dug farther through the box

until he found the custom-made holster. The leather had been specially cut to fit around the tiny nipple on the front of the Glock's trigger guard that housed the laser bulb. Extra magazines and an ample supply of .45-caliber ammunition in both 230-grain Hydra-Shok hollowpoint and armor-piercing rounds were also in the box.

Bolan hadn't specified the solid, pointed Ap rounds. But knowing the Desert Eagle was temporarily out of commission, and that he might need the impressive penetration the .44 Magnum bullet had provided, Kissinger had included them.

The Executioner dug deeper and came across a black-and-blue box displaying a sword embedded in stone, reminiscent of the legend of King Arthur. Gerber Legendary Blades read the end of the box, and beneath that was Applegate Combat Folder. He opened the box and pulled out the knife and a nylon sheath with a holsterlike thumb-break retainer. Stripping the protective plastic cover from the knife itself, he examined the weapon.

Like the full-size Applegate-Fairbairn fighter he now carried, the liner-locking folder possessed a handle frame and spring made of an aircraft-grade titanium alloy. The scales, complete with the traditional Applegate longitudinal grip grooves, were of black linen Micarta. Bolan pressed his thumb against the large checkered thumb stud and flicked the blade open with his fingernail. On one side of the blade were the engraved signatures of Rex Applegate and W. E. Fairbairn. On the other were the words First Production Run.

Bolan nodded his approval. He had wanted this smaller and foldable fighting knife to use in plainclothes. The new knife had only recently come on the market, and Bolan knew the weapon would be in high demand. Kissinger had done his job well in procuring it.

Glancing at his wristwatch, Bolan realized the fax had had more than enough time to reach Stony Man Farm. He leaned forward, lifted the cellular telephone from its clip on the control panel and punched in one of Barbara Price's numbers. To guard against curious ears that might try to tap into Stony Man conversations, the phone was programmed to automatically bounce the connection to numbers on four different continents before it finally reached the Blue Ridge Mountains.

"Akira's looking at the fax now," the mission controller told Bolan. "I'll connect you."

Bolan heard a series of clicks, then Aaron Kurtzman's familiar voice said, "Bad news, Striker."

"What is it?"

"Let me put you on speakerphone so Akira can tell you himself."

The Executioner heard another click, then Akira Tokaido said, "Actually there's both good news and bad news. Here's the skinny. The character is definitely Japanese *kanji*. The bad news is it means 'box' or 'crate'. It simply reinforced the obvious. It's a container."

Bolan let his breath out in disappointment, then forced his brain into a more positive mode. "Okay," he said. "It would have been useful if it had been a name or address, but the reality of the situation is it's not. What's happened here is that the company that makes the crates made up a special order—for a client that didn't want that company's name, or anything else, on the crate that might eventually be traced back to him. But somehow one of the characters in their stamping or logo accidentally got on the wood. Maybe whoever was in charge didn't get it off the regular assembly line fast enough and didn't notice it. Maybe he did see it but thought since it said only 'box' it wouldn't matter. There are a million explanations as to how the thing got on the crate. But that's not what's important. What is, is whether we can make use of it." He waited a moment, then said, "So. Can we?"

"There may be hope, however slight, Striker," Tokaido replied. "We *do* know that it is Japanese *kanji*, so you're at least heading to the right country. I'll enter the character into my files, tap into the computer records of Japan's major box and crate companies and begin looking at their labels and other logos. Who knows? We might get a match.''

"Okay, I'm heading on to Tokyo. Bear, see what you can come up with on the steel angle. Akira, go ahead with what you just suggested. It's as good as any other lead we've got right now. I'll get back to you as soon as we touch down and see if either of you has come up with something.'' He tapped the button, ending the call and replaced the cellular phone in the clip.

Bolan leaned back, closing his eyes for a few moments. Grimaldi continued to whistle, the soft music and the hum of the jet engines almost putting the Executioner to sleep. When they hit an air pocket and dropped sharply, he opened his eyes again. "Jack, once we touch down, I don't know where I'll be going or how long I'll be.''

Grimaldi stopped whistling. "So what else is new?'' he said. "Same song, verse 547.''

"I'll take this cellular with me.'' Bolan unclipped the phone again and dropped it into a pocket. "You still have another one in the back?''

Grimaldi nodded as he began dropping the aircraft through the clouds again. "In one of the lockers.''

"Okay. Keep the phone with you. I'll call you if and when we need to take off again. And stay close enough to the airport that you can have this bird warmed up and ready to go by the time I get here.''

''You got it,'' Grimaldi agreed.

Bolan glanced over his shoulder toward the rear of the plane. ''By the way,'' he said. ''Do we have any yen on board?'' Along with weapons, extra clothing and other equipment, Stony Man's air fleet tried always to carry a reasonable amount of currency for the major nations of the world.

''Try locker number 6.''

The jet dropped back through the clouds. Far below, Bolan could see the blue waters of the Sea of Japan. Beyond on the horizon, and slightly to the west of their flight path, were the tops of the undersea mountains known as the islands of Kyushu and Shikoku. Dead ahead lay Honshu, with Tokyo approximately halfway up the east coast of Japan's largest island.

Also ahead, the Executioner hoped, lay the answer to where the steel that made up the Eliminators, and the crates in which they were packed, came from.

Northern Ireland

BOBBY MCHIGGINS SEEMED unable to take his eyes off Calvin James, T. J. Hawkins observed during the drive from Dunluce Castle into Londonderry. Except, of course, when James happened to glance the IRA man's way. Each time that happened, McHiggins would quickly avert his own gaze, usually looking straight down at the floor of the minivan.

Hawkins chuckled under his breath. James had put on quite a performance.

Hawkins settled in against the seat as the minivan moved through the night. As usual O'Prunty was behind the wheel with McCarter riding shotgun. In the middle seat, McHiggins was squashed between Manning's powerful shoulders and the impetus of his terror, Calvin James. Hawkins and Rafael Encizo occupied the vehicle's rear seat.

Hawkins watched through the windows as O'Prunty guided the minivan into the city, turning onto a winding lane that took them through the nighttime traffic and past the lighted windows of the Georgian and Victorian buildings in the main business and shopping district of the town. Leaving the original walled area, they crossed Cragavon Bridge, where modern Londonderry had grown up along the River Foyle to be ten times as large as the old city.

They were headed, Hawkins knew, to the home of Damon O'Keefe.

"Tell me when to turn," O'Prunty said behind the steering wheel.

McHiggins nodded. Two miles later he said, "Here. To the right."

O'Prunty made the turn and drove slowly up a steep hillside into an older residential section of Victorian houses. Thatched roofs covered some of the homes, which were all crowded tightly together. McHiggins guided them through several more turns, then finally past a small frame dwelling painted a soft shade of green. The paint was fresh, the yard immaculate. Hawkins was mildly surprised at the up-keep—it wasn't the run-down warren he'd have expected an IRA weapons procurer to live in. Two vehicles were parked in the driveway: a plain Ford hatchback and a small, 50 cc Yamaha motorbike.

O'Prunty drove two more blocks, then pulled over to the curb in front of a small neighborhood park.

O'Prunty shifted the minivan into Park and killed the engine. "That's it, then, is it?" he said.

"Aye," McHiggins answered in a wavering voice that proved he hadn't yet recovered from Calvin James's wild interrogation. "O'Keefe lives there with his mom."

"What?" O'Prunty said as he stomped the parking brake. "You said nothing about his mom!"

"I didn't think to tell you," McHiggins said

shakily. "Didn't know it was important." He glanced at James.

"Not important!" O'Prunty shouted in disgust.

"It does throw a little different light on things," McCarter said from the passenger seat. He turned in his seat and rested one arm over the back. "Could you tell who was home when we went by?" he asked.

McHiggins coughed nervously. "By the car and motorbike, I'd say they both were," he said. "Damon rides the Yamaha, although he'll drive his mom's car on occasion. Though I can't be sure."

McCarter turned back to the front and took a deep breath. McHiggins started to speak again, and the Phoenix Force leader cut him off. "Shut up," the Briton said. "I need a minute to think."

Hawkins waited patiently along with O'Prunty, McHiggins and the rest of Phoenix Force as the seconds turned to minutes. Finally McCarter turned to face the rear of the van again. "T.J.," he said, "we've got to get her out of the house somehow. Do you still have that silly-looking book bag in your gear?"

Hawkins laughed. What the Phoenix Force leader was referring to wasn't really a book bag—it was a backpack in which he sometimes carried odds and ends to keep them from getting lost at the bottom of his larger duffelbag. "Got it."

McCarter nodded. "Okay. Get it out and get into some jeans and a T-shirt and anything else you've got that'll make you look like the typical American college kid who cut classes this semester and is thumbing his way across Europe on Daddy's money. You're the youngest. You've got the best chance of pulling it off."

Hawkins opened the duffel in the storage area just behind him and began to rummage through his personal gear. Two minutes later he was dressed in baggy blue jeans, a T-shirt bearing the emblem of Munich's famous beer hall, the Hoffbrau Haus, and worn running shoes. He piled several other shirts and items into the backpack to fill it out, slipped his Beretta 92 beneath the T-shirt and looked up for further orders.

"Blimey!" O'Prunty said in a loud, mirthful voice. "You're perfect—I've seen a million of you polluting the roads and overflowing the hostels. All ye need is a Swiss Army knife!"

Hawkins laughed, pulled one from his duffel bag and slid the pouch onto his belt.

O'Prunty grinned, shaking his head in disbelief.

McCarter handed a map over the seat to James, who passed it back to Hawkins.

Hawkins glanced down and saw it was a map of Ireland.

"We're going to wait awhile," McCarter said. "Let them get good and tired around the TV. Then I want you to go up to the front porch and knock. If O'Keefe's mother answers, point at the map and start asking directions. As soon as you hear us kick the back door, grab her, pull her outside and take her to the ground. Stay on top of her until one of us comes out and gives you the all-clear. I want to make sure this woman doesn't get hurt, and I don't want O'Keefe dead, either. We need him alive."

"Gotcha," Hawkins said. "And what if O'Keefe answers the door himself?"

"Grab him the same way. Do your best not to kill him." Even in the semidarkness, Hawkins could see McCarter frowning in concentration.

The men of Phoenix Force settled in to wait. Most of them closed their eyes, and a few minutes later Hawkins heard the sound of snoring as they took advantage of the short downtime to get some rest. He tried to sleep himself but found he was too wound up waiting to play the part McCarter had assigned him.

Finally McCarter said, "All right, everybody up."

Eyes began to open around the minivan.

"Walk slowly, T.J.," the Phoenix Force leader said. "Give us time to get set up in back."

Hawkins nodded as he slipped the backpack

straps over his shoulders. "Affirmative. Anything else?"

McCarter shook his head. James slid the door open, and Hawkins stepped out into the night.

As he'd been ordered, the Phoenix Force warrior walked slowly back along the street, looking at the map in his hands in case any curious eyes might be on him. He heard the rest of the team get out and close the doors, then saw them jog past and cut around the block to the narrow alley that ran behind the houses with Manning holding McHiggins by the arm. When he was certain that they'd had time to reach the rear of O'Keefe's home, he picked up his pace and mounted the steps to the porch.

Hawkins shifted the open map to his left hand, readjusted the Beretta between his belt buckle and navel, then reached up and rapped on the freshly painted wooden door frame.

A moment later the door opened. Hawkins looked up from the map and tried to keep hidden the surprise that suddenly tightened his chest. The person standing just inside the door wasn't Damon O'Keefe or his mother. It was a burly red-haired Irishman with tattoos covering muscular forearms. Behind him, stretched out on the couches and slumping in chairs, were at least ten other men who might as well have had Irish Republican Army signs hanging around their necks.

And each and every one of them had a pistol on his belt or a rifle or submachine gun within reach.

Brooklyn, New York

THE TIME for action had come.

Carl Lyons exited the Chevy van, slid the side door open and climbed into the back where Schwarz and Blancanales had already opened the equipment lockers and were suiting up for the battle about to take place. Quickly doffing his sport coat, shirt, slacks and street shoes, he slid into the blacksuit handed to him by Schwarz.

Out of the corner of his eye, he saw Eddie Caveretti staring in amazement. "Who in hell *are* you guys?" the Falcon hit man asked. "You don't look like Family anymore."

"We're not," Schwarz said. "We're worse." Then, in his best Rambo voice, he added, "We're your worst nightmare."

Lyons wrapped the black nylon equipment belt around his waist and slid the .357 Magnum Colt Python into the holster on his hip. Transferring four speedloaders into the caddie just in front of the revolver, he slid his arms into the black leather shoulder rig and cinched the keepers to the gun belt on both sides. Lyons's Colt Gold Cup pistol, complete with sound suppressor, went into the holster under his left arm. Two extra 10-round magazines filled with .45 Hydra-Shok bullets were snapped in the carrier under his right. Hanging under the mags was a sheathed Applegate-Fairbairn Mini-Smatchet boot knife.

The Able Team leader pulled a long trench coat from a hanger inside one of the lockers and shrugged into it. His Atchisson 12 automatic assault shotgun came down off the rack, and he looped the sling around his neck, then slid it under the tail of the long coat. It would bulge, and anyone looking closely would know he was carrying something. But it would take only a few seconds to get from the van to the tenement house.

Besides, he wasn't going undercover. The men of Able Team were going to war.

Schwarz looked up as he tied the laces at the tops of his black nylon combat boots. Like Blancanales, he wore a blacksuit, a Beretta 92 and a shoulder rig that held a 50-round Calico M-950 A machine pistol on a sling under his right arm. The same rig carried an extra 100-round cylindrical drum mag on the left. Able Team's electronics man nodded toward Caveretti. "What do you want to do with Eddie boy, Ironman?" he asked. "We can't leave him here."

"No," Lyons agreed. "We'll take him with us."

"No!" Caveretti shouted. "Shit, no! They see

me with you, I'll never be able to walk the streets again!"

"Hey," Blancanales said as he pulled a box of shotgun shells off a locker shelf and tossed them to Lyons, "look on the bright side. You probably won't even live through the night."

Caveretti's lips clamped shut.

Lyons caught the box and looked down at the label, which read 12-Gauge, #8 Birdshot. It certainly wasn't what he'd usually stoke the Atchisson with for combat, but this was a special situation. Blancanales had explained about the thin walls on two sides of Bobby the Deuce's apartment, and the fact that stray rounds or overpenetrations focused on the other two directions might fly through the windows and onto the streets. So the men had replaced their usual high-speed 9 mm rounds with subsonic frangible bullets. Lyons had mild .38 Specials in his .357, and replacing his double-aught buckshot with the dove and pigeon loads was the final step. No, he thought again, the #8 birdshot was hardly his favorite load. But at the close quarters at which they'd be working, the miniature BBs would be deadly if shots were properly placed.

The Able Team leader racked the buckshot out of the Atchisson and inserted the lighter shells. That was what it was all about after all, he knew. Shot placement. You could argue 9 mm versus

.45 all day long if you wanted. A .22 Long Rifle round in the heart or head stem still beat a .44 Magnum bullet in the toe.

"Ready?" Lyons asked the rest of the team.

Schwarz and Blancanales both nodded.

"Hey wait...listen..." Caveretti pleaded.

Schwarz threw open the sliding door, and Lyons grabbed the Falcon by the arm and threw him out. Caveretti landed on his belly and sucked air.

"Keep your mouth shut, Eddie," Lyons ordered. "You're a street punk who kills innocent people for a living." He dropped to the pavement, reached down and jerked the man back to his feet. "You're a hit man. Not a very good one, maybe, and not nearly as tough as you think you are, but a murderer nonetheless. If you live through this, we'll let you go. If you don't—" the Able Team leader shoved Caveretti down the street in front of him "—you deserve anything you get."

Taking up a swift pace, the three men in trench coats and the one in the bright green Falcon jacket walked down the street toward the front door of the brownstone. They mounted the crumbling concrete steps, entered the hall and made their way up the stairs to the fourth floor. The deafening rock music Blancanales had warned them of still blasted into the hall, and the sweet aroma of marijuana smoke filled the air.

Three trench coats fell to the moldy carpet as they approached apartment 411.

"Kick it?" Schwarz asked in a normal voice as they stopped just outside the door. Considering the pandemonium that came from Bobby the Deuce's, there was no need to whisper.

Lyons shook his head. "I've got a better idea." Pulling the Atchisson from around his neck, he grabbed Caveretti by the back of the collar of his Falcon jacket and slammed the hit man into the door with all his strength.

Caveretti's nose made first contact. Blood spurted onto the wood as the lock snapped and the door swung open. The human battering ram screamed as he was propelled into Bobby the Deuce's living room and fell to the floor.

Lyons and Schwarz went next, followed by Blancanales. The Able Team leader moved immediately to the left, covering that half of the battle area, while Schwarz took the right. Blancanales would work the back, covering their rear and giving both men backup and support.

For a brief second, the mouths of all eight men lounging around the filthy living room fell open. Then a man in a ragged blue chair drew a Browning pistol from his belt, leaned forward and aimed at Lyons.

As he heard the Browning's hammer cock back, Lyons pulled the Atchisson's trigger. A load of birdshot struck the Falcon squarely in the chest from a distance of less than five feet. With no time to spread into a pattern, the tiny grains of lead, many of the gases generated by the explosion and even the wadding from the shell entered the man's chest almost as one unit.

A gaping black hole appeared as the gangster was thrown back against the chair.

The sounds of subsonic 9 mm gunfire met the Able Team leader's ears as Schwarz and Blancanales opened up with their Calicos. In his peripheral vision, Lyons saw three men on the other side of the room go down, jerking against the automatic fire like marionettes on the strings of a mad puppeteer. He swung the shotgun toward a man with a long knife scar on the side of his face, who was bringing a sawed-off double-barreled shotgun into play.

Lyons seriously doubted that the double-barrel was filled with the low-penetrating birdshot. If the man got off a round, it would likely go through the wall behind the Able Team leader and all the way into one of the apartments on the other side of the hall.

He couldn't afford to let that happen.

Stroking the Atchisson's trigger once more, Lyons felt the mild recoil of the light load. Dozens of tiny holes appeared on the shotgunner's face around and over the knife scar. The Falcon's head snapped back as if pulled by the long dirty-blond hair that hung from the back of his head. His face turned red from the blood seeping out of the many minuscule holes.

Lyons took two steps forward, lowered his weapon and pulled the trigger again. At the closer range, the Atchisson's next round hit the man in the chest with almost as much force as the load that had taken out the Falcon on the chair. He dropped to the floor as the Able Team leader saw a short man who looked like a power-lifter. The man had no gun, and he had more guts than sense. Instead of taking cover, he sprinted across the room with a butcher knife in his hand.

The former LAPD detective let him get close enough for the birdshot to do maximum damage, then cut loose with two rounds. The first hit the muscle boy just above the heart, ruining a pectoral that had to have taken years to build. The second load caught him squarely between the eyes, blowing off the top half his face and the greasy hair atop his head.

The Calicos continued to chatter on the other side of the room. A few rounds from various Falcon weapons exploded, and Lyons silently prayed that none of them had struck Schwarz or Blancanales or exited the walls to harm innocents in the other apartments.

The Able Team leader turned the Atchisson toward the final man in his sector, a tall man who appeared to be a little older than the others. The man had produced one of the Eliminator .45 autos and was turning it toward Lyons.

The former LAPD cop took him out with one fast round to the chest, another to the face. He went down as the chatter from the Calicos ended, and suddenly the apartment fell silent.

Lyons turned toward Blancanales. "Which one was Bobby the Deuce?" he asked.

Blancanales walked to a corpse wearing a blood-splattered white T-shirt. A burning cigarette had fallen from Bobby the Deuce's mouth and lay smoldering on the carpet next to his head. He stepped on it as he said, "This outstanding citizen here."

Lyons shook his head. "We won't be getting any information out of him. Okay, Gadgets, get across the hall and see if anybody in the other apartments took a hit. You should be able to see the entry rounds in the outside walls if there are any. You find a hole, knock. You get no answer, kick it in and see if anyone needs medical attention."

Schwarz nodded and disappeared through the front door.

"Where's Eddie?" Lyons asked, then answered his own question by looking down at the floor where Caveretti had first fallen. The Falcon hit man hadn't moved since, and he never would again.

The back of Caveretti's bright green Falcon jacket was now bright red. He had either taken a wild round from one of his brother Falcons, or they had intentionally put a bullet into him for bringing in the heat.

"There goes our only snitch," Blancanales said.

Lyons nodded. "Yeah, but I think we already had everything he knew about the Eliminators." He looped the Atchisson back around his neck and looked down at the ground. The front room of the apartment was in total chaos. Broken furniture, glass from lamps, stuffing from the chairs and papers of every kind littered the squalid carpet. "Okay, Pol," Lyons said, "we're running on borrowed time. Somebody's bound to have called the cops. Start sifting through this mess for anything that looks like it might be a lead. I'll start in the back."

Lyons moved through the kitchen into the bedroom. Starting on the left side of the room, the former detective systematically searched every nook and cranny in the disheveled cubicle. He found nothing of interest until he came to the closet.

Opening the door, he looked down to see three wooden crates. Bobby the Deuce had made no attempt to hide the two boxes of single-shot pistols or the third crate of .45 imitations. Lyons was about to call Blancanales when he heard the phone in the living room ring.

The Able leader reached the front room just as Blancanales picked up the receiver. "Yeah?" Pol said.

There was a brief pause, then he said, "He can't talk," adopting a strong Brooklyn accent. After another pause, Blancanales said, "Why? 'Cause the Deuce is fuckin' dead, man, that's why. Stupid fuck ODed." Silence fell over the apartment once more as the Able Team commando listened to whatever was being said at the other end of the line.

"Yeah, I got 'em. You want 'em, you gotta deal with me...yeah, yeah...okay. See you there."

He hung up and turned to Lyons. "Biker gang called the Road Kills. Ever heard of them?"

Lyons nodded. "Small club, but up-and-coming. Vicious."

"Anyway, it sounds like they were supposed to buy Eliminators from the Falcons. Guy I talked to called himself Turtle. He's willing to deal with me. Think they might know anything that would help us?"

Lyons shrugged. "I doubt it. Sounds like it's Bobby the Deuce who had the Eliminator connection, and the throttle jockeys are just customers.'' He paused, then shrugged again. ''But we might as well give it a try—unless we want to hunt up the rest of the Falcons. And I doubt they know any more than we do.'' He glanced at Bobby the Deuce lying dead on the floor. ''We've hit a dead end here.''

Blancanales stooped, found a clean green Falcon jacket next to one of the chairs and picked it up. ''Think we can get Cowboy to send us some of the sample guns that've been coming in so we can do the deal?''

Lyons shook his head. ''We won't need to.'' He led Blancanales into the bedroom to the closet.

As they started to lift the crates, Schwarz came back in from the hall.

''Any problems?'' Lyons asked.

Schwarz lowered his gaze to the floor. ''One casualty.''

Lyons felt as if he'd just swallowed a ten-pound rock. It was the nightmare that all of the men operating out of Stony Man Farm constantly lived with—that they would someday be responsible for the death of an innocent citizen who happened to be in the wrong place at the wrong time. He and Blancanales followed their teammate out through the living room and into the apartment directly across the hall.

Schwarz pointed to a corpse in the middle of

the living-room floor, then suddenly his "face of shame" relaxed into a grin. The man had been shooting up with what looked to be heroin when death had claimed him. His arm was still tied off with a bandanna. A dirty spoon, a syringe and other drug paraphernalia littered the carpet next to him. The stray bullet had taken him in the left temple.

And he still wore a bright green jacket with a swooping falcon on the back.

"The Lord do work in mysterious ways," Pol intoned.

Lyons gave Schwarz a stern look, then led the way back across the hall. "You're a barrel of laughs today, Gadgets," he said humorlessly. "But if you think you can stop rehearsing your comedy routine for a little while, I'd like to get the crates out of the closet and down to the van before the cops show up."

Footsteps sounded on the steps in the hallway. Schwarz stuck his head outside for a second, then pulled it back in. "Looks like we're a little late for that."

Lyons blew air through his clenched teeth. "Pol, this kind of situation is your specialty," he said. "Handle it." He turned to Gadgets. "Help me load the weapons."

Blancanales was pulling his Justice ID out of one of the slit pockets of his blacksuit when

Lyons led Schwarz into the bedroom. They found a dolly in the closet next to the crates and loaded them, one on top of the other, into the rack. Both men reached into pockets of their blacksuits, produced their own Department of Justice credentials and clipped them to their chests before wheeling the crates out.

Blancanales was talking to four blue-suited NYPD officers when they hit the living room. With his own ID on the upper left breast of his blacksuit, he looked like he could be a member of any SWAT team, local or federal, in the country.

"Yeah," a young officer said, "now I remember seeing you guys. With Sergeant Waters, right?"

Blancanales glanced at Lyons. He had no choice but to agree. "Yeah. Waters," he said.

"What's in the crates?" a middle-aged sergeant with a beer belly asked as Lyons and Schwarz stopped in front of the door.

"Evidence," Lyons said. "Sorry, we aren't at liberty to divulge what it is just yet."

The sergeant scowled with the jealous anger many local cops had for Feds, but it didn't make any difference.

"Look, guys," Blancanales said, "this is an ongoing investigation. We've got to get to the next stop before word leaks out about what happened here.'' He rubbed his chin as if in deep thought. ''How about we stop by your office later today and give you our reports?''

The middle-aged sergeant nodded, but he didn't like it. ''Okay. We'll seal off the scene and call in the lab techs. We can contact you through Waters if we need to?''

Blancanales glanced at Lyons again before he said, ''Sure.''

Lyons made a mental note to call Hal Brognola. After he, Schwarz and Blancanales left in a few moments, the four officers standing in front of them now weren't likely to ever see the men of Able Team again. Elmo Waters would be taking the heat over it unless Brognola, through his position at the Justice Department, intervened.

Which he would. Waters was a Stony Man blacksuit graduate, and the Farm looked after their own.

''Coming through,'' Lyons said, then pushed the dolly across the threshold as the cops moved away from the door. The elevator was broken, so he and Pol lifted the dolly into the air and carted it down the four flights of steps. They loaded the crates into the back of the van and got in.

''I didn't get a chance to ask you,'' Lyons said as he pulled the van away from the curb. ''You find anything of interest in the living room?''

''Yeah.'' Blancanales grinned as he pulled out

a slip of paper from a pocket and held it where Lyons could see it.

As he turned a corner, the Able Team leader looked down to see the stub from a welfare check.

"These things were all over the place," Blancanales said. "All the Falcons were on the dole." He grinned as he settled back into the passengers' seat. "Never let it be said that the men of Able Team don't do their fair share for welfare reform."

CHAPTER SIX

Tokyo, Japan

Although the Executioner looked at most things a little differently than the rest of the world, his first impression of Tokyo was always similar to any other human being's. A city swarming with people and automobiles traveling bumper to bumper at maniacal speeds, it was a concrete jungle that seemed to extend forever.

Dressed in a conservative blue pin-striped business suit that hid the Beretta under his arm, the laser-equipped Glock on his right hip where the Desert Eagle usually rode, and the Applegate Combat Folder in the horizontal sheath on his belt, Mack Bolan stood more than a head taller than anyone else in Shinoku Station as he made his way through the pushing and shoving horde toward the open doors of the subway train.

As luck would have it, Grimaldi had touched down just in time for Bolan to get caught up in the breakneck morning scramble from the suburbs to the offices. Like the rest of the men and women chatting in Japanese and other languages, he moved with the flow of the crowd, being propelled sometimes right, sometimes left, as the human tidal wave gradually swelled toward the subway train.

Bolan got through the doors, found a tiny corner to squeeze into and reached overhead to grab a strap as the throng continued to jam into the car. When the train finally looked like a college fraternity's attempt to set the record for the number of people in a phone booth, the doors closed while the unfortunates who hadn't boarded pounded the windows and howled curses.

Bolan shook his head. Anyone who still regarded the Japanese as terminally formal and polite had never been to Shinoku, he mused as the train took off.

The Executioner swayed with the rhythm of the train as it moved along the tracks. He had called Stony Man Farm again before leaving Tokyo's Narita International Airport and learned that Kurtzman was still searching for the manufacturer of the steel used in the Eliminators. Tokaido, however, had matched the *kanji* character to the logo used on the boxes of the Takahata Box, Crate and Container Company. With a clear-cut destination now, Bolan had used a taxi to get him from the airport to the station, a little over an hour from Narita.

The train finally came to a stop, and Bolan let himself be pushed through the doors to the platform. The situation at Ueno Station, the city's third-largest and located just northeast of the Imperial Palace, was hardly less crowded. The boarding spot for all trains headed for northern Japan, and the disembarkment point for the cultural and natural attraction center of Ueno Park, it looked like a human ant-farm gone wild. Outside the station, men wearing thousand-dollar suits and carrying computers that sold for five times that much behaved like common street ruffians in their battles to outmaneuver each other for taxis.

The last cab was pulling away when the Executioner exited the station. The only transport left was one of Tokyo's famous luxury *haiya*—or "hire"—cars, and he slipped into the back seat. The driver, dressed immaculately in a Western chauffeur's suit and cap, took off as soon as Bolan gave him the address.

The industrial area of Koto Ward sat southeast of Asakusa near the Sumida River. They crossed the Komagata Bridge, then passed the Kiyosumi Garden before finally coming abreast of a huge manufacturing building. The sign atop the structure was in both *kanji* and English. It read Takahata.

The driver drove on, stopping two blocks farther down at the address the Executioner had given him. The *haiya* car drivers were known to be not only more careful and polite than Japanese cabbies, but they also kept immaculate records of their fares. If any violence broke out at the crate manufacturer's, Bolan didn't want the police tracing him back to the scene. He paid the driver and got out, finding himself in front of a textile factory.

Bolan waited until the car was lost in heavy traffic again before turning and heading back in the direction from which they'd just come. He walked briskly, imitating the fast, on-the-way-to-do-important-business pace of everyone else in Tokyo. He slowed slightly as he reached the front of the box company, eyeballing the strengths and weaknesses of the building and mentally noting soft targets of entry, as well as potential escape routes. The offices looked to be in the front of the building, and the actual manufacturing plant in the rear.

Bolan mounted the steps, then entered the front door and found himself in a reception area. Barely visible above a sea of computer terminals, adding machines, electric typewriters and other office equipment, a petite Japanese woman with jet black hair sat behind a semicircular desk.

Bolan walked up to a break in the electronic forest and smiled. "*O-hayo gozaimasu,*" he said. "English?"

The woman smiled, exhibiting a perfect row of white teeth. "Only what I learned at Brown," she said, giggling, "but I think you'll be able to understand me. And good morning to you. May I help you?"

The Executioner reached into the handkerchief pocket of his suit coat and pulled out a business card he had found in the stack kept aboard the Stony Man Learjet. He handed it to the woman and said, "Morris Hart, Matthews Import and Export, Los Angeles and Tokyo."

The woman barely glanced at the card. "Yes, Mr. Hart. And how can I be of service?"

"We're looking for a new container company," the Executioner said. "I'd like to speak to someone about setting up an account."

The woman's expression hardened ever so slightly. "Do you have an appointment, Mr. Hart?"

"No. I'm sorry. The fact is, I'm in Tokyo on other business and just happened to pass by here in a cab yesterday. Had a little spare time today and thought I'd check things out. You know, do a little extra for the company. Go the extra mile and get a few feathers in my cap, so to speak.''

''Yes, I understand.'' The woman turned to her side, partially hidden behind a computer monitor, and Bolan heard a click.

''Ohara-san,'' her voice said, then she spoke rapidly in Japanese. After several verbal exchanges, she pushed the button again and turned back to Bolan.

''I am sorry,'' she said, ''but the man to whom you should speak will be busy until tomorrow. Is it possible you could—?''

The woman was interrupted by a slender Oriental man who entered the reception area from a side door. In an agitated condition, he immediately calmed when he saw Bolan. ''Excuse me,'' he said, bowing slightly as he stepped up next to the Executioner. ''I do not mean to interrupt. But we are encountering a minor emergency in the labeling section. Would you mind if I spoke with Yoshiko? It will only take a moment.''

''Of course not.'' Bolan smiled like any other pleasant business rep trying to con his way into a meeting without an appointment.

The slender man was dressed in chocolate brown slacks and a white shirt with an open collar. His sleeves had been rolled up to a point just below the elbow. He leaned forward, placed both hands on the edge of the circular desk in front of the receptionist and spoke in a hushed tone. As he did, the sleeve on his left arm rode up slightly higher.

Again Bolan couldn't understand the words. But the quick glance the woman called Yoshiko shot his way before shaking her head made him certain the man had just asked if the foreigner spoke Japanese.

The two conversed for a few moments, then Yoshiko nodded, pressed the intercom button again and spoke while the man hurried back out the way he'd come. A moment later the woman turned back to the Executioner. "Please forgive our rudeness," she said. "As I was about to say, is it possible that you could return at three tomorrow afternoon?"

"Certainly," Bolan said. "And thank you very much." He turned, walked out of the building and down the steps.

The salesman smile faded from Bolan's face as he turned and started along the sidewalk once more. He wouldn't return the next day; he would return that night. The time for con jobs was over, and it was time for an after-hours soft probe of the Takahata Box, Crate and Container Company.

He no longer doubted he was at the right place. He might have seen only the lower half of the tattoo on the forearm beneath the rolled-up sleeve, but that had been enough.

He had seen the tattoo many times before.

It was the mark of the Yakuza, the Japanese Mafia.

The Caribbean

COLONEL HAROLD MADDOX could remember an old expression his first-grade teacher used to use: "When you're angry, the poison flows all through your body."

Right now, Maddox knew, if he bit anyone they'd die faster than if they'd been struck by a cobra.

He turned away from the stack of newspapers on his desk and looked out the window. In the early-morning sun just beginning to rise over the Caribbean, two dozen men were wheeling crates across the ramp from the dock to one of his cargo ships. The crates contained the last shipment of his single-shot pistols. He had phased them out to provide tooling and manpower for the more elaborate weapons—the .45 clone and the new submachine grease guns. The ship would stop to off-load in Miami, New Orleans and finally Houston before it made its way back to Mad Dog Island to take on more freight.

The order was the biggest he'd received yet. It had come in through his front man in the U.S. the week before, during the height of the newspaper publicity the Eliminator had been getting.

The former Army colonel turned back to the newspapers. New stories filled the front pages. Opinions on issues other than the Eliminator and his guns had invaded the editorial columns. The only story relating to him in any of the rags on his desk was the brief account of some damn fool who had committed suicide with one of the single-shots.

Maddox pulled a cigar from the humidor and took his time lighting it. Perhaps Andy Warhol's prediction had been right, he thought. Considering the capabilities of the new information age, everyone would be famous, but only for fifteen minutes.

The phone buzzer next to the papers sounded. Maddox lifted the receiver to his ear and listened. "Yes, Gladwyn," he said a second later, "send him in."

The door opened and Randolph Staggs walked into the office. "Good morning, Colonel."

"Good morning." Maddox waved at the chairs in front of his desk. "Have any trouble last night?"

Staggs took a seat and shook his head. "I waited until after the men were all in the barracks. The tide was still going out." He chuckled and glanced at his watch. "Right about now, anything the sharks didn't get of Donalds ought to be washing up on shore in Panama or Costa Rica."

"Very good." Reaching into the humidor again, he said, "Cigar?" He had never offered any of his expensive Cubans to his men before, and he saw the look of surprise register on Staggs's face.

"Why...sure, Colonel. Thanks." Staggs leaned forward and accepted the long Churchill cigar and a lighter.

Maddox tried not to smile when Staggs lit the cigar exactly the way he would have predicted. Rather than light it slowly and evenly like any man who appreciated fine tobacco, Staggs bit off the end, stuck it in his mouth and held the flame directly against the end. As the cigar began to burn, he would get runners going down the sides that would ruin the evenness of the smoke.

When Staggs was puffing away like the smoke stack on a freight train, Maddox said, "Have you seen Morrison since we met here yesterday afternoon?"

Staggs shook his head. "No, but there's nothing unusual about that. When he's not working, he just disappears into the trees. I know he's good at what he does, but I got to tell you, Colonel, that man's strange with a capital *S*."

Maddox laughed. "You understate, my dear boy. You could capitalize all of the letters of that word, and it would still not come close to doing justice to our Native American friend.''

''Well, anyway,'' Staggs said, letting smoke curl from the corner of his mouth, ''he gives me the creeps.''

Eerily, almost as if Shawnee Morrison had heard them talking about him, the phone buzzed again. Maddox gave the go-ahead to Gladwyn, and a moment later the man walked in and took a seat next to Staggs. Morrison wore his blue jeans tucked into high-topped moccasins constructed of thick black leather. The medicine bag hung around his neck under the collar of a faded work shirt. No weapons were visible.

But Maddox knew they were hidden all over his body.

As usual Morrison seemed to feel no compulsion to speak.

''I take it all went well with you, too?'' Maddox said.

Morrison nodded. ''Denard's body will not be found.''

''Good. I'm afraid I have some rather bad news,'' he said. ''Our friend Donalds is dead.''

Morrison's expression didn't change.

Sometimes Maddox found the Indian's detachment intriguing, other times, like now, it became annoying. ''You don't seem surprised.''

Morrison shook his head. "I knew you had killed him."

"What?"

"I knew you had killed him," Morrison repeated. "Then Staggs dragged him to the south side of the island and let him go out with the tide."

"You saw that?" Maddox asked angrily. If Staggs had been careless enough that Morrison had witnessed his actions, some of the workers might have seen it, as well. The last thing he needed right now was some half-assed peasant uprising....

"No," Morrison said, "I saw blood in the sand and tracks."

He turned to Staggs and said, "You wrapped your arms under Donalds's chest from the back, then you walked backward, dragging him into the sea."

Maddox looked to Staggs, who shrugged, then nodded.

Turning back to Morrison, Maddox took a puff on his cigar and said, "How do you know it was me who killed him? And how do you know it was Staggs who dumped him in the ocean?"

"He wasn't killed on the beach. Not enough blood."

"That doesn't answer my question."

"And I recognized the imprints of Staggs's

boots. I know how Donalds was carried because his heels dug into the sand while Staggs dragged him. They made furrows all the way to the water.''

''That still doesn't tell me why you think *I* killed him and not Staggs.''

Morrison shrugged slightly, his first movement since sitting down. ''Why would Staggs kill him somewhere else, knowing he would have to transport the body all that way?'' he asked. ''He could have easily persuaded Donalds to go down to the beach on some pretense, killed him there and saved himself a lot of trouble. And he wouldn't have risked one of the men seeing him with the body.'' He stopped talking for a moment, then added, ''Which means you did it. Probably in a moment of anger. If you hadn't lost your temper, you'd have had Staggs do it.''

''Hot damn,'' Staggs said, shaking his head in genuine amazement. ''Colonel, we got us a regular Sherlock Holmes here.''

Maddox lifted his humidor and held it out toward Morrison. ''Take *two*,'' he offered.

Morrison took four and stuffed them into the pocket of his work shirt.

Maddox set the humidor back on his desk. ''Donalds was working with Denard.''

Morrison looked him impassively in the eye. ''No, he wasn't.''

The colonel returned the stare. Out of anyone else, it would have appeared to be insolence. But Maddox knew it was just Morrison's way. "Okay, tell me why you think that."

"Because before I killed him, I asked Denard if anyone else on the island was working with him. He said no."

Staggs snickered. "And you don't think he could have lied to you?" he asked.

Morrison turned to face the man. "No," he said. "I don't. I'm known to be very persuasive when I question a man."

"Go ahead," Maddox prompted. "Finish the story."

"Denard told me that by coincidence Donalds had been his college roommate. He had recognized the man immediately but didn't think Donalds remembered him. He thought it better, under the circumstances, to leave it that way."

"And you're sure he was telling the truth?" Maddox asked.

The man's indifferent face suddenly stretched into an enormous, toothy, almost profane smile. His eyes glowed like fiery embers of charcoal as he leaned forward. "Colonel," Morrison said, "by that time, there wasn't enough left of the man to lie."

Then, even faster than it had appeared, the

smile was gone and the apathetic expression fell over Morrison's face once more.

The sudden passion, after all the months of watching the man deadpan his way through events so gruesome most men would have vomited, sent a sudden chill down Maddox's back. He looked at Staggs out of the corner of his eye and saw that Morrison had produced the same result in him.

Suddenly Maddox realized for the first time just what an elaborate and efficient killing machine he had on his hands.

And at the same time, he realized what Randolph Staggs had meant when he'd said that William "Shawnee" Morrison gave him the creeps.

New York City

CARL LYONS HAD DEALT with outlaw bikers ever since his first day as a rookie Los Angeles patrolman. The radio had advised of a disturbance at a residence in south L.A., and he and his partner had quieted the ruckus between a Satan's Saint and the man's slovenly, needle-tracked wife without violence.

But Lyons had left the scene with a definite distaste for the dirty, long-haired man dressed in foul-smelling leather and denim. And it was a first impression that had stayed with him, and been reinforced, ever since.

Night had fallen by the time Able Team pulled into the parking lot of Miss Carriage's Public Tavern just off Flatbush and Atlantic Avenues. At least two dozen Harley-Davidsons were lined up in front of the door, with more in the parking area to the side of the brick building.

Lyons, behind the wheel of the van, shook his head. One thing you had to give the biker rogues of America, he thought—they were patriotic. There wasn't a Japanese motorcycle or a machine from any other country parked on the premises.

The Able Team leader looked up at the flashing sign atop the one-story frame structure. It showed a cartoon mouse dressed in biker regalia seated at a table. One moment the mouse would be sitting there in front of a frothing mug of beer. Then the sign would go dark, and when it reappeared the rodent's head would be tipped back with the mug to its lips. Then the minidrama would begin all over again.

"Cute," Blancanales said from the shotgun seat. "Very cute."

"Not to mention classy," Schwarz said behind him.

Lyons turned in his seat so he could see both men. Like himself, they wore blue jeans and Falcon jackets they had taken from Bobby the Deuce's apartment. Their weapons were hidden beneath the green nylon.

"It occurs to me," Schwarz said, "that we could have trouble in this little hellhole."

"The idea *had* crossed my mind," Lyons told him.

"We taking the Calicos?" Blancanales asked.

Lyons pondered the idea for a moment. The submachine pistols were far too large to be hidden beneath the waist-length Falcon jackets. Maybe the Falcons themselves would abandon their colors in a situation like this in order to carry heavy artillery, but Lyons's gut level feeling was that Able Team needed the props to be convincing. He, Blancanales and Schwarz were all older than the average Falcon, and none of them had had time to get filthy enough to look the part. Maybe there was a way to compromise.

"Gadgets," the Able Team leader said, "slip into your subgun and throw one of the trench coats over the top. Make sure the green jacket can still be seen underneath. You'll be our backup. Pol and I will have to make do with side arms."

Schwarz slid his arms into the nylon harness and then the sleeves of his black trenchcoat. He left the longer coat unbuttoned, with the green lapels of the jacket below on display in the gap.

Lyons, Schwarz and Blancanales exited the van and started toward the front door of the bar. "Nothing like walking right into the mouth of the lion to wake you up," Blancanales said.

"Beats a double espresso any day," Schwarz agreed.

Lyons jerked open the door and led the way inside. He stopped five feet inside the tavern and surveyed the interior of Miss Carriage's as his eyes grew accustomed to the lighting.

The repugnant stench of cigarette and marijuana smoke, mixed with stale beer and body odor, filled the Able Team leader's sinuses. Just to his right was a series of pinball machines and video games, complete with the sounds of buzzers, bells and the explosions of planets blowing up on-screen. A long wooden bar started ten feet in front of him, running almost the entire length of the room. It stopped twenty feet from the back wall, where several green-felted tables stood. Tattooed men in Road Kill colors with loud voices moved about the tables drinking beer as they shot pool.

One man, a fat-faced character with a scraggly beard, sat by himself in a corner. Lyons eyed him briefly, guessing him to be a mental case. His expression kept changing from one of delight to one of pain. Occasionally he closed his eyes and grunted.

Biker gangs had been known to occasionally adopt retarded or mentally ill people, treating them much like mascots, and Lyons wondered if this might be the case here.

Lyons led his teammates up to the bar and ordered three beers. They had just arrived when a clean-shaved biker stood up from one of the tables and walked forward. He had the massive shoulders and chest of an Olympic weight lifter, which threatened to rip his cutoff jean jacket down the back. But unlike most serious muscle men, a long thin neck led from the muscle up to an undersized head. He stopped two feet in front of Lyons and smiled, displaying a row of teeth that should have been used in all grade-school hygiene classes as an example of what happens to those who don't brush.

"You must be Turtle," Lyons said.

The man frowned. "How'd you know?"

Lyons looked at the head, neck and shoulders again. He got the definite feeling that Turtle might just have the ability to pull his head down and make it disappear somewhere inside the overdeveloped trapezius muscles. "Lucky guess," the Able Team leader said.

"What happened to the Deuce?" the biker asked.

"My man here told you this afternoon," Lyons said. "OD."

Turtle nodded. "Too bad. We don't care too much for you street-walkers, but the Deuce had some damn fine connections."

"Yeah, well, we can eulogize him for a while

if you want," Lyons said. "Maybe get a minister in here or somebody to sing 'Amazing Grace.' But I'd just as soon get our business done and go out and 'street-walk' some more. You see, we don't think too much of you bastards, either."

A wicked smile came over Turtle's face. "You got the guns, tough guy?"

"I got the guns."

"Good. We'll take them."

"You got the money?" Lyons had no idea what price Turtle and Bobby the Deuce had agreed upon, or how many of the guns in the van were supposed to go to the Road Kills. But it didn't matter. He didn't plan to let the deal get that far.

As it turned out, Turtle had the same idea.

Two hulking bikers suddenly appeared at Turtle's sides. Both men were well over six feet tall, and each had to weigh more than three hundred pounds. Their smiles were almost as evil as Turtle's.

"I asked you if you had the money," Lyons repeated.

The taller of the two bearded hulks leaned forward slightly and smiled. Breath from hell hit the men of Able Team in the face as he said, "No, we don't have the fuckin' money. But we don't need any, neither."

Turtle turned partially, giving Lyons a view behind him again for a moment. The Road Kill leader pursed his lips and whistled. All of the bikers at the tables stood and began to close in on the bar.

Turtle showed Lyons his cavity-ridden teeth and rotting gums again. "Before we kill you and take your guns," he said, "you want to know why?"

Lyons glanced at his watch. "We've got another stop to make tonight so make it brief."

"Like I said," Turtle went on. "Bobby the Deuce was a good connection. But I know for a fact that none of the other Falcons had any idea where the Eliminators were coming from. So with Bobby dead, the connection dies, too." An Eliminator .45 semiauto suddenly appeared in his hand. "We, on the other hand, *do* have another Eliminator connection. Not as convenient as the Deuce, maybe, but one where we can score when we need to. And with Bobby dead, that leaves no reason in hell why we shouldn't just rip you off of this last load of bang-bangs and go do business with our other friend."

Turtle reached out and jammed the gun into Lyon's forehead.

The big ex-cop didn't hesitate. With a lightninglike movement, he reached up and snatched the weapon out of the man's hand. Turtle's face turned to one of total astonishment, and for a moment no one moved.

Then other guns began to come out.

Lyons spun the Eliminator in his hand and pumped two rounds into Turtle's belly. He had already turned the stamped-out .45 to the biker on the right before the Road Kill leader hit the ground. Another duo of .45s blasted from the Eliminator's barrel, both entering just under the giant's chin and traveling up into his brain.

Next to him, Lyons sensed movement and knew Schwarz and Blancanales were drawing their weapons. Screams filled the room as the biker mamas ran for the doors. The Able Team let them go.

Lyons swung the Eliminator to where Turtle had stood only a second before, shooting the last three rounds in the cheap gun into the other giant biker's chest.

Beside him, he heard the sound of Blancanales's Beretta 92 and the full-auto staccato of Schwarz's Calico. The explosions of other weapons around the room threatened to deafen him as two bullets whizzed past at belt level and drilled through the wooden bar to his rear.

Lyons heard a scream behind him and knew that the bartender had been hit.

The Able Team leader had drawn the Colt Python with his left hand as he pulled the Eliminator's trigger the final time. He wasted no time switching hands as the .45 fell from the fingers of his right. Shooting left-handed, he double-actioned two 125-grain semijacketed hollowpoint rounds toward a Road Kill biker wearing a black eye patch and gold earring. The man-stopper rounds found their target, and the quasipirate slumped to the floor.

A one-armed biker four steps from Lyons turned a stainless-steel S&W Model 66 his way. The man got off one round that sped past the Able Team leader's ear and into the mirror over the bar before Lyons double-tapped him with Magnum bullets. The first .357 round shot into the biker's throat, severing the carotid artery and sending a spray of crimson jetting forth. The second round fell lower, penetrating a heart already emptying of blood.

Out of the corner of his eye, Lyons watched two men drop to Blancanales's Beretta, then saw four more hit the floor after Schwarz had sprayed them with a figure eight of 9 mm rounds.

The Able Team leader turned his attention to a biker in his late teens. The man's face was a combination of ripe acne and the scars of pimples come and gone. He aimed what looked like a Charter Arms Bulldog .44 Special at the bar.

Lyons drew the sound-suppressed Government Model pistol from shoulder leather as he double-actioned the Python dry. The last two .357 Magnum rounds both hit the X-ring in the pimple-faced biker's chest, throwing him backward to the floor. By the time a tall thin Road Kill biker with long, blond, Vikinglike hair had turned the Browning Hi-Power in his hand Lyons's way, the Able Team leader had thumbed the manual safety down on the Colt and had the sights on his sternum.

The sound-suppressed pistol coughed, almost seeming silent compared to the Magnum roar of Lyons's Python. The round hit the bull's-eye, and the Viking went limp, dropping his Browning and slithering to the floor like a dying viper.

Lyons turned, seeing Blancanales drop a man firing a Star semiauto. Schwarz cut loose with another burst from his Calico, and two more bikers' lives came to an abrupt halt. The Able Team leader swung his Government Model back and forth across the room, searching for targets, but none remained.

As the roar in Lyons's ears began to die down, he heard Schwarz's voice. "Lady luck isn't smiling on us these days, Ironman. Again we've got nobody who can talk."

Lyons's gaze moved back to the retarded man at the corner table. The man had remained detached throughout the firefight and hadn't made a move toward Able Team. It wasn't likely that he even knew his own name, let alone anything about the Eliminators.

Then, suddenly, the man let out a scream, followed by a low guttural groan. His face relaxed, his shoulders slumped and he closed his eyes.

Lyons started toward him, the Government Model leading the way. He was three feet from the man's table when the guy looked up.

His gaze moved over the bodies littering the floor, and he shook his head in disbelief. "Who the hell are you? What's going on?"

Before Lyons could comment, a pair of denim-clad buttocks appeared at the side of the table. Next came the red-splotched skin of a bare back wearing a short orange tube top. Finally a face wearing far too much makeup looked up at Carl Lyons.

The woman crawled the rest of the way out from beneath the table and ran a hand across her chin as she rose to her feet.

CHAPTER SEVEN

Londonderry, Northern Ireland

Gary Manning watched T. J. Hawkins get out of the minivan dressed like an American college student and walk toward Damon O'Keefe's house as the rest of Phoenix Force got out and moved to the rear of the vehicle.

Manning opened the swing-out door and reached in, handing a Heckler & Koch MP-5 subgun to Felix O'Prunty and the other members of the team. He started to take one of the German submachine guns for himself, thought a moment, then decided on the Winchester Model 1200 riot gun instead. He dug through an equipment box until he came to a nylon belt with shell loops. The loops were filled with 12-gauge rounds that would be devastating at the close fighting range they were about to encounter. The big Canadian looped the belt over his head.

A moment later Phoenix Force and O'Prunty

were jogging toward the intersecting street at the side of the block that would lead to the alley behind the O'Keefes' house. Manning's eyes fell on the MI-6 man as they ran. The Irish operative was a good man, but Manning could see that the combination of whiskey, inactivity and age were beginning to take their toll. O'Prunty was huffing and puffing furiously after the first half block while the men from Stony Man Farm were not yet even into their stride.

Hawkins disappeared as they made the turn, and Manning fell in behind McCarter. They entered the alley, and a dog began to bark. The Briton motioned for an immediate halt and turned to Manning. "Gary, go ahead and take care of that."

Manning handed McCarter the riot gun and hurried forward, seeing a small hairless form jerking spasmodically just behind the chain-link fence in the backyard next to the O'Keefes' house. He ran forward, vaulted the fence and reached into his pocket at the same time.

The Chihuahua was too startled to move as the big Canadian reached down and grabbed him under the belly, sweeping him off his feet. The shock didn't last long, however, and the dog suddenly howled in fear.

Manning plunged the syringe through the short

fur covering the dog's body. A second later the yapping little dog was sleeping soundly.

The big Canadian laid the dog gently on the ground, then climbed back over the fence and joined the others at the mouth of the alley again. They gave it another thirty seconds to make sure no one would come out of the houses to check on the Chihuahua, then moved on to the rear of Damon O'Keefe's house. Manning followed McCarter to the back door with James, Encizo and O'Prunty right behind.

What they found they hadn't counted on. A glassed-in porch had been built along the entire width of the rear of the dwelling. Through the glass they could see potted and hanging plants, an iron patio table and chairs and the door leading into the house. The storm door to the porch was propped open with a brick, but the screen door in front of it was closed. McCarter tried the latch, which was locked. It would be easy enough to penetrate but there was no way they'd be able to hear Hawkins knock on the front door from inside.

McCarter stopped them again. "Cal," he whispered, "stay outside and motion to us when you hear T.J. knock and the door opens."

James nodded as McCarter turned back to the porch door. He unclipped his Spyderco Military

Model knife from his belt and sliced through the screen, reached through and opened the door.

A moment later McCarter, Manning and Encizo stood at the rear door of the house, watching James. The seconds clicked away, then James held up his hand and punched it forward in the air, indicating that Hawkins had knocked. A few more seconds went by, then the black Phoenix Force warrior reached forward in front of his belt, grasped the knob of an imaginary door and jerked it open.

McCarter kicked. Wood splintered and steel screeched against steel as the lower hinge broke and the door swung awkwardly open on the top joint. Manning waited during the split second it took his teammate to follow his kick, then, shotgun at the ready, he followed the Phoenix Force leader into the house. Behind him he could hear Encizo.

The Phoenix Force warriors found themselves in a hall leading toward the front of the house. At the end they could see the kitchen and, through the tiny patch of visibility created by a slightly offset door, the commotion that was just beginning in the living room.

Two doors were set in the wall off the hallway before the kitchen, one on the right, the other on the left. Ahead of Manning, McCarter went left, ducking into what the big Canadian assumed was a rear bedroom.

Manning took the right door, speeding into the room low and racking the pump gun's slide at the same time. He found an empty bed, dresser and chest of drawers. Spotting the walls were newspaper clippings, which he assumed related to IRA activities.

McCarter's voice boomed from the bedroom across the hall as Manning exited the room again. But the Briton's voice didn't sound like he'd been hurt, and Manning didn't have time right now to find out what it was all about.

By the time he reached the kitchen, Encizo was already there. Manning stepped off the hall carpet onto the white tile just in time to see an IRA terrorist bolt through the door from the living room, a British Webley revolver clutched in his right hand.

But he never got a chance to use it.

Encizo stitched him groin to throat with a full-auto spray of 9 mm rounds. Bullets blasted through the wall between the kitchen and living room just above Manning's head. Holes appeared in the wallboard, and white dust filled the air. The big Canadian ducked lower, coming up alongside Encizo. They moved cautiously on to the doorway, seeing men rushing back and forth through the opening, some with weapons already in hand, others making mad dashes toward guns scattered across the living room.

Manning knelt next to the doorway and risked one eye around the corner. He saw Hawkins blasting away in the door leading to the front porch and wondered what had gone wrong. Hawkins, who might have been Phoenix Force's newest member, had nonetheless proved his fighting ability and judgment dozens of times since coming to Stony Man Farm. He wouldn't have disobeyed McCarter's orders without a good reason.

Manning picked out a man wearing a black T-shirt. The sleeves had been rolled up, and a package of cigarettes was gripped in the cuff. The IRA terrorist had just reached an AK-47 leaning against the wall by the television set. Manning pumped a round of double-aught 12-gauge buckshot into his back, taking him down.

Encizo opened up with a series of 3-round bursts from his H&K. Manning pumped the slide of the Winchester, the sound drowned out by the louder roar of gunfire. Encizo stood on the other side of the door, and as Manning prepped the scattergun for a second shot, he saw the little Cuban take out a shooter with a flopping handlebar mustache.

The 12-gauge ready again, Manning swung the front bead sight toward an IRA gunner with long wavy hair. But before he could pull the trigger,

Hawkins dropped the man with a double-tap from his Beretta.

Manning heard glass crash at the side of the room and swung the shotgun in that direction. He came close to shooting Calvin James, who had evidently circled the house on the outside and now jabbed the barrel of his MP-5 through the window. James opened up on full-auto, making an IRA terrorist wearing a Dallas Cowboys football jersey jerk in a dance of death.

Next to the cavorting football fan, another of Damon O'Keefe's cohorts was firing an old Ingram MAC-10 submachine gun. Manning aimed the Winchester his way and pulled the trigger.

The double-aught buck struck the man in the neck, nearly decapitating him. Both his carotid artery and jugular vein took the hit and he had almost bled out before he hit the ground.

Manning racked the slide, fired, racked the slide again and fired again. The first round struck the shoulder of a man wearing a tweed hat with the brim turned down. The force of the buckshot spun him in a full circle, bringing him back to face the big Canadian as Manning pulled the trigger the second time. This blast caught the IRA terrorist squarely in the chest, and he fell over the wavy-haired man Hawkins had downed only seconds earlier.

For a brief second Manning thought of Mc-

Carter. The Phoenix Force leader hadn't appeared from the rear bedroom, and the big Canadian wondered just what it was that had delayed him. Then a stray round from someone struck the television screen and the box exploded, sending sparks and smoke into the air.

Next to Manning, Encizo continued to fire the H&K. Rounds continued to fly through the broken glass of the side window as James pumped more bullets into the enemy gunners.

A short wiry man dressed in khaki pants and a cutoff sweatshirt turned toward the door to the kitchen. He got off one wild round from his .357 Colt Trooper, then Manning took him down with another blast from the 12-gauge.

A terrorist firing an Uzi opened up from the corner to Manning's right, and the big Canadian heard a grunt across the room. He saw Hawkins go down, and anger filled his soul.

Twisting awkwardly through the door, Manning pumped the shotgun. The IRA man saw what was coming and raised his arms instinctively to protect himself. Manning squeezed the trigger, and the small balls of lead struck the Uzi, flattened, glanced off and spread out around the gunners body. Racking the slide, he sent another blast of buckshot into the man's face.

Hawkins was on his feet again by the time Manning turned back to him. The left calf of his blue jeans had been torn away, and blood ran down his leg onto his hiking boot. The wound had done little but knock the young warrior off his feet, however. He moved as if nothing had happened.

Manning pulled back around the corner into the kitchen, speed-loading a shell from the belt carrier around his neck directly into the chamber of the Winchester. He slammed the slide forward to load the gun, then looked up briefly to check his surroundings. Gunfire still sounded on the other side of the wall, but it was dwindling. In the doorway he saw the empty brass flying from Encizo's Heckler & Koch. Satisfied that the Cuban warrior had things covered for the time being, he loaded the rest of the shotgun's magazine, then peered around the corner again.

He needn't have bothered. The last IRA man fell to a double-tap from Hawkins's Beretta as his eyes swept the living room.

Manning didn't wait around to congratulate himself or the others. He rose to his feet and headed back down the hallway to the bedroom where McCarter had disappeared. As he neared the door, he heard a screeching string of what could only have been curses in a language he had never before encountered.

Sprinting up to the door, the big Canadian

aimed the shotgun into the room. What he saw made him stifle a laugh.

McCarter was on all fours on the four-poster, a small, wriggling form beneath him. McCarter had the woman pinned to the bed with his body. His hands held hers, outstretched above her head. Manning looked down. Another of the Webley revolvers lay on the floor next to the bed, evidently having been knocked from Mrs. O'Keefe's hands or nightstand during the struggle.

Manning lost the battle to keep the grin off his face. "Need any help, O fearless leader?" he asked.

McCarter turned to face him as another string of profanities escaped the woman's lips. "It wouldn't hurt," he said. "This one's a regular wildcat." He paused, then his own smile crept across his face. "By the way, the language is Gaelic. I don't know what it means, but I'm sure our ears would burn from now until eternity."

Tokyo, Japan

THE OVERSIZE soft-side briefcase slung over his shoulder on a leather strap, Bolan walked casually down the sidewalk toward the Takahata Box, Crate and Container Company. Although it was getting late, people came and went and traffic was still moderately heavy. Still dressed in the business suit he had worn that afternoon when he reconned the offices, he caught a glimpse of his reflection in a window as he passed.

He looked bulkier than he had that afternoon, as if he'd have gained twenty pounds or so in the few hours since. But no one would notice, and even if they did, they'd just take him to be another overweight American businessman on his way back to the hotel for the evening.

The Executioner passed the Takahata building looking straight ahead. But in his peripheral vision, he studied the front office area. The lights were out for the night, and that part of the manufacturing company appeared to be vacant.

Strolling across the street and on another block, he passed a cleaner's, bakery and finally a pharmacy on the corner. He turned on the side street running along the pharmacy's side and continued at a leisurely pace until he reached the alley behind the buildings.

At which point he disappeared.

Bolan moved faster now, walking briskly down the litter-scattered brick walkway to the opposite corner. He stopped briefly, looking both ways to make sure there were no curious eyes, then crossed the street and ducked into the alley behind the Takahata building.

Heading directly to the shadows behind a large trash container, the Executioner opened the briefcase and withdrew the Beretta 93-R, the Glock 21 with the Aro-Tek laser sight and the holsters and rigs for the weapons. He would be returning to the fixed-blade Applegate-Fairbairn knife for combat dress, and it came out next, followed by his black nylon combat boots. Last he withdrew a leather pouch with a belt clip attached to one side, then set his gear and the empty briefcase on the ground and unknotted his tie. His coat, shoes, shirt and slacks came off in that order and went into the briefcase.

The Executioner glanced down the alley, reaffirming that he was alone, then he slipped the Beretta's shoulder rig over his blacksuit. The gun belt with the Glock went around his waist. It also held a small laser flashlight, extra magazines for the .45 and various other pieces of equipment in nylon and leather carriers. The fighting knife was suspended from the Beretta's shoulder harness under his right arm. He clipped the leather pouch to his side in between the other equipment.

Bolan stuffed the briefcase inside the trash bin and moved along the rear of the building. Through the windows he could see men working the machines that made the various shipping receptacles the Takahata Company manufactured. As he watched through the glass from the alley's shadows, he saw a man in green work clothes operating a machine that stamped out cardboard boxes. He moved silently on along the outer brick wall, seeing another man operating a saw and cutting wooden crates.

Across the room the Executioner could see several men around a conveyer belt that was moving the completed crates toward a stamping machine. The boxes moved into an area beneath a large sealer, paused long enough for the steel plate to descend onto their lids, then moved on with the company's markings imprinted.

Bolan couldn't see the imprint being left on the wood from where he stood. But he knew what at least one of the characters looked like. And it meant "box."

Stealing on through the shadows, the Executioner came to the corner of the building. The plant section of the structure was too heavily populated to risk entry to the building that way. Somehow he had to penetrate the office area where no one was likely to be. That was the part of the company in which he was interested, anyway.

Dropping to all fours, Bolan used a short hedge that ran along the sidewalk to conceal himself from passersby on the street. He reached the front corner and looked out to the sidewalk.

People still walked along the pathway. He'd be seen if he tried to go in the front.

Turning back in the direction he'd just come

from, the Executioner retraced his steps to the last window outside the office area. He knew there would be an alarm—he was in Japan after all, the electronics capital of the world. It would be a sophisticated device, as well, and it would be hidden. Not being trustworthy themselves, the Yakuza would be sensitive to the fact that others might break in on them.

Bolan glanced at the window as he rose to a squatting position. He felt certain he could deactivate the alarm, but finding it would be the problem. That would take time. In fact it might take all night, and he didn't have a whole night to spare.

Glancing up the wall, the Executioner saw more windows on the second story and the top, third level. To save expenses, many people didn't wire the upper floors. Had the Yakuza? He didn't know, but he was about to find out.

Unzipping the leather pouch he had added to his belt, the Executioner produced an electric drill gun and several large bolts. He had returned to their jet at the airport immediately after reconning the box company and found the drill in one of the lockers at the rear of the plane. Now he inserted one of the bolts into the drill's magazine and twisted it into place.

Reaching overhead, Bolan pressed the sharp tip of the bolt against the bricks and pulled the trigger. The hand-held machine buzzed for a half second, and the threaded end of the bolt drilled into the brick. The rest—approximately two and a half inches—extended from the wall.

Bolan repeated the procedure two feet to one side of the first bolt, then returned the drill gun to his pouch. In the alley behind the manufacturing division, he searched through the trash bins until he came across what he needed. One of the wooden crates had been defective and dumped into the trash.

The Executioner hauled the crate to the side of the building and stood it on end. His eyes searched the ground until he found a chunk of concrete roughly the size of his fist. He dropped it into a pocket of his black suit, then, using the bolts already drilled into the building to pull himself up, he stood briefly on the crate, then stepped up onto the bolts.

Working quickly, Bolan drilled another pair of footholds into the brick. They were less than six inches from the bottom of the second-floor window, and he used them to pull himself up, then reached out and grasped the concrete sill. A moment later he had dragged himself up the brick and stood on the sill itself.

The Executioner considered going in the second-floor opening, then discarded the idea. It might be wired into the alarm system. But the third floor was even less likely to be wired, so he repeated the process with the drill gun up to the next level.

Balancing now on the concrete just below the glass, the Executioner peered inside. He saw a dark office area that had been converted into a break room. Couches and chairs lined the walls, and a coffee machine and teapot sat on a table in the corner.

Opening one of the small leather pouches, the Executioner pulled out a roll of tape. Quickly he ran stripes across the window both horizontally and vertically. Returning the tape to his pocket, he drew the Beretta and used the butt to tap the glass.

The window broke with only a few telltale shards of glass falling the three stories to the ground.

Bolan reached in, unlocked the window and opened it. A moment later he closed it behind him. He couldn't hear an alarm, which meant nothing. The system could easily be silent, clandestinely alerting either the police, the Yakuza or both.

The Executioner peeled the tape away from the glass and scattered the shards across the floor. He stuffed the sticky strips into his pocket, then dropped the chunk of concrete on the floor several feet in from the wall. With any luck, whoever discovered the broken window in the morning would assume some kid or street punk had simply thrown the concrete through the window.

Bolan moved quietly across the carpet to the door. The hall was dark, the only illumination being what light filtered in from the office windows. Somewhere he could hear the hum of a computer that hadn't been turned off. The clicking of a clock from one of the offices echoed hollowly along the corridor. Behind him, through the walls, he could feel the vibrations of the machines in the manufacturing division and hear their muffled roars.

Moving silently along the hall, Bolan came to the stairs. He suspected what he was looking for would be on the ground floor, but he checked the offices along the way just in case. Each of the small cubicles held a desk, various pieces of other furniture and a computer. He was looking for a computer, all right, but he suspected that none of these was the right one.

Bolan moved on. The second floor proved just as unlikely to contain what he was looking for, so the Executioner descended the steps to the ground. He made his way down another dark hall, past offices and storerooms, until he reached a large room with several desks and computers—a secretarial pool.

This was where the sales records would be kept.

Bolan chose one of the computers randomly and turned it on. As he listened to the machine warm up, he flipped on the fax machine and printer next to it. Taking the cellular phone from his blacksuit, he tapped in Kurtzman's number at Stony Man Farm.

The computer man answered on the second ring. "Kurtzman."

"It's me," Bolan said. "I'm going to need Akira."

"Hold on."

A moment later Akira Tokaido's familiar voice said, "Hello, Striker."

"You got your fax warmed up and ready?" Bolan asked.

"Sure do. What have you got?"

"I'm inside the offices of Takahata Box, Crate and Container. I've got a computer warming up to check their files. Just one problem I can think of."

"And that would be…?" Tokaido said.

"I don't read Japanese."

"But what is the fax for?"

"I figured I'd copy down the file lists as best I could and send them to you. Let you interpret them and tell me where to start."

"That would take far too long, and we might

still miss the pertinent data. Let Bear establish a link into their hard drive, then simply send all of their files to us. We'll copy them and do the searching ourselves."

"Good plan."

The young man guided the Executioner through the process of linking the hard drive into Stony Man's computer network, and a few minutes later the files of the box company were crossing the Pacific on their way to the Blue Ridge Mountains. Bolan waited.

Finally Tokaido came back on the line. "The transfer and copy is complete," he said.

"And they won't be able to tell here that anything has happened?" Bolan asked.

"Not when Bear gets finished," Tokaido assured him.

Bolan hung up, taking a brief moment to go over his escape plan as he shut down the machines around him. He needed to return to the third floor and exit through the same window he had come in. He would pull the bolts as he went down the wall by reversing the drill gun, carry the box back to the trash bin, change back into his clothes and be gone.

It all sounded easy as he went over it in his head.

But the Yakuza gunmen who suddenly burst through the door changed those plans.

The Caribbean

AN UNUSUALLY COOL night breeze blew through the unscreened window into the shack. Somewhere in the distance a bird called to its mate, and closer to the tiny one-room building, a choir of crickets began to sing.

Colonel Harold J. Maddox came awake with a start. Still half asleep, he nevertheless knew immediately where he was. He rose quietly to a sitting position on the bed, looking at the woman next to him. She lay on her side, faced away from him, snoring softly. Moonlight filtered through the window, illuminating her round bare buttocks and showing the goose bumps on the white flesh brought on by the breeze. He reached across the bed, stroking her flesh until the bumps disappeared, then pulled the covers up over her.

Maddox stood and glanced down at the luminous hands of his wristwatch on the nightstand. It was almost 0200; he had to have dozed for a couple of hours. Reaching for his T-shirt on the chair next to the nightstand, he slipped it over his head and looked back to the woman in the bed.

He was glad he had brought Gladwyn to the island from Jamaica. She was not only a loyal and efficient secretary, but she was also a damn good lay. And there was nothing like getting your rocks off on a regular basis to keep your head clear. Did he love her? No, of course not, Maddox thought as he stepped into his camou fatigue pants. But he sure *liked* the hell out of her.

It was a damn shame he'd probably have to kill her someday.

Maddox sat down gently on the edge of the bed and began to strap on his leather sandals. Gladwyn knew too much, and when he was finished making a killing with the Eliminators, he planned to spread his money around the banks in the Cayman Islands and live a life of legitimate ease. And Gladwyn, quite simply, didn't fit into that plan.

The former U.S. Army colonel sat motionless for a moment, thinking of the word he had just spoken in his mind. "Legitimate," he whispered out loud, and the sound brought a smile to his face. After all these years, would he even know how to go legit? The son of gunsmith, he had grown up around firearms. His first paying job had been slipping into his father's workshop after hours and making zip guns, which he sold to his friends. During his thirty years with the Army, he had found plenty of time to carry ordnance out the back doors of armories and had built up quite a fortune through other schemes. Always he had escaped detection, and his record was clean.

Buckling his sandals, Maddox stood, slipped his watch over his wrist, then lifted the Smith & Wesson 645 pistol from the nightstand and shoved it into his belt beneath the T-shirt. Careful not to awaken Gladwyn, he opened the thin plywood door of the shack and started across the grounds toward his office. The breeze bit into him now, raising goose bumps on his own arms and shoulders. He thought back on his father, realizing that the man had instilled far more than just the art of making guns into him. Harold Maddox Sr. had constantly harped that the greatest business profits always came from the domains with which the worker was both familiar and interested. That philosophy might not have worked for the father, but it had been invaluable to his son, and after the real estate and other investments, it was finally guns to which Harold Maddox had returned.

Maddox walked on toward his office. As a U.S. Army small-arms expert, he had always been impressed with the simplicity of the quickly mass-produced World War II weapons. When it had come time to retire from service, he had decided to go for what he thought of as his big and final sting before he also retired from business. It was then that he had realized this same philosophy of *fast* manufacture could be used to construct similar firearms cheaply.

The island was quiet as Maddox neared the small office building, the workers asleep in their barracks. He encountered two guards on the way, both alert and challenging him as he neared. Good. The men were doing their jobs.

Inserting his key into the door, Maddox hurried through Gladwyn's office, switched on the light in his own and dropped into the chair behind his desk. He took time to light one of the huge Churchill cigars from the humidor, then opened his desk drawer and found a pen and several sheets of clean white paper. His first instinct was to slip into a pair of gloves to avoid leaving prints on the paper, but that wasn't his goal. Leaving at least one print was imperative to the sense of drama he wanted to create for the media to expound upon, and he reminded himself his prints weren't on file. Just before retirement he had conveniently slipped into both the actual files in the Pentagon and computer records of his military prints and destroyed them. The only place his fingerprints had been recorded since were in Walla Walla when he'd been arrested on the impaired-driving charge.

Maddox grinned as he entered the date at the top of the page. Police fingerprint searches in real life weren't like they were on television and in the movies. Electronic-age Sherlock Holmeses didn't simply enter a print into the computer and sit back while the machine kicked out a name. In reality, additional leads were necessary to narrow the search, and a technician might spend years looking for an isolated print. But even in the unlikely event that that happened, he was covered. Since misdemeanor arrests weren't recorded by the National Crime Information Center, there was no way anyone would ever locate the isolated set of records in Walla Walla.

It would be like looking for the proverbial needle in a haystack—when you didn't even know a haystack existed.

Confident that he was safe, Maddox began to write.

To whom it may concern:
It has come to my attention that you no longer feel I am fit for headlines in your newspaper. This deeply saddens me. In retaliation, after a three-day grace period beginning at the time I mail this letter, I shall have to kill one journalist a day for every day I do not appear on the front page. You may feel free to reprint this communiqué if you like, and make copies for any police agency who is interested. They will not catch me as I am far and above their intelligence.

But let's have some fun with them, shall we? Directly after my signature you will find a thumbprint.

I intend to step up production and increase both the volume and types of weapons I manufacture. Only when the oppressed of the world are armed will they be able to rise up and overthrow the tyrannical regimes of the United States government and its puppet states the world over.

All power to the people!

Catch me if you can.

Sincerely,
the Eliminator

Maddox sat back in his chair and laughed out loud. Then, the smile still on his face, he leaned forward and pressed his thumbprint onto the page beneath the words *the Eliminator*.

CHAPTER EIGHT

In the Air above Louisiana

"So," Carl Lyons said from the copilot's seat of the Learjet 60. "I take it McCarter and company are busting heads in Ireland?"

Next to him, behind the controls of the plane streaking through the sky, Charlie Mott shrugged. "Don't ask me, Ironman. My orders were to drop them off and head back home in case you guys needed a lift. You know me—I just run a taxi service."

Lyons nodded and glanced behind him to where Schwarz and Blancanales sat with their two new passengers: the Road Kill biker Lyons had originally thought was a mental case, and the woman who had been hiding under his table during the firefight. The overly made-up woman sat quietly, staring into space with a blank expression.

The biker's name, they had learned, was Tap Dancer. His girlfriend was called Dime.

"Tell us where we're going again, Tap Dancer," the Able Team leader demanded.

"I done told you three times already."

"So do it again," Schwarz urged. "We all enjoy seeing how your story changes each time."

"It don't change," Tap Dancer argued. "I just tell it different."

"Then let me see if I can paraphrase it for you into words we, who actually passed second grade, can understand," Schwarz said. "Besides the Falcons, the only other gun connection the Road Kills had were the skinheads in New Orleans?"

"Yep," Tap Dancer said. "Guy used to be a Road Kill. Moved down to the Big Easy about a year ago and hooked up with the 'heads. He's a bouncer in a place on Bourbon Street."

"What this guy's name?" Lyons asked.

"Guy."

"Yeah," Blancanales said, nodding, exhibiting the patience one usually reserved for a child learning to tie his own shoes. "What is the guy's name?"

"Guy. His name is Guy."

"Is that his real name or one of the cute little labels you bikers came up with?"

"Hell, I dunno," Tap Dancer said. "I just

know we say 'Guy,' and he'll look up at us. And he can get guns through the 'heads.''

"And you know where to find him?" Schwarz asked.

"Sure."

Mott cleared his throat.

Lyons turned to look at the pilot.

"I hate to interrupt this highly enlightening and intellectual conversation," Mott said, "but you might want to get your new buddy's straitjacket ready. We'll be touching down in roughly ten minutes." He sniffed through his nose and frowned. "And not a moment too soon if you ask me. I'm going to have to disinfect the cabin and run one of those air-freshener things through the air-conditioning system to get this stench out."

Neither Tap Dancer nor Dime seemed to notice the insult.

A few minutes later they had acquired clearance to land at Moisant International Airport in Kenner. Five minutes later the wheels hit the tarmac, and Mott rolled the Learjet to a halt.

Lyons turned his attention back to Tap Dancer and Dime. "I'm not going to cuff you," he said, "because I don't want to draw attention." He smiled in a way that Barbara Price had once told him looked like a cross between the Marquis de Sade and a hungry wolf, and added, "but if either of you tries to rabbit on us, or pulls anything else,

I'm going to put a 125-grain, semijacketed Federal .357 Magnum slug right between your ears. Do I make myself clear?''

Both Dime and Tap Dancer nodded, fear on their faces.

The men of Able Team bade Mott goodbye and left him to do the paperwork. They stepped down out of the Learjet with their prisoners, Lyons leading the way into the terminal, then out the front to a line of cabs. They crowded into one of the yellow vehicles, and the Able Team leader told the cabbie to take them to the French Quarter.

Reggae music blasted from the radio as the driver started the engine and pulled away from the curb. Lyons got a dirty look when he reached forward to the dash and turned it off.

A half hour later they had covered the seventeen miles to world-famous Bourbon Street. The mixed aromas of garlic, strong roasted coffee beans and the musty age of the buildings filtered through the closed windows of the cab even before the driver pulled up to the curb and stopped. Lyons handed him a fistful of small bills and got out.

The Able Team leader gathered the rest of the party on the sidewalk as the cab picked up another fare and pulled away. ''What's the name of the club where Guy works?'' he asked Tap Dancer.

''Uh, Guys and, uh, Guys and, uh, something.''

"Guys 'n' Dolls," Gadgets said, pointing across the street.

"The place belong to him?" Lyons asked.

"Nah, he just works here."

Lyons glanced down the street as they reached the opposite curb. He had been in the French Quarter of New Orleans many times, but he'd never gotten over feeling that he'd just walked onto the Hollywood movie set of some historical film. Iron rails, many two and a half centuries old, framed the overhanging galleries and balconies up and down the street. Many of the sidewalks were in dire need of repair, and made walking difficult for the people who used them.

Schwarz opened the door and stepped back, ushering the rest of them into the darkness. Lyons nodded for him to go ahead, then followed. He took a breath of the clammy air mixed with the smells of alcoholic beverages and cigarette and cigar smoke, then glanced up at the stage. A stripper, down to her G-string, was gyrating suggestively to the brassy jazz blasting from a sound system. Men were seated in the chairs around the stage and runway, their eyes popping out as they stuffed dollar bills into the woman's abbreviated underwear.

Blancanales found a table large enough to seat them all and led the way to the chairs that circled it. They sat, and a moment later a young blond woman wearing little more than the dancer came to take their orders.

"I want a Hurricane!" Dime shouted with glee.

Lyons tried to make himself comfortable as he waited for the beer he'd ordered, watching the dancer enough to keep from looking out of place but averting his eyes now and then to search the room for Guy. Seeing no sign of anyone even close to having a shaved head, he turned to Tap Dancer seated at his side. "Where is he?"

"Search me," the biker replied as the waitress returned to place a beer in front of him. "I'm pretty sure this was the place."

Lyons restrained the impulse to grab the man by his shirtfront. His first impression of Tap Dancer at the biker bar had been that the man was an imbecile. Then, when he spoke somewhat coherently, he had changed his mind. But now, after getting to know the man, Lyons was no longer so sure that the loony looks on his face hadn't been insanity after all. The man was obviously a little touched.

The Able Team leader grabbed the waitress's arm gently as she set a beer in front of him. "Honey, is there a guy *named* Guy who works here?" he asked.

The blonde smiled. "Sure. He's the bouncer. Want to talk to him? I can get him."

As it turned out, she didn't need to.

A scream suddenly came from the stage, and Lyons looked up to see one of the men up front trying to tug off the dancer's G-string. A split second later a bald-headed man wearing an olive drab tank top appeared from out of nowhere. Reaching up with both heavily muscled arms, the man jerked the guy's hand away, slipped him into an arm lock, and applied pressure.

Another scream, this time from the grabber, broke the silence that had fallen over the club. A second later a loud snap sounded as the man's elbow broke.

The guy was crying as the bald-headed bouncer escorted him out the front door and yelled, "Don't come back!"

"That's him!" Tap Dancer said excitedly. "That's Guy!"

"Call him over," Lyons said.

Tap Dancer waited until the bouncer was walking past them, then said, "Hey, Guy! It's me, Tap Dancer!"

The burly bald-headed man stopped and squinted through lashless, piglike eyes.

"You remember me, don't you?" Tap Dancer asked, some of the excitement and confidence seeping from his voice.

"I remember *her*," Guy said, turning his gaze toward Dime. "Damn, honey, you're good."

Dime beamed at the compliment.

Tap Dancer began to sulk.

"Why don't you introduce me to your friends and then tell me what you're doing this far from Bed-Stuy," Guy suggested as he dropped into the last vacant seat at the table.

"Well, uh..." Tap Dancer said, obviously trying to remember what Lyons had told him to say. "This is, uh, Ironman. These other guys are his buddies. You remember the Falcons?"

"Sure," Guy said.

"Well, they're, uh, Falcons."

Guy squinted harder. He wasn't as dumb as Tap Dancer—that was clear. "A little old to be Falcons, aren't you?" he asked.

"Yeah," Lyons agreed, "we are. Tap Dancer's forte never was brainpower. What he meant to say was that we used to be Falcons. We've moved on in the world—kind of like you."

This made more sense to the man in the tank top. "So," he said, talking to Lyons now and ignoring Tap Dancer, "you guys in town to have a little fun? Want me to set you up with some pussy? I'll get you the best beef prices in town."

"Maybe later," Lyons said. "Right now we're here on business." He paused. "*Family* business."

Guy leaned in. "I see. What can I do for you?"

Lyons glanced around for curious ears, then dropped his voice to a whisper. "We need firepower. Enough to take out a half-dozen boys who've made our employer in the Big Apple a very unhappy man.''

Guy was suspicious. "How come you didn't bring your own hardware with you?" he asked.

Lyons made a steeple out of his fingers and rested them on the table in front of him. "This was a hurry-up job, and we had to fly down commercial. Tap Dancer assured me he had connections who could supply the pieces."

Guy looked back to the biker. "You hookin' up with these guys, are you, Taps?"

"I'm, uh, tryin', Guy. Sure."

Guy turned back to Lyons. "Okay, I can help you out. But if you plan to use the guns I get you around here, they're going to cost double. You know, shitting in your own backyard and all that? It could bring on some extra heat."

Lyons nodded. "I understand," he said. "No problem—we've got the bread."

"So, what did you have in mind?" Guy asked.

"Something with firepower," Lyons said. "And stuff that can't be traced. We're going to drop the things right after it goes down. We don't want to be hauling shooters around with us afterward."

Guy smiled and stood. "I got just what you need. I'll make a couple of calls and have them for you by tonight."

"Here?" Lyons asked.

"Not only no, but *hell* no," Guy said. "This place is my straight gig. Legitimate. I book out of here but I always do the serious stuff someplace else."

"Where, then?"

Guy squinted his pig eyes in thought again, then finally said, "You know where Shorty's Sail Rentals is on Pontchartrain Beach?"

"No, but we can find it easy enough."

"Okay, show up there around nine tonight. If I'm not there yet, I'm on my way. Or I'll leave word with Shorty where to meet me."

Lyons nodded. "Fair enough. You're sure the equipment you'll be bringing doesn't have a paper trail somewhere?" he asked again to make sure. "Like I said, we're going to dump them just as soon as we're done."

Guy waved a hand in front of his face to dismiss the idea. "Paper trail?" He laughed. "Paper trail? Hell, to have a paper trail there would have to have been some *paper* on these things, right? Well, there never has been—not when they were manufactured and nothing since." He paused, then leaned in closer. "You've read the papers?"

Lyons nodded. He knew what Guy's last comment had meant.

The Eliminators.

Northern Ireland

"AH, YA BLOODY BASTARDS!" Brigette O'Keefe screamed, changing from Gaelic to English as soon as McCarter dropped her hands and stood up to move away from the bed. "You've killed him! You've killed my only child!" With a quickness that belied her age, the small, frail woman sprinted past Manning and out into the hall.

McCarter and Manning followed her into the living room. The Phoenix Force leader's first sight was of McHiggins, curled in a fetal position on the floor. Blood still dripped from the IRA man's mouth but his eyes stared blindly in death. He had caught a round from one of the other IRA men during the firefight, whether by accident or because they realized he had brought the intruders to the house, the Phoenix Force leader would never know. But McCarter felt his heart sink at the realization that their only link to the IRA was dead.

The former SAS man's heart sank still farther as Brigette O'Keefe knelt next to her son and cradled his head. "You've killed my boy!"

Hawkins knelt next to her. "We're sorry, ma'am," he said in his Southern drawl. "We wouldn't have done it if there'd been any other way."

Hawkins got a hard slap across his face for the words.

Brigette O'Keefe looked up at McCarter, her face reflecting the hatred in her soul. "May you rot in hell for all eternity!" she cried. "May you smolder and burn and may the devil cut out your hearts and feed them to his demons!"

McCarter didn't know what to say. One of the few constants in life was a mother's love. Regardless of how malevolent a woman's son turned out to be, his mother still loved him. It was no different with Mrs. O'Keefe, and the Phoenix Force leader wished there had been another way to handle the situation—or at least that the woman hadn't been home to see what had happened.

But Brigette O'Keefe wasn't finished. She spit forth another tirade in Gaelic, then returned to English once more. "You bloody Brits!" she screeched as she hugged Damon's head to her breast. "You take over everything, and you kill anyone who doesn't fall in line! Well, you'll be gettin' your just deserves some day!" She paused long enough to take a deep breath, then blurted out, "And one of you'll be gettin' it in the morning!"

A silence fell over the room as they waited for her to go on. But Brigette O'Keefe realized the mistake she'd made, and her lips clamped tightly together.

"How?" O'Prunty asked quietly. "How will they be gettin' their just deserves in the morning?"

"And you!" the woman screamed. "You're worse than the rest! An Irishman by birth, are you? Well, you be no Irishman at heart. A bloody traitor to your own kind, that's what you are! Workin' for the bloody enemy as you do!"

"What did you mean about tomorrow morning?" McCarter asked.

Daggers of fire shot from Brigette O'Keefe's eyes to the former British SAS commando. "I'll say no more about it," she said, then hugged her son's body closer and began to weep.

McCarter stared at the woman for a moment. Something was about to go down. She knew what it was, but she wasn't about to talk. He glanced quickly to Calvin James, then averted his eyes. No, he couldn't ask James to interrogate her like he had McHiggins. The good guys of the world had to draw a line somewhere or they'd be no better than the scum they went after. And scaring the wits out of a little old lady didn't fall under what McCarter believed appropriate behavior, especially right after they'd killed her son.

Besides, the Phoenix Force leader thought, still watching James out of the corner of his eye, he doubted his teammate would do it even under direct order. Calvin James was a highly moral man, as were all of the members of Phoenix Force.

It was what separated them from the animals they hunted.

"Gary," McCarter said quietly, "look after Mrs. O'Keefe. The rest of you stay here with them. Felix, I'd like to see you for a few minutes in the other room." He turned on his heel and led the MI-6 operative back into the bedroom.

As soon as they were out of view, O'Prunty pulled a pocket flask out of his coat, unscrewed the cap and held the flask to his lips for several seconds. His eyes watered slightly, but they also glowed with the adrenaline still coursing through his veins. He extended the metal container to McCarter. "Hell of a little donnybrook, eh, mate?" he said. "Want a taste?"

McCarter smiled but refused the drink. "You get the same take on what Mrs. O'Keefe just said that I did?"

Screwing the cap back onto the flask, he stuck it back inside his coat. "Somethin' big goin' down. But I'm damned if I know what, and I suspect it would take bamboo shoots under the old lass's fingernails to get it out of her. Think there's any chance of sweet-talking her?"

McCarter let out a sardonic chuckle. "After we just blew away her son and all his friends? Not a chance in bloody hell."

"We didn't take out *all* of his friends," O'Prunty said. "There's plenty more of those Molotov-cocktail-hurling bastards where these came from. And it's no doubt they who are up to whatever devilment the old missus was talking about."

McCarter nodded. "But we're at a dead end, Felix. O'Keefe and McHiggins are dead. There's no one left to make talk, and you're right—I've got no intention of hurting the old lady." He blew air through his clenched teeth. "I suppose the only thing to do is for you to get on the horn to London. See if your boys have any intel we might match up to what she said. It's a long shot, but we've got nothing else."

O'Prunty nodded, then moved to the telephone on the nightstand next to the bed. He lifted the receiver, got an operator, gave her a credit-card number, then had her ring the MI-6 offices on the other side of the Irish Sea.

A few seconds later he said, "O'Prunty here. Code number 614375635. Connect me to intelligence." There was a pause during which he looked at his watch. "Yes, Ian, I know it's late. Maybe no one has put you on to the fact yet, but we don't keep bankers' hours in this business. So get someone out of bed if you have to and tell them to call me back at this number. Now!" He read the O'Keefe's telephone number off the phone, then slammed the receiver back into the cradle.

Turning to McCarter, he said, "Bloody lazy civil servants," and shook his head.

McCarter smiled at the fact that O'Prunty himself was a civil servant, then a screech of rage came from the living room. The Phoenix Force leader turned instinctively on his heels and hurried out of the bedroom and down the hall. He saw Gary Manning, who could bench-press more than any other two men of Phoenix Force combined, fighting for his life as he struggled to control, without injuring, Brigette O'Keefe.

The old woman's temper had flared again, and she had bounded to her feet. She was striking Manning across his broad chest with her bony fists.

Encizo, Hawkins and James stood in a ring around the combatants, offering no help and trying not to laugh. Manning caught a glimpse of McCarter and turned to him as he finally got Mrs. O'Keefe's arms pinned to her sides. The barrel-chested Canadian's face begged to be relieved of the assignment McCarter had given him.

The Briton ignored his expression and started back toward the bedroom. The phone started had just started to ring when he reached the door.

"Yes?" O'Prunty said into the instrument. "Yes, hello, Niles. It's O'Prunty." He recited the code number again, then quickly explained what had just occurred at the O'Keefe residence. He went on to reveal that Mrs. O'Keefe had accidentally spouted off about someone getting their "just deserves" in the morning. "What we're needing," he stated, "is for you to cross-reference all current IRA intelligence to see if we can add it to this and make some sense out of it." He paused, then said, "All right, I'll wait."

Holding the phone away from his mouth and covering the mouthpiece with his hand, he looked at McCarter. "He's checking now."

The seconds ticked away in the quiet house, the only sound being the soft sniffles that came down the hall as Brigette O'Keefe continued to mourn her son. Finally O'Prunty said, "Yes Niles, of course I'm still here. Did you think I might have gone for a pint at the local pub?"

He listened a moment, then turned to McCarter. "There's rumor of something brewing with the IRA," he said, "but they've got little else. None of our informants seems to know exactly what it is."

McCarter scratched his head. "The old woman said one of them would be getting what he deserved," he said. "One. That sounds like an assassination rather than a bomb or machine gunning or something that might result in multiple casualties. Emphasize that and see what your man says.''

O'Prunty relayed the information and waited for an answer. Finally he said, ''It doesn't change anything, David, but it doesn't contradict anything, either.''

McCarter frowned in thought. ''I assume MI-6 keeps an up-to-date itinerary of the prime minister and other government dignitaries?'' he asked.

''Of course,'' O'Prunty said. He relayed McCarter's words into the phone, then the two men waited again. Suddenly O'Prunty's normally red face went white. ''You're sure?'' he asked. ''Okay, Niles. Thanks. I'll keep in touch.''

The blood had only slightly returned to the MI-6 man's face when he turned to McCarter. ''It's one of the royals,'' he said, ''who will be speaking to a group called Parents of Disabled Children at 0800.''

''Where?'' McCarter demanded, already starting to move back toward the living room to round up the others.

''Back at the distillery,'' O'Prunty said. ''If we leave now, we can just about make it.''

Tokyo, Japan

BOLAN DROPPED behind the desk where he'd been working as the first full-auto burst from a 9 mm

Japanese Shin Chuo Kogyo submachine gun flew over his head like a supersonic swarm of angry bees. Plastic burst as the rounds struck the computer, and smoke and flames shot from both the monitor and hard drive. A piece of the keyboard rolled back over the edge of the desk, falling onto the Executioner's arm as he hit the floor.

He drew the Glock 21 and adjusted his grip on the weapon, making sure the web of his hand fit securely against the activating button on the Glock's back-strap as more bursts from the Japanese submachine guns struck the desk.

But the heavy oak construction stopped the penetrating parabellum rounds. The gunfire stopped, and as the Executioner's ears cleared from the blasts he could hear the shuffling of feet as his adversaries moved to circle the desk.

Bolan took advantage of the lull to lean around the side of the desk, spotting a Yakuza gunner dressed in a conservative gray European suit. The Japanese gangster aimed a subgun at the center of the desk. Before the man's eyes could shift to the Executioner's position, Bolan pointed the Glock his way, tightened his grip to activate the laser and saw it fall on the man's tie a foot below his chin.

The Executioner squeezed the trigger, and the gun jumped in his hand. The necktie seemed to cave in, and a moment later the Yakuza hardman lay dead on the floor.

Shifting his aim to a gunman three feet to the right, Bolan swung the laser's red dot to the center of the man's V-neck sweater. The Executioner's second .45 hollowpoint round drilled through the fuzzy wool and sent the Yakuza mobster to meet his Maker.

A volley of rounds from an unseen machine gun sent Bolan ducking back behind the safety of the desk. He waited while hundreds of rounds peppered his cover, wondering how many it would take before even the sturdy hardwood began to give way. He couldn't stay where he was forever—that was clear. And diving out into the open to seek new cover was an engraved and embossed invitation to meet the Grim Reaper. But his only course of action from where he now knelt was to continue to lean around the corners or over the top of the desk. And it wouldn't take much more of that before he found a 9 mm bullet streaking his way.

A creak sounded in the desk over the blasts of the rounds, and Bolan looked up to see the pointed nose of a 9 mm hardball bullet staring him in the face. The round had found a trail blazed by former bullets and almost made its way through the wood into his face.

The desk was weakening; time was running out.

Glancing to his right, the Executioner saw another desk similar to the one behind which he crouched. It would eventually weaken, too, but it might buy enough time for him to reduce the number of Yakuza assailants. With a deep breath he dived from hiding into the open.

A gangster swung his weapon toward the Executioner as Bolan flew through the air. Jerking the Glock into target acquisition, Bolan tapped the trigger as soon as the red dot fell on the man. The round struck the gunman in the shoulder, spinning him in a full 360-degree pirouette as the subgun fell from his fingers. He was facing the Executioner again, a shocked look on his face, when Bolan's shoulder struck the carpet.

The Executioner's second round entered the Yakuza's face just below the nose and wound upward into his brain, taking a good deal of that organ with it as it blasted out the back of his head.

Bolan got his bearings behind the new desk. Glancing right and left, he could see none of the Yakuza men. He looked over his shoulder. Reflections in the glass windows on the outside wall of the building revealed three assailants crouching behind other desks and easy chairs. Bolan picked the closest one—a man kneeling behind a desk and firing a .32 caliber Nambu Type 57B pistol at the Executioner's position. The man's entire right side was visible in the glass.

Keeping his vital parts safe behind the desk, Bolan extended only his wrist and the hand holding the Glock around the corner. He estimated the angle of fire and got as close to target acquisition as possible before squeezing the pistol grip to activate the laser. The red dot suddenly appeared, not on the Yakuza gunner but on the desk directly in front of him. Watching the man's reflection in the window, Bolan adjusted his aim until the red dot fell on the side of the gunner's face like some giant glowing blemish.

The men of the Yakuza had seen the red dot already, and there was a split second of recognition in the gunner's eyes as the light struck his face and he realized what was about to happen.

Bolan pulled the trigger, and the side of the gunman's head exploded. He pulled his hand back a split second before a 3-round burst struck the side of the desk where his hand had been. He looked back at the window and saw the angry face of another Yakuza gangster run his subgun dry and reach for a fresh magazine.

The Executioner didn't give him time to reload.

His back against the desk, Bolan continued to watch the man fumble with the magazine as he twirled the Glock in his hand. Holding the semi-auto pistol backward now, his middle finger f over the laser's activation button as his thumb found the trigger. The Executioner raised the weapon over the desk, watched in the window until the red dot had centered on the Yakuza gunner's chest and squeezed.

With the strange grip, the Glock bucked unfamiliarly in Bolan's hand. The recoil from the man-killing round sent the weapon up and to the left, but it mattered little.

The hollowpoint round streaked straight down the path of the laser beam to the red dot and struck the gangster squarely in the chest. A soft, muffled groan escaped the hardman's lips as he slithered to the floor.

The magnitude of the gunfire had died down considerably as Bolan decimated the enemy force. Now it was almost nonexistent save for what sounded like a lone man firing occasional volleys. In the window reflection Bolan could still see a Yakuza gangster hiding just to the side of a desk near the front of the room. He was armed with what looked like a Nambu Model 60 .38 pistol.

But he wasn't responsible for the periodic shooting. The bullets still striking the desk bore the distinctive sounds of the Japanese subguns. Besides, he was too petrified to pull the trigger anymore, the gun frozen in his hand.

Bolan crawled quietly to the other end of the desk, keeping the paralyzed man in sight in the window as he moved. This desk, like the one that he had hidden behind initially, was finally beginning to splinter as he hooked the Glock around the corner. Centering the laser beam on a spot just below his target's arm, he began to squeeze the Glock's trigger.

The man holding the revolver looked down and saw the red dot on his side. His mouth dropped open in terror as he looked up and saw Bolan's own reflection in the window. But his fear lasted less than a second.

The .45-caliber round from the Executioner's Glock 21 saw to that.

The autofire from somewhere else in the office suddenly quieted. Bolan heard the distinctive sound of a magazine dropping from a Shin Chuo subgun. A split second later metal scraped against metal as a fresh box mag found purchase. The Executioner's last remaining adversary now had a new load of thirty rounds of 9 mm parabellum ammo at his immediate disposal.

His eyes still glued to the windows behind him, Bolan took advantage of the opportunity to drop the partially spent Glock magazine and insert a full one up the plastic grips. He pocketed the half-full clip as he continued to scan the glass.

There was no sign of the remaining Yakuza man's position.

Bolan waited patiently, his back to the desk and

the Glock still in the reverse, thumb-on-the-trigger grip. Seconds turned to minutes as the deadly game of cat-and-mouse continued. Finally the Executioner heard the soft sounds of movement on the carpet, sounding as if they were directly behind him.

Frowning, Bolan stared into the window immediately in front of him. He could see nothing. Then the reality of what was happening struck him like a lightning bolt between the eyes.

The final Yakuza man had figured out that the Executioner was using the window reflections in conjunction with a laser sight. He had dropped below the glass and was crawling toward the desk.

Slowly, silently, Bolan twisted around and returned the Glock to a proper grip. Now facing the desk, he inched his way into the chair well, beneath the surface. The front board on the other side of the well appeared to be plywood rather than oak, and he moved closer, pressing his ear against the flat surface.

Ever so softly, the Executioner heard breathing on the other side of the desk.

Moving back slightly, Bolan aimed the laser's red dot at the center of the plywood board and pulled the trigger. Holding the weapon steady, he emptied ten of the Glock's fourteen rounds into the composite wood, scattering them at different angles.

He heard a scream.

Crawling backward out of the chair well, the Executioner rose over the desk with the Glock aimed toward the floor. He needn't have bothered.

Below, bleeding profusely onto the expensive carpet, lay the final Yakuza gunman. It was impossible to tell how many of the Executioner's blindly fired rounds had found their target.

But whatever the number, it had been enough.

Somewhere in the distance, Bolan heard the wail of police sirens. He hadn't had time since the Yakuza hardmen burst through the door to wonder how they had discovered his presence. But now he realized that the third-floor windows *had* been wired for security. He had tripped that wire when he'd broken the glass, sending one silent alarm to a central security station somewhere within the Takahata building, and another to the police.

The Executioner wasted no time. He couldn't leave by the ground floor—the only exit he knew was the front and he might run straight into the men in blue on his way out. Exiting through the same door he had entered earlier, he sprinted up the steps to the window he had broken. Lowering himself onto the highest set of climb bolts, he retraced his way down the side of the building, then jumped to the ground between the building and hedge when he reached the second floor.

Bolan hit the sidewalk in "parachute" mode, rolling down onto his legs, then his side and popping back to his feet. He saw the flashing red-and-blue lights of several cars as they pulled to a halt in front of the building. Ducking low, he rounded the corner back into the alley behind the manufacturing area.

Sprinting through the darkness past the trash receptacles and other debris, the Executioner ran toward the trash bin where he had hidden his briefcase. He might need to change back into civvies to facilitate his escape.

He had reached the trash bin when the first car, lights flashing and siren screaming, turned into the alley.

Bolan ripped open the bin's lid, reached in and grabbed the handles of the briefcase. Drawing the Glock, he activated the laser and centered the dot on the right front tire of the vehicle racing his way. A squeeze of the trigger brought on a blast of gases and a streak of muzzle-flash from the barrel of the .45.

The Japanese squad car skidded, then fishtailed into the side of the building.

Bolan could already hear the doors opening. Excited voices screamed in Japanese as he turned toward the other mouth of the alley.

As he did, two more patrol units turned the corner to cut off that avenue of escape.

The Executioner lifted the Glock again, aiming for a front tire of the lead vehicle. This car skidded, as well, coming to a halt in the center of the alley. The police vehicle behind it crashed into the rear bumper.

Bolan glanced quickly to the opposite side of the alley. The stone edifice of some other building ran the length of the alley. The only means of escape possibly still open was back through the Takahata building itself.

As more car doors slammed shut and voices again barked orders in a flurry of words he couldn't understand, the Executioner dropped the red dot on the lock to the nearest door leading into the manufacturing division of the box company and fired.

A second later he had entered the production area and was sprinting past the startled crate makers.

CHAPTER NINE

New Orleans, Louisiana

Carl Lyons watched the people around small campfires in the sand as he led Schwarz, Blancanales, Tap Dancer and Dime down the beach. Men, women and children laughed and chattered as they roasted hot dogs and marshmallows on straightened clothes hangers over the open flames. Here and there a young couple could be seen kissing as they reclined on blankets. A few of the couples had progressed past the kissing stage.

In addition to the families and couples, muscular men in swimsuits and bikini-clad women who looked like they'd just stepped out of the centerfolds of *Playboy* and *Penthouse* walked up and down the beach in the twilight falling over Lake Pontchartrain. Not wanting to draw undue attention, Able Team and their newly found informants had stopped at a shopping mall on the way to the lake and outfitted themselves with beach wear. Schwarz had also bought a cheap, soft-sided nylon briefcase, which he hoped his contact would think was stuffed with money.

Trudging through the sand, Lyons led his team on toward the sea of masts that extended out of the water in front of the sign announcing Shorty's Sail Rentals. The only downside to their clothing was the fact that weapons were nearly impossible to conceal. But in this case, it didn't matter. Guy was bound to shake them down, and they'd told him they couldn't bring their guns along since the trip from New York had been a hurry-up affair on a commercial airline. Besides, if they already had guns, why would they be wanting to buy them from the skinheads?

Dinghys, catamarans, trimarans, motor crafts, sailboards, paddleboats and other small vessels had been chained to the dock around the shack that served as Shorty's office. Lyons let his hand fall briefly to the crotch of his swimsuit to make sure the Spyderco Military Model folding knife was still clipped to his jockstrap, out of sight beneath the trunks. Constructed of crucible CPM 440V steel and coated with Blak-Ti to prevent corrosion, the Military knife was one of the sturdiest folding fighter knives on the market. It could cut tin cans all day, and the serrated edge would still shave the hair off a man's arm.

The Able Team leader stopped at the counter

of the open window at Shorty's. A man wearing a brown warm-up jacket, with thinning gray hair and permanently suntanned skin, stood facing him just inside the booth. His eyes were down, engrossed in the photo of a bikini-clad woman on the page of a surfing magazine that lay open on the counter in front of him. On racks behind the man were rows of candy bars, crackers, potato chips and other snacks, and next to the food was a board holding dozens of keys.

"You Shorty?" Lyons asked.

The man took his time looking up from the magazine. "Who wants to know?" he asked.

"Me," Lyons said. "My friends and I were supposed to meet somebody here. If we didn't see him, we were to ask for you."

"I'm Shorty, then," the man said, dropping his eyes back to the picture of the girl in the bikini.

Lyons watched a young blonde wearing a thong walk past the shack and smile at him, wondering how Shorty could be so absorbed in a picture when there was so much of the real thing visible all around him. "You seen Guy tonight?" he asked, turning his attention back to the man in the window.

"Nope."

Lyons waited for more of an answer. When he didn't get one, he said, "Did he call?"

"Yep."

The Able Team leader was losing patience with Shorty. Fast. "What did he say?"

"Not much," Shorty said, and turned the page.

Lyons reached forward, grabbing the front of the man's jacket with a fist. He lifted Shorty onto his tiptoes, then said, "Friend, I don't like playing games, and I don't like your attitude. Is Guy coming here, or are we supposed to meet him someplace else?"

Shorty got the point. "Guy told me to give you one of the boats," he said. "Take it out. He'll find you." Lyons let him back down, and he cleared his throat. "And don't turn the lights on. Guy doesn't like to take chances when he does business."

"Then give me a key," the Able Team leader said, letting go of the man's jacket.

Shorty reached behind him and pulled a key off the rack. "Number 6," he said. "Trimaran docked on the other side. It'll seat six, but be careful. The sail's a little low, and it'll bust a hole clean through your head if you don't duck when you come about."

Lyons nodded and took the key. As he started to leave, Blancanales stepped up to the window.

"You just met our public-relations man," he said. "He got the job because of his patience and sweet disposition. Be glad you didn't have to deal with one of us."

A confused expression came over Shorty's face, then he went back to his magazine.

They walked away and found the trimaran docked along the shore on the other side of the shack. A padlock secured the chain looped through a steel ring on the dock. After Lyons unlocked it and pocketed the key, they boarded the small craft and shoved it out into the lake.

"The man wasn't kidding when he said to watch your head," Blancanales commented as they raised the trimaran's lone sail. "One mistake and you could have your teeth smashed out by this baby."

The men of Able Team and their two Road Kill informants had to fold themselves at the waist as they came about and the sail whipped over their heads in the evening breeze. Lyons manned the line, tacking through the head wind out into the dark waters. Slowly the campfires along the beach changed from brightly glowing flames to mere pinpoints of light. The quarter moon overhead provided the only illumination on the lake.

When they were approximately five hundred yards from shore, Lyons trimmed the sail, tossed the small anchor over the side and let the trimaran bob slowly with the waves.

"What now?" Blancanales asked. "Throw in a few lines and hope for bass?"

Lyons ignored the comment, letting his eyes

roam through the darkness and across the waves. He saw nothing. But somewhere in the distance he heard the soft purr of an outboard motor. As he and the others waited silently, the hum grew louder. A few minutes later the dark shadow of a twenty-five-foot cabin cruiser appeared on the horizon. As it neared, Able Team saw the boat's light flash on, then quickly off again.

Twenty yards from the trimaran, the cruiser cut its engine and turned broadside, gliding through the gentle waves until it came abreast of the smaller craft. The dark shadows of several men could be seen on deck, but none of the faces was recognizable.

"Ahoy." Lyons recognized the voice as Guy's. "Come aboard."

A ladder was dropped over the side of the cruiser, and Lyons watched as a dark set of hands secured the rubber-coated hooks at the top over the rail. He reached out, grabbed one of the steps and pulled himself up. Schwarz followed, then Blancanales shoved Tap Dancer and Dime up the ladder before bringing up the rear.

A kerosene lamp stood next to the ladder that led down into the cabin. Lyons counted six men on deck—all of them with cleanly shaved heads—and wondered how many more might be below. All of the skinheads wore side arms on Sam Browne police-style belts wrapped around their swim trunks, and three of them, including Guy, gripped full-auto Eliminator grease guns.

Guy stepped forward out of the bunch. Gone was the friendly disposition he had displayed at the club earlier that day. It had been replaced with a stern, businesslike attitude that bordered on the surly. "You bring the money with you?" he asked Lyons.

"Sure," the Able Team leader said, hooking a thumb toward the briefcase in Schwarz's hand. "You got the guns?"

"You're lookin' at 'em," Guy said. He held out the grease gun for Lyons's inspection.

Lyons dropped the magazine from the weapon, noting it was empty. He worked the bolt. The chamber was empty, as well.

Guy cleared his throat.

When Lyons looked up, he was staring into the big bore at the end of one of the Eliminator Government Models. The two men who still held grease guns had swung them around to cover the rest of Able Team, Tap Dancer and Dime. The other three had drawn their pistols.

"Now, *these* guns are loaded," Guy said, grinning like a cat holding the gun on a mouse. "But in case you have any doubts..." He twisted suddenly, popping three rounds into the lake next to the hull. The bullets made tiny plops in the water as they hit.

Guy turned back to Lyons. "You see, sport," he said, still smiling, "I got to thinking after you left. Tap Dancer never was the brightest son of a bitch in the world, and his woman here's even dumber than he is. And you guys, well, you just flat don't look like Falcons or Road Kills or Mafia like you tried to tell me you were. Fact is, you look more like cops." He paused, drew in a long, dramatic breath, then said, "But even if you are who you claim to be, it doesn't matter. Nobody's gonna know what happened to you but a few hungry fish."

Lyons remained calm. He had known what was happening was a possibility and had prepared for it. "So what you're telling me, Guy, is you're going to rip us off, kill us and dump us into the lake?"

Guy rubbed the back of his free hand across his forehead. With a look of mock amazement covering his face, he said, "Whew! Nothin' slips past you, does it, sport?"

"Very little," Lyons agreed. "But you've made one mistake."

"Oh, really?" Guy said, smirking. "And what might that be?"

Now it was Lyons's turn to smile. "I lied to you about the money."

Schwarz opened the briefcase, pulled out the newspaper and let it flutter in the breeze onto the deck. The sides of the nylon bag hung limply from his fingers.

A look of pure rage fell over Guy's face. He stepped forward and shoved the Eliminator .45 into Lyons's nose. "Then you better know how to take us to it," he said in a low, threatening tone of voice.

Lyons wasted no time. He knew it was now or never. He swept the gun away from his face with his left hand. At the same time his right dug the knife from inside his swimsuit. Inserting his thumb into the opening hole on the blade, he flicked the Military Model open as a .45 round blasted from the Eliminator past his neck.

The Able Team leader watched Schwarz and Blancanales draw their own knives as he sliced the ragged edge across the tendons in Guy's wrist. The serrated blade fairly "rended" rather than cut, and the pistol fell out of the skinhead's life-less fingers and clattered onto the deck of the cabin cruiser.

As he drew the knife back over his head, Lyons caught a glimpse of Blancanales driving his own weapon through the thin T-shirt covering the chest of one of the other bald men, ripping the grease gun from the man's fists a moment before the guy fell to the deck.

The Able Team leader brought his knife around in a lightning-fast hammer-hand blow. The hard pommel end of the folding knife struck Guy in the temple, causing him to slump forward into Lyons's arms. As he caught the unconscious man, Lyons saw Schwarz slice the throat of another skinhead. Blood gushed from the gash like a broken fire hydrant.

Twisting Guy to face the others, Lyons wrapped his left wrist around the skinhead's throat and grabbed the opposite ear. Crossing his right hand over the choke-hold, he worked the tip of his knife under the restraining arm and dug the serrated blade lightly into Guy's throat.

He didn't want the man dead, just under control. At least for now.

"All right, freeze!" The Able Team leader shouted at the top of his lungs, "or I'll turn this good ol' boy into a bald-headed pork chop!"

The remaining skinheads froze in place. Schwarz had already pried the Eliminator pistol from the dying fingers of the man with the slashed throat, and Blancanales swept his grease gun in a menacing circle.

The skinheads dropped their guns.

"Frisk them," Lyons ordered.

Schwarz and Blancanales patted the men down and came up with two knives and a hideout .25. They threw these weapons, along with the ones they hadn't commandeered for their own use, over the rails into the water.

Guy had begun to come around. "What...huh? What's, uh, happening?"

"The tables turned while you were napping," Blancanales said. "You can't expect to keep up with all the little minidramas that go on if you're going to sleep all the time."

Guy got his bearings and felt the serrated edge of Lyons' knife against his throat. "What are you gonna do with us?"

"That depends on what you do for *us*," the Able Team leader told him. "But first we're all going to sit down on the deck and have a nice friendly little chat."

Northern Ireland

THE TRIP BACK to the distillery took roughly half the time it had taken to get from the whiskey-manufacturing site to Londonderry. McCarter, a longtime race-car driver and auto-rally contestant, took the wheel of the minivan, coaxing the maximum amount of speed from the sluggish vehicle, which had been designed more for comfort and transport than swiftness.

The men of Phoenix Force and Felix O'Prunty arrived at the distillery at 0735 hours. Already a crowd of parents and disabled children was heading from the parking area toward the rows of wooden folding chairs that had been set up near the bank of St. Columb's Rill. A stage, complete with podium, bunting and more chairs, stood in front of where the audience was gathering.

McCarter pulled the van to a halt in the last open parking space at the rear of the lot. Behind him, in the rearview mirror, he saw the cars that had followed the minivan off the highway as they pulled over and parked on the side of the road. He turned, resting an arm over the back of his seat.

The men of Phoenix Force had changed into turtleneck sweaters, casual slacks, tweed jackets and leather or tweed driving caps and hats. Individually they now looked as if they'd fit right in walking along the streets of Belfast or sitting at the corner table of one of the local pubs. But as a group, they still looked like what they were—hard men bent on a mission. McCarter's biggest fear was that they'd draw the attention of the royal's executive security team from Scotland Yard and be mistaken for IRA terrorists themselves.

"We're going to split up," the Phoenix Force leader said as more vehicles pulled in along the road behind the minivan. "We'll leave separately. Anybody think to pick up one of the maps of the grounds when we were here before?"

Encizo reached inside his sport coat and pulled

out a folded page, opening it before handing it over.

O'Prunty handed McCarter a ballpoint pen, and McCarter quickly divided the site into sectors. "Rafe," he said, "take the area around the chairs. Cal, move into the main building and check it out. T.J., I want you over by the Pagoda Towers, and Gary, try to position yourself somewhere behind where the speaker will be. That'll take a little thought and creativity to keep the boys from the Yard from spotting you."

He took time for a breath, then added, "In fact I think you ought to go with him, Felix. You've got the credentials to keep a scene from taking place if there's trouble."

O'Prunty nodded his agreement. "Haven't worked with the Yard chaps for some time," he said. "But last time I did, I knew several who were assigned to the royal-security detail. If we're lucky, there might even be one of them along."

The sarcasm in his voice didn't escape the men of Phoenix Force.

"I'll be the rover," McCarter said, finishing up the assignments. "Get your radios clipped to your belt and the earpieces fitted. If anything looks suspicious, get on the air with it."

His teammates nodded. Hawkins opened a hard plastic case and passed out the walkie-talkies and earpieces. Battery operated and connected by remote, there was no exterior wiring between the belt-clipped main unit and hearing piece to give them away. The earpieces looked like ordinary hearing aids, and anyone curious would have to look closely to even spot them in the first place. To speak they would have to unclip the belt unit and hold it to their lips, but that should be a one-time operation if one of the warriors spotted a threat, and by then it wouldn't matter.

Events would be unfolding.

Hawkins left the vehicle first, checking to make sure his tweed jacket covered the weapons hidden beneath. Encizo gave him a sixty-second head start toward the towers, then got out and headed toward the chairs that were already almost filled. McCarter saw him slip into the last empty seat at the back where he could view the entire audience, as well as the rostrum.

Manning and O'Prunty got out next, walking casually toward a grove of trees on the other side of the stage. That left only James and McCarter.

"Cal," the Phoenix Force leader said as his teammate started to open the door, "I don't have to tell you that you're going to stand out a little more than the rest of us in this horde of redheaded light-skinned sons of the Blarney stone. Be careful."

James grinned. "What's wrong, David?" he said. "You never heard of the Black Irish?"

McCarter chuckled. "Get out of here."

The Briton watched James cross the grounds and enter the distillery building. He took a moment to stare through the windshield, surveying the general area. As rover, with no particular zone with which to be personally responsible, he would be free to follow his instincts as to where trouble might brew. But right now he saw nothing suspicious among the crowd or anywhere else in the area.

McCarter exited the minivan, strolling casually toward the folding chairs. He made his way to the far northern edge of the property, letting his eyes roam over the horizon. Seeing nothing out of the ordinary, he turned back toward the distillery itself and scanned the grounds around him. Secure in the belief that no land mines, trip wires, or other traps had been set in the area, he entered the building itself with the strong but not unpleasant odor of peat fires in his nostrils once more.

Only a skeleton crew was on duty, the rest of the employees having left to await the royal's arrival, which would take place any minute now. All tours had been canceled until after her address, but a scant few tourists roamed the distillery on their own. McCarter found James in the room where the Old Bushmills Millennium Malt was maturing in bourbon barrels. The rest of the room was deserted.

James was staring down at one of the barrels.

"Find something?" McCarter asked.

James took a moment before answering. "Maybe."

McCarter followed James's line of sight to the barrel. The seal on the lid read Distilled 1975, Millennium Irish Whiskey.

"You see what I see?" James asked.

McCarter shifted his gaze from the seal to the rest of the barrel, but he saw nothing to make it stand out from the other whiskey containers. He shook his head.

James leaned in and pointed to a spot on the left-hand side where the lid convened with the barrel's trunk. The edge of the lid was slightly ajar, with perhaps one-thirtieth of an inch extending up over the lip. McCarter leaned closer and saw that the tiny ring was wet. The odor of the peat fires from outside left his nostrils and was replaced by the smell of finely aging whiskey.

"When was the last time they opened these things to sample them?" he asked James.

"September, last year. I remember reading it in the brochure."

"Let's get the top off and have a look," McCarter suggested. "I'll watch the door." He moved to the entryway and positioned himself so he could see both James and the hallway.

James drew the modified Crossada fighting

knife from the back-rig beneath his tweed coat, and jammed it between the lid and barrel. Slowly he began to pry upward. When the gap was large enough, he shifted the knife to another spot and pried some more. He had almost gotten the lid completely off when he said, "Oh-oh."

McCarter took a quick glance up and down the hall, then hurried to James's side. He needed no explanation as to why the Phoenix Force warrior had stopped.

The edge of a bright red electrical wire could be seen just under the lid.

"It's a trip wire," James announced. "Lift the lid, and whatever little surprise O'Keefe's buddies planted in here will go up."

McCarter stared at the whiskey barrel. Something didn't jive. Old Bushmills was a Northern Ireland landmark, a symbol of all the IRA held dear. It was metaphorical of the days before the English had conquered the Emerald Isle, and it didn't make sense for the Irish to blow it up.

Besides, if it was the royal they were after, the odds of the blast getting all the way out to the podium were negligible unless they had planted enough explosives inside the barrel to take out the entire grounds. And if they'd done that, they'd also kill the Irish men and women who had come to hear the speech, many of whom would be IRA themselves, or at least sympathizers.

They'd also be killing children, disabled children at that. And that simply wasn't their style.

McCarter had no love for the IRA, but he had to admit that this sort of behavior didn't fit the profile of their usual attacks. They might indiscriminately blow up people in London, but not here where their friends and relatives lived. Most of all, however, a bomb inside the building seemed to go against what Mrs. O'Keefe had let slip about one person getting "just deserves" this morning.

McCarter contemplated the discrepancies as he pulled the walkie-talkie from his belt. First things first, he thought. "Phoenix One, Phoenix Four," he said into the microphone. "Come in, Gary."

A moment later Manning's voice entered McCarter's earpiece. "Four here," the big Canadian explosives expert said. "Shoot."

"We've just found something that falls into your area of expertise," McCarter said. "I need you inside, in the Millennium Malt room. *Now.* I'm sending Cal to take your place. Tell O'Prunty to stay put."

"Affirmative, One," Manning replied. "I'm on my way."

James nodded that he had understood his orders and left the room. A minute later Gary Manning walked in.

McCarter pointed to the half-opened lid but

said nothing. He didn't have to. Manning took it in and summed it up with one glance.

"My guess would be Semtex," he said more to himself than McCarter as he pulled a multipurpose tool from his pocket. He opened the knife blade from the tool and gently inserted it between the lid and barrel. "You got a flashlight handy, David?"

McCarter pulled a miniflashlight out of his pants pocket, stepped forward and shone its beam into the gap around Manning's blade. The big Canadian bent down and looked inside.

"Still can't see what it's made of," he said, standing up. "But it doesn't look like there's any backup wire to blow if I snip the trip."

"Doesn't *look* like there is doesn't sound like a certainty to me."

Manning chuckled, then shrugged. "There are no certainties in life, fearless leader," he said. "Especially in our line of work, and particularly when it comes to explosives. You have to play the odds and even your hunches sometimes." Without further hesitation, he used the multipurpose tool's wire cutter to sever the red wire.

McCarter felt a moment of relief when the room didn't blow up around him. He watched Manning lift the lid the rest of the way off. "Whew!" the Canadian said, looking down into the barrel. "Talk about booze that'll take the top of your head off."

The Briton shone the flashlight into the barrel. Just below the surface of the whiskey, attached to the side of the barrel with wood screws, he could see the bomb. "Semtex?" he asked.

Manning shook his head. "I was wrong. It's C-4." He chuckled. "Hey, one out of two ain't bad. Be glad I wasn't wrong about a backup trip wire."

McCarter was. "How hard is it going to be to defuse?"

"Piece of cake," Manning said. "I'll have it out of here and the barrel put back together before you can say 'boom.'" He had stuck the wire cutter into the whiskey when they heard the voice behind them.

"What in bloody hell do you two think you're doing?"

McCarter and Manning turned to see a man wearing a charcoal gray suit staring angrily in their direction.

"We're taking a bit of the bite out of your brew," McCarter said. He pointed to the barrel. "Come have a look."

The man in the suit walked forward, looked down into the whiskey and turned a ghostly pale.

"Is that what I think it is?" he asked in a trembling voice.

"That depends on what you think it is," Manning replied as he went to work, wrist deep in single-malt whiskey. "But if you think it's a bomb, then yes, it's what you think it is."

The man's pale complexion went even whiter. "My name is Galway," he said. "I'm the managing director of the distillery. May I ask who you gentlemen might be?"

"We might be anyone," McCarter said as Manning continued to work. "But who we are is a specially trained team of counterterrorists currently working with MI-6." He paused. "Any more 'might's or 'maybe's?"

"No," Galway said.

"Then I suggest you go back to your office and leave us to our work. Otherwise this four-hundred-year-old company just might not get to finish aging its Millennium Malt. And keep this under your hat, won't you, old chap? I doubt that public knowledge of this incident would help sell whiskey."

Galway took another quick look at the bomb, then said, "I believe I'll go listen to the oration." He turned on his heel and was gone.

"Bingo," Manning said a moment later. He pulled the dripping bomb up out of the barrel and showed it to McCarter. "Safe out of the water—or should I say whiskey."

The sound of whirling helicopter rotors flopping somewhere in the air nearby met the ears of the men from Stony Man Farm. "Not a moment too soon," McCarter said. "Sounds as if the royal is arriving."

"Well, it is safe to speak now," Manning stated. He set the bomb on top of the neighboring barrel and replaced the lid. Picking up the bomb again, he said, "I'll take this with us and—" The Canadian stopped himself in midsentence.

McCarter had raised his radio to call the rest of the men in. He stopped. "What's wrong?"

Manning's gaze was locked on the bomb. "I was wrong again," he said. "This isn't C-4." He squinted at the pliable claylike substance.

"Then what is it?" McCarter asked.

"I don't know," Manning said, shaking his head. "But it's not C-4, and it's not Semtex. In fact it's not even an explosive material." He tore his eyes away from the bomb and looked over to McCarter. "This thing's a dummy, David. It was put here with the lid left ajar to waste the time of anyone looking for such things."

McCarter started to speak but was stopped by Hawkins's excited voice in his ear. "Phoenix Five to One. I'm over at the Pagoda Towers and I can see heads in both of them.'' There was a long pause during which radio static replaced his voice. When he came back on he added, ''At least one of them's got a rifle. Looks like a scoped 8 mm Mauser from here.''

CHAPTER TEN

Tokyo, Japan

With the briefcase containing his civilian clothes slung over his shoulder, the Executioner raced past the surprised crate makers and assorted machinery like a tailback who had broken through the line and hit open field. He was halfway to the inner door—a door he hoped led out of the Takahata manufacturing shop and back into the office area—when one of the men, dressed in white coveralls and a matching work cap, overcame the shock of seeing a heavily armed man in black enter the workroom and decided to be a hero.

Jumping out from behind a drill press, the box maker assumed a classic martial-arts stance and let out a blood-curdling *kiai*. Again like a football player, Bolan's right hand shot out in a stiff-arm. His open palm struck the martial artist squarely on the chin and sent him staggering back to perform a backward jackknife over the base of the drill press.

Without breaking his pace, the Executioner lowered a shoulder and hit the door. The frame splintered and sent the door flying from its hinges. Bolan ran down the hall, listening to the screams of sirens on all sides of the building. If the police hadn't already entered the doors, he knew it would only be seconds before they did.

The Executioner came to a door at the end of the hall and paused to look through the diamond-shaped window near the top, seeing another hallway that looked deserted. He glanced over his shoulder to make sure none of the other production workers had decided to play superstar and give pursuit. None had.

Silently Bolan opened the door and entered the adjacent hall. He sensed more than heard the presence of other men somewhere close. Ducking into the first office he came to, he opened the door a crack and peered back into the hallway.

Soft footsteps sounded on the tile floor. A moment later a uniformed Japanese police officer appeared. The man shuffled awkwardly down the hall, trying to maintain a Weaver shooting stance and keep his department-issue 9 mm Glock 17 ready in a two-handed grip. The stance wasn't compatible with movement, nor was he able to keep the barrel of the Glock from bobbing up and down with each step.

Bolan waited as the Japanese officer neared the door. Killing cops had never fit into the Executioner's creed, and he didn't plan to start changing doctrines now. The man in black had always believed that he and the men in blue were on the same side in the war against crime and unjustified aggression. If necessary, he would bluff, frighten and even inflict minor injury upon any of the cops who stood in the way of his escape. But he would kill none of them.

If it came down to him or them, the Executioner had decided long ago he would take a bullet himself before he sent some honorable law-enforcement official to an early grave.

He let the man get a foot from the door before he made his move. Timing his actions so the bouncing Glock would be pointed down, away from vital areas of his body, he swung the door open, reached out and grabbed the barrel of the weapon.

Bolan tugged the pistol toward him, twisting the barrel so it pointed out and away from his side. The jerk brought the officer's head snapping forward, and the Executioner sent a hard right cross into the man's face. Blood spurted from the cop's nostrils as he released his grip on the Glock and fell to the floor.

The Executioner dragged the body into the office and shut the door. Searching the unconscious man's gun belt, he found a collapsible steel baton and a small pepper-spray dispenser. He snapped his wrist, bringing the club to its full length, then aimed the pepper canister away from himself and gave it a test squirt. With the baton in his right hand, the small canister in his left, he exited the room before the spray could affect him in the confined area.

Moving silently down the hallway in his rubber-cleated nylon combat boots, Bolan reached the corner of the hall and stopped. Just out of sight, on the other side of the wall, he heard voices whispering in Japanese. He dropped to one knee and slowly edged one eye around the barrier.

Two more officers, their Glocks hanging limply from their arms and aimed at the ground, stood quietly arguing over some aspect of the building search.

The Executioner didn't figure he'd get a better chance.

Rising to his feet again, he stepped around the corner and sent a second-long spray of pepper gas into the face of the nearest man. A scream erupted from the officer's mouth, and he dropped to his knees as the other cop, a step or so behind him, started to raise his Glock.

Bolan stepped in quickly, rapping the baton on

the wrist behind the pistol. The blow jarred the weapon from the man's hand and he, too, let out a scream of pain. But it was nothing compared to the continued shrieks of the man with a face full of cayenne-pepper resin.

The Executioner hurried on, knowing that the howls of pain from the temporarily incapacitated men would bring more of the Japanese cops to the scene. It was his hope that they all would hear the noise and come to investigate, creating a window of escape in the perimeter defense he was sure had been set up by now.

Bolan cut down two more halls, encountering no more resistance and gradually making his way through the unfamiliar labyrinth toward what he hoped would be the front of the building. When he finally came to a familiar hallway, he knew he was close and stopped long enough to open his briefcase and pull on his slacks and jacket over the blacksuit. A moment later he stepped into the same secretarial pool from which he had transferred the Takahata files to Stony Man Farm.

The large room was dark, as he had left it. Unless he missed his guess, the front reception area where he had been that afternoon lay just on the other side of the far wall. Making his way quietly across the carpet, he cracked the door and peered through the opening.

The reception area stood where he'd suspected

it would be. An overhead light had been left on, and he saw it was less than twenty feet to the front door. Through the glass he could see the whirling lights of two squad cars but no officers could be seen in or around the vehicles. In civvies now, once safely through the lobby and onto the sidewalk, he could sprint to the more heavily populated area a block away and stand a decent chance of getting lost in the crowds on the sidewalk.

The only problem was that three Japanese cops, Glocks up and ready, stood covering the lobby.

Bolan decided on what appeared to be the only tactic available. It was a long shot, but he didn't have time to sit down and figure out a plan to shorten the odds. Soon the other officers searching the building would begin to double back and come up on him from the rear.

Then they'd have him trapped, and all chance of escape would be erased.

Drawing the Glock 21 from his hip holster, the Executioner aimed it at the floor to test the laser. The dot glowed brightly on the tile in the semidark room. Then, grasping the doorknob with his left hand, he suddenly threw the door open and stepped into the lobby.

All three cops turned toward him.

Bolan dropped the red-orange dot on the face of the nearest man and yelled, *"Koko de ii desu!"* using up most of the conversational Japanese he knew in one sentence. It might have been his words that caused the men to obey and freeze, but the Executioner suspected that the laser dot in the center of the officer's forehead had something to do with it, as well.

Bolan kept the laser on the man as he motioned for the other two to drop their weapons. They recognized the red dot and what it meant, and didn't hesitate. The man in Bolan's sights, however, had been forced to close his eyes against the intense illumination from the five milliwatt beam. "Tell him to drop his gun, too," the Executioner barked at the others in English.

One of them understood. He spoke a few words in Japanese, and a moment later the Glock in the hand of the blind man fell to the ground.

The Executioner moved in swiftly, keeping the laser dot centered on the officer's forehead. He twirled the cop away from him, wrapped his left arm around the man's throat, then shoved the gun up under his chin. The laser was still activated by his grip on the backstrap, and the red light splashed off the cop's skin to create an eerie red-orange glow around his face.

Bolan motioned for the other two men to get on the floor. They complied, falling to their faces and spreading their arms and legs. With the third cop in tow, the Executioner moved sideways toward the front door, keeping the men on the floor in his field of vision.

When he reached the door, Bolan pulled his arm away from his hostage's throat long enough to push open the door, then returned to the choke hold. Using the same crablike sidestep, he descended the concrete stairs to the cars parked along the curb.

As they had appeared to be from inside the building, neither of the vehicles with the flashing red lights was occupied. The officers had left the engines running and the doors open as they piled out to converge on the Takahata building. Bolan dragged his hostage to the nearest car, shoved him in and pushed him across the seat to the passenger side before slipping behind the wheel and killing the bar lights on top of the roof.

The Executioner transferred the Glock to his left hand and centered the laser dot on the man's chest. With his right hand, he threw the transmission into Drive and pulled away from the curb.

Two blocks later, when he was sure none of the other Japanese officers had seen his escape and followed, he pulled over to the side of the street.

"Get out," the Executioner ordered.

The Japanese cop evidently didn't speak English. He stared at Bolan with a mixture of anxiety and puzzlement covering his face.

Bolan reached for the handle of his own door

and mimed opened it, then stabbed a finger at the cop's chest before hooking a thumb past him to the sidewalk. "You," he said. "Out." At the same time he relaxed his grip on the Glock, and the laser dot disappeared.

The uniformed man got the message. Slowly, probably wondering if he was about to be shot, he unlatched the door. A moment later he stood on the sidewalk staring back at Bolan in disbelief at his good luck.

The Executioner watched the Japanese cop in the rearview mirror as he drove away. The man shrunk to a tiny dot of blue, then disappeared altogether in the distance.

CHAPTER ELEVEN

Pittsburgh, Pennsylvania

Dr. Glenn Barrister leaned back from the desk in his study and took off his glasses. He rubbed his eyes, both from fatigue and irritation. Bill paying was such a boring chore. He glanced over the itemized power bill, then started to write the check. Gradually the pile of envelopes on his desk began to grow smaller. He was just about to open the envelope of the last bill when the doorbell suddenly rang.

The research specialist jerked in his chair, glancing up at the clock. It was nearly 11:30 p.m. Who could it be? He lived alone and had few close friends. Those he saw socially he met away from his house, and he *never* had drop-by company, particularly at this hour.

The doorbell chimed again, and fear shot through him. Slowly he opened the bottom drawer of his desk and pulled out the aged revolver that had been passed down through his family. He stared at it, trying to remember if it was loaded.

The ring from the front doorbell was now accompanied by a loud pounding. Barrister jumped from his seat, then walked toward the hall, his legs feeling leaden. He passed through the darkened living room with the gun dangling at his side, then realized he shouldn't let it be seen and hid it behind his back.

"Who is it?" Barrister asked when he reached the door, surprised that his voice didn't crack from the terror coursing through his body.

"Dr. Barrister, we need to talk to you," a calm, even friendly voice said on the other side of the wood.

"Who are you?" Barrister asked. The voice sounded friendly, but wouldn't a criminal who wanted to trick you make sure to sound unthreatening? He suspected they would, but the world of thieves and killers was something totally outside his frame of reference. Barrister had grown up in a nice upper-middle-class family, then gone straight through three universities to gain his bachelor's degree, then master's and finally a Ph.D. He had landed a teaching assignment immediately, and even *he* knew he had never been exposed much to life off campus.

Particularly the ways of criminals.

"Dr. Barrister," the friendly voice said again,

"please open the door. It's imperative that we speak with you."

Barrister's mind continued to race, fixing on details of the man's words and trying to rationalize himself into a more tranquil state. The voice had used the word *imperative,* which Barrister didn't think would be in the vocabulary of many crack-smoking robbers. The man on the other side of the door had also used correct grammar, saying *speak* rather than *talk* as the metallurgist suspected a street criminal would have done.

Barrister took a deep breath. He was overreacting, he was sure. It was probably the police. And besides, if anything went awry, he had his grandfather's gun behind his back. "Are you the police?" he asked.

"Federal agents, Dr. Barrister. U.S. Department of Justice. Please open the door."

Barrister felt a wave of comfort rush through him as he unbolted the door, then twisted the knob. He felt even better when he saw the four men standing on his front porch under the light. The one closest to the door wore a conservative gray suit like the metallurgist imagined an FBI agent would wear, and the other three were obviously some sort of special police officers. They were dressed in tight black jumpsuits, black caps and strange gun belts were attached to holsters strapped around their lower thighs.

If Barrister had been a Hollywood casting director, he wouldn't have been able to do a better job of finding men to portray federal agents, and he breathed a sigh of relief.

Remembering the gun behind his back, Barrister realized suddenly that greeting police officers with a gun—regardless of whether they were local or federal—might get one shot. He stuck the revolver in the back of his slacks as he opened the storm door.

The man in the gray suit, evidently the one who had spoken to him, smiled. "May we come in, Doctor?" he asked.

"Certainly, officers," Barrister said as he stepped back and held the door open. It occurred to him that he had seen no badges or shoulder patches on the men in the tight black jumpsuits and that he should have asked that the man in gray present some credentials.

The thought brought on another short burst of fear. But why? he asked himself. The way they looked, what else could they be but police officers?

Barrister made sure the gun in the back of his belt was hidden from the men as they entered the house. Still facing them, he shut the door behind him. "What can I do for you gentlemen?" he asked.

"Dr. Barrister, we have need of your specialties," the dark-complected man in the gray suit said. "We'd like you to come with us."

Barrister looked instinctively at his watch. "At this hour?"

"I'm afraid so. We have an emergency situation on our hands."

The word *credentials* entered the metallurgist's mind again. He wasn't going anywhere with anyone unless he knew for certain who they were. "I'd like to see some identification."

The leader smiled and reached into the inside pocket of his jacket.

A moment later Barrister held in his hand an identification card that identified the man as Special Agent Leo Turrin, U.S. Department of Justice.

"Can you tell me what this is all about?" Barrister asked, handing the card back.

"Not yet, I'm afraid," Turrin replied.

Now certain that the men in his living room were all police officers, Barrister found new courage and bristled slightly at Turrin's refusal. "I believe I am still living in the United States of America," he said, "not Nazi Germany, where men dressed in black entered your home at odd hours and hauled you away without any explanation." He paused to take a breath, then puffed his chest out in defiance. "I'm sorry, gentlemen. I'll be happy to help. Why don't you call me at my office in the science building tomorrow morning?''

The man named Turrin lowered his gaze to the floor and shook his head sadly. ''I really am sorry to have to treat you like this Dr. Barrister, but you're going to come with us tonight. One way or the other, you're coming with us.''

The fortitude Barrister had felt for an instant evaporated even faster. These men might look like federal agents, but they weren't acting like them. Could Turrin's credentials be counterfeit? It dawned on Barrister that he had never seen a genuine Justice Department badge or identification card and wouldn't know a fake from the real thing. And the men in black— he looked at them closer now—no, he had been right the first time. They had no badges or patches.

''I'd like to see identification from *all* of you men, then I'm going to make some phone calls to verify who you say you are,'' the metallurgist said.

Again the man calling himself Turrin shook his head. ''I'm sorry, Doctor, we simply don't have the time for all that.''

''This is outrageous!'' Barrister shouted, surprised at how loud his voice was. ''I have no intentions of—''

Turrin took a step toward the metallurgist, and before he knew what he'd done, Barrister had jerked the revolver from the back of his slacks. He aimed it at the man in gray, who was less than an arm's length away from him now. The man stopped in his tracks.

"Dr. Barrister," Turrin said, "please put that thing away."

"I will not!" Barrister shouted. "And if you take one more step, I will shoot."

Turrin smiled. "Dr. Barrister, the gun is pointing directly at me, and I can see into the cylinder. You're not going to shoot me or anybody else with it in the condition it's in. The gun isn't loaded, Doctor."

Barrister felt a surge of foolishness move through his body to accompany the terror in his heart. Without thinking, he turned the gun toward his face to look for himself.

The man in gray took the step the metallurgist had ordered him not to take and reached out, seizing the revolver from Barrister's hand.

Later Barrister would remember that the movement was done smoothly, and not even particularly fast.

Turrin opened the gun and dumped the cartridges onto the floor. He tossed the revolver over his shoulder to one of the men in the jumpsuits, who caught it and placed it carefully on the lamp table next to the couch.

The man in gray looked Barrister in the eyes.

"Now, Doctor," he said, "is there anything you'd like to pack before we go? We could be gone for several days."

Stony Man Farm

AARON KURTZMAN TURNED and looked down the ramp at Akira Tokaido. The young Japanese hadn't quit typing, nor had his head quit bobbing, since the computer files of the Takahata Box, Crate and Container Company had come across the wires to Stony Man Farm.

Kurtzman had wheeled down the ramp as soon as they'd arrived and taken a quick look for himself. As he'd known they would be, the files were all written in *kanji,* meaning he hadn't a clue as to what he was seeing on-screen. So he'd wheeled back up to his own work and left Tokaido to his. Kurtzman liked to supervise his people at arm's length once an assignment had been given out. Breathing over somebody's shoulder produced negative returns, splitting that person's attention between the computer and his or her supervisor. Split attention, he didn't need.

And besides, all of the members of his cybernetics team were self-starters, and once they'd begun a task they were like dogs holding on to a bone. They didn't give up until the job was complete. Tokaido, Wethers and Delahunt weren't just experts; they were the top of the crop.

If they hadn't been, they'd never have been recruited to Stony Man Farm.

Kurtzman's phone rang, and he turned back to his console. Lifting the receiver to his ear, he automatically turned toward the glass wall that divided the computer room from Barbara Price's mission-control area. He saw Price looking back at him through the glass, and in his ear heard her voice say, "Bear, you've got visitors." She glanced toward the door to the computer room as she hung up and reached for a button on her desk.

Stony Man Farm's computer wizard followed Price's gaze to the door as he heard the electronic lock buzz. Just on the other side of the glass stood Leo Turrin, three blacksuits and a small man wearing dark blue casual slacks and a short-sleeved white shirt with the collar unbuttoned. The man looked frightened as Turrin pushed the door open and ushered him through before falling into step behind him. The blacksuits brought up the rear.

Turrin took the arm of the small man and escorted him gently up the wheelchair ramp to Kurtzman's bank of computers. The man looked not only frightened but confused.

"Aaron," Turrin said as the party reached the

top, "I'd like you to meet Dr. Glenn Barrister. Doctor, this is our cybernetics expert."

"Pleased to meet you, Dr. Barrister," Kurtzman said, extending a hand.

Barrister shook it with a weak grip as his eyes circled the room in amazement. "Do I call you...Aaron?" he asked.

Kurtzman nodded.

Barrister released his hand and pulled his eyes back into his head. "Quite a setup you gentlemen have here. But I've got to tell you, I'm a little perplexed. I'm starting to relax because it's evident that you work for the government in some capacity."

Kurtzman chuckled. "I'm not sure that's a very good reason to relax."

Turrin and the blacksuits laughed quietly, and the joke even brought a feeble grin to Barrister's face. "Yes, quite true," he said. "But at least you aren't the Mafia hit men I imagined when these men with the guns and jumpsuits blindfolded me and put me on the airplane. By the way, can you tell me where I am?"

Kurtzman shook his head. "I'm sorry, Doctor, I can't tell you where you are or who we are. But I can tell you that we're a top-secret installation of the United States government and we're the good guys."

"How can I be sure of that?" Barrister asked.

"I think that you'll be certain when you find out what we wanted you here for," Kurtzman said. "Leo, could you wheel one of the chairs up the ramp for the doctor?"

Turrin turned to descend the ramp, but one of the blacksuits had already gone down to get the chair. As he pushed it up the ramp, Barrister spoke again. "Then I suppose when all this—whatever it is—is over, I'll be free to go?"

Kurtzman's head bobbed again. "Most assuredly."

"But I also assume that I'll be expected to keep it all to myself?"

This time Kurtzman shrugged. "That would be nice, Doctor. But even if you get windy, it's been our experience that no one will believe you. You might as well tell your associates that you were taken aboard an alien aircraft and subjected to a humiliating medical examination by little green men with oblong heads."

"Yes," Barrister said, "I see your point. But I do have one problem."

"And that would be...?"

"I'm expected to teach two classes tomorrow and meet several colleagues in the laboratory. My absence will be noted and unexcused."

"That's already been taken care of," Kurtzman replied. "There'll be a letter waiting at the science building from the President. It will explain that you've been called away for an emergency assignment."

Barrister frowned. "The university president?" he asked. "Dr. Campbell and I have never seen eye to eye. I doubt he would—"

"I didn't mean the *university* president, Dr. Barrister."

Barrister's eyes opened as wide, and Kurtzman could see that the enormity of the Stony Man operation had finally sunk in.

The blacksuit pushed the chair next to Kurtzman and the computer genius said, "So, Doctor, shall we get busy?"

Barrister nodded, finally relaxed and comforted by the knowledge that he wasn't going to be killed or made part of some criminal scam. "Yes, why don't we?" he said, dropping into the chair. "But I do have one last problem."

Kurtzman waited.

"Why don't you call me Glenn?" Barrister said with a smile that was now genuine rather than nervously affected. "If you continue to call me Dr. Barrister, I'll feel compelled to call you Dr. Bear, and that borders on the ludicrous."

CHAPTER TWELVE

The Caribbean

Colonel Harold J. Maddox was always amazed at how easily, and for how little, members of the underworld would sell out their partners. Forget the code of *omertà*. Forget loyalty or "honor among thieves." That was all archaic bullshit—if it had ever been the norm. Be they mafiosi, bikers or street gangs, ten or twenty thousand dollars dropped here and there could do wonders when it came to getting the inside scoop on how his weapons were being used. To date, however, he hadn't learned anything of importance from his spies, and he had even begun to wonder if the expense was necessary.

This morning he no longer doubted that it was.

"Damn, sir," the voice in New York said into Maddox's ear. "I couldn't fuckin' believe it. Here they came, asking to do a deal and all of a sudden they open up with these *Star Wars* guns and kill everybody in the place.''

Maddox glanced at the row of lights on his phone, double-checking to make sure the trace-jamming device was in operation so neither the caller nor any other curious parties could track the connection. And the biker on the other end had no idea to whom he was talking. He was safe. ''What did the guns look like, Bongo?'' Maddox said patiently. He found the stupidity of the Road Kill biker repugnant, and couldn't wait to get the necessary information from him and get off the line.

''Big, long, pistollike sons of bitches,'' Bongo said. ''They had these round-ass things on top that looked like black plastic logs or something. I think that was the magazine.''

''Calicos,'' Maddox said. ''Probably the Model 950. A fine machine pistol. But tell me again, Bongo, how did you keep from getting killed yourself?''

''Luck, sir, pure, dumb, fuckin' luck. I'd gone in the men's room to take a piss when all the shooting started.''

''Then how do you know what happened?''

''I cracked the door at first. Then I saw what was happening and closed it fast. Sat down on the shitter and prayed like hell that God wouldn't let them come check the bathroom when they were finished.''

"Well," Maddox said, "I'm sure you've always been one of the Lord's favorite creations.''

The biker didn't catch the sarcasm.

"Who do you think these men with the Calicos might have been?" Maddox asked.

"I dunno," Bongo said. "Cops of some kind. Undercover cops. Hell, who knows? Maybe Feds.''

"And you say that two other Road Kills survived?"

"Yeah," Bongo said. "Guy named Tap Dancer and his bitch.''

"Tell me about Tap Dancer.''

"Not much to tell. He's not real bright but no eggplant, either.''

"These men—the ones who raided Miss Carriage's," Maddox said. "They took Tap Dancer and his girlfriend with them?"

"Yeah. Don't know why.''

"Bongo, I suspect they're planning to have Tap Dancer lead them to other customers of mine. Where would Tap Dancer take them?"

"I dunno.''

"Think hard. There's another five thousand in it for you if you can put me on their trail.''

"Tap Dancer had been real tight with a Road Kill named Guy," the biker said immediately.

"Guy moved down to New Orleans. Word has it he's in with the 'heads."

"You mean drug abusers, as in acid-head?" Maddox said.

"No, no, man. *Skin*heads. You know, the guys who shave their heads and hate—"

"Yes, I know what skinheads are," Maddox said. "Do you have an address or phone number on this Guy?"

"No, but I might be able to get one. I do remember somebody saying he was a bouncer at a club on Bourbon Street. Guys 'n' Dolls is the name of it. You know, like the movie? Funny, ain't it?"

"What's that?" Maddox asked.

"Well, this guy's name is Guy and he works at Guys 'n' Dolls. Sort of—" Bongo paused, searching for the right word "— ironic. Yeah, that's it, it's ironic."

"Yes, Bongo," Maddox said patiently, "it's very ironic. See if you can get Guy's home address and phone number. Then call me back. Immediately."

"Er, the five grand you was talkin' about, sir..."

"There'll be a check in the mail as soon as I hear from you again."

"Yeah...okay."

Maddox hung up, relieved to be rid of the imbecile. But he had no more than dropped the receiver into the cradle than the same line rang again.

The former Army colonel raised the phone to his ear once more. "Yes?" he said.

"It is Hiroshi," the voice said in fairly good English.

Maddox let out a minor sigh of relief. At least the Yakuza man was more intelligent than Bongo. "Yes, Hiroshi. What can I do for you?"

"Someone broke into the Takahata offices last night. There was evidence he had been in the room where our files are left on the computer."

Maddox thought a moment, frowning. "Did he get into the files that connect our transactions?" he asked.

"We do not know," Hiroshi replied. "Possibly. The computers were badly damaged when we arrived."

"The man got away?"

"Yes. There was a running battle with the police who answered the alarm. But he escaped."

"How easily could he have discovered that we had done business if he *did* access the files?" Maddox asked.

"Not easily," Hiroshi said. "But with time, it could be done. Some records must be kept."

Maddox grew silent for a moment. The crates he had purchased from Takahata had always gone to a front company he owned in Jamaica, Island Produce Distributors. If this mysterious burglar was hunting the source of the Eliminators, and had learned of the transactions between the produce distribution company and Takahata, he'd head to Kingston.

"All right, Hiroshi," Maddox finally said. "Thank you."

"There will be a bonus for this information, I assume?" the Yakuza man said.

Maddox sighed. Everyone had their hand out these days. "Five thousand," he said. "I'll wire it to you tonight."

"Thank you," Hiroshi said, and hung up.

Maddox replaced the receiver and sat back in his chair, turning to look out the window at the bright morning sun reflecting off the soft waves. Problems were beginning to arise. The Road Kills had been slaughtered and the Takahata offices broken into. Had only one of these two occurrences happened, he might have written it off as coincidence. But not both.

Someone—some agency, actually—was on the trail of the Eliminators.

Well, Maddox thought, turning to face his desk once more, when you faced a problem, you dealt with it. Whether it was a military dilemma, a business problem or some snooping bunch of U.S. government bureaucrats sticking their noses where they didn't belong, you found a way to solve your problem.

And he knew exactly how to solve this one. When you were being hunted, you eliminated the hunter.

Maddox lifted the telephone and tapped a pager number into the instrument. There was no need to enter his own number for a return call—there was no one else on the island with a phone. As soon as he heard the beep that signaled his page had been received, he hung up and tapped another number. When it beeped, he returned the receiver to the cradle once more.

Morrison arrived first. Maddox pointed to the chairs in front of his desk as he drew a big Churchill cigar from the humidor and began the lighting ritual. The man sat, as usual, without a word.

Staggs came in two minutes later. Maddox finished lighting the cigar as the man dropped into the vacant chair.

Taking two puffs from the cigar, Maddox turned the tip to his eyes to make sure the cigar was burning evenly. Then, resting it in the marble ashtray, he looked up at his two top men.

"A minor obstacle is trying to block our path, gentlemen, and I'd like you two to take care of it."

Morrison remained silent, but Staggs said, "What is it, Colonel?"

Quickly Maddox gave them a summary of the information he had just received during the two phone calls.

"So, exactly what is it you'd like us to do, sir?" Staggs asked, leaning forward in his chair.

"Take as many of the guards as you think you'll need," Maddox said, picking up his cigar again and sticking it into his mouth. "Find the men responsible for these acts and try to learn who it is sponsoring them. Then eliminate the problem for me, won't you?"

"Sure, Colonel. Where you want me to head?"

"New Orleans."

Staggs thought a moment, then said, "Sounds like there's three of these guys. I'll pick up the trail, then find a good place to snipe their asses."

"Fine," Maddox said. "However you like. Just kill them." He turned his eyes to Morrison. "Shawnee, that leaves you with Jamaica. Do you need any backup?"

Maddox had rarely seen the Indian smile and never heard him laugh. That ended now, as Morrison suddenly let out a cackle that told Maddox his question sounded as absurd to the mysterious Native American as some of those Bongo had asked during the earlier phone call.

The cackle ended abruptly, then Morrison crossed one leg over the other and let his black moccasin dangle in the air. "You said it was only one man who broke into the Takahata building?" he asked Maddox.

The colonel nodded.

"And it will be only one man who heads for the fruit company in Jamaica?"

"That's my educated guess."

"Then I'll need no one else," Morrison said in a low, almost inaudible voice. "I'll find him, torture the truth from him and kill him myself."

In the Air above Alabama

CARL LYONS LOOKED down through the sky as Charlie Mott slowed the Learjet. Below, he could see the twisting waters of the Tallapoosa River. Farther north was a heavily wooded area, with a clearing standing almost dead center. In the clearing he could see a tiny flicker of flame.

That had to be the Ku Klux Klan site of which Guy had informed them, and Lyons was ninety-nine percent sure that man hadn't lied. Guy had felt the serrated edge of Lyons's knife pressed into the flesh beneath his chin, and there had been no question in the thug's mind that even the hint of a lie would bring about a very bloody death.

"So," Mott said, "want a couple more flyovers to get your bearings, or you ready?"

"I've seen enough," Lyons replied. "Just give us time to slip into our chutes."

"I'll circle wide, then. Dress warmly, boys. We don't want you catching the sniffles, now, do we?"

Lyons moved to the back of the plane where Schwarz and Blancanales were already slipping into the straps of their parachutes. He found his own where he had left it on the floor, and lifted it to his back over the small equipment backpack he already bore. The big ex-cop also toted the 50-round Calico 950 and an extra 100-round cylindrical magazine. On his belt was his Colt Python, and stuck into the back of his pants, secured in a custom-made thumb-break inside-the-waistband strap holster, was the Colt .45 automatic with the sound suppressor.

The Able Team leader's mind traced back over the steps that had led them to this Ku Klux Klan meeting just north of Montgomery, Alabama. Guy had been hesitant to say where the Eliminators had come from, but a little extra pressure of the knife on his throat—just enough to start a thin trickle of blood dripping down his chest—had persuaded him.

The skinhead had spoken at first slowly, then faster as Lyons increased the pressure. Lyons could feel that the blade had dug under the skin, and had to be less than a centimeter from the man's carotid artery.

More importantly, Guy could feel it.

Lyons slipped the chute straps over his arms and secured the belt at his waist. Guy might or might not know it, but his words had saved both his own life and those of his men. Instead of turning their bodies into fish chum, Able Team had left them tied and bound in the alley behind New Orleans's police headquarters. They had also left some of the Eliminators and a note saying Merry Christmas and signed A friend.

A short, anonymous phone call to the desk sergeant had alerted the New Orleans men in blue as to what lay out back waiting for them.

"You guys ready?" Lyons asked as Mott banked the plane toward the clearing.

Both Schwarz and Blancanales nodded.

"I'll try to get her over into the wind," Mott said. "Give you plenty of time to get to the ground before you reach the woods." He adjusted something on the instrument panel, then added, "Wait until I give the word, then all of you get out as fast as you can. You should land within a hundred yards of the trees."

The seconds of another minute ticked by as Mott forced the Learjet into the heavy head wind. Then he said, "Okay, gents, get ready."

Lyons opened the aircraft's door.

"Jump!" Mott yelled.

Lyons dived first, and was whipped behind the plane as soon as he hit the wind. For a moment it felt as if he would move laterally forever, without falling, but a few seconds later he began to descend. He looked up as he free-fell, seeing Schwarz shoot out of the doorway. A second and a half later, Blancanales followed.

He looked down through the night, counting off the seconds before finally pulling the rip cord. The chute spilled out, caught the air and shot him suddenly upward again. When the opposing forces of wind and gravity had neutralized, he began to descend once more.

The former L.A. detective glanced over his head to see that the two other chutes had deployed successfully, then grasped the static lines and glided down to the ground.

Schwarz landed a few seconds later, ten yards to the Able Team leader's left. Blancanales came to the ground a second after that, landing twenty yards closer to the trees. All three men hauled in their canopies and weighted them down with rocks.

Lyons reached over his shoulder, unzipping his backpack and ripping out a white sheet and a pointed white hood. He threw the sheet over his shoulders and stuck his head through a hole cut in the center, then dropped it down to cover his weapons. The hood went over his head, and he stared through the eyeholes as he walked toward Blancanales.

Schwarz, now dressed identically as a Klansman, fell in next to him.

Blancanales had already slipped into his sheet and was putting the hood on as they approached.

"We go through the trees just like we belong here," Lyons said. "We'll just hang around and listen to their propaganda speeches while we get a make on who the leaders are."

"I'll try not to puke," Blancanales said.

"Good idea," Lyons countered. "Guy told us they always have a party after the meeting, drink beer and watch the cross burn out. As soon as they're drunk enough, I want both of you to zero in on a leader and get him off to the side for a little talk. Any questions?"

When he saw there was none, Lyons led the way into the trees. In their Klan sheets there was no reason for stealth, so they found a path and began to follow it. A few minutes later the fire appeared. When they stepped into the clearing, they saw the burning cross.

Perhaps a hundred men, all dressed in sheets and hoods, stood around the cross, which was just behind a short platform. Here and there Lyons could see pistol belts strapped over the sheets. Other men carried rifles or submachine guns in the crooks of their arms or slung over their shoulders.

Many of the weapons were Eliminators.

As Able Team took up spots at the rear edge of the crowd, they looked up to the podium on the stage and saw a tall hooded man screaming his hateful doctrine:

"We all remember the yellow menace!" he shouted at the top of his lungs with the fervor of a tent revivalist. "But I'm here to tell you, what we got now is a multicolored menace! We got a black menace sweeping this nation, robbing and killing our boys and raping our daughters! We got a red menace claiming we stole their land, land they was stealing back and forth from each other before we even got here."

His words were met with a round of applause. When it quieted, the speaker went on. "I just paid my income taxes for last year like the rest of you—at least *most* of the rest of you."

The line brought a few chuckles.

"Four figures it was!" the speaker screamed. "And four times what I paid the year before!"

Murmurs of acknowledgment could be heard throughout the crowd.

"Well, let me tell you something, my white brothers!" the man behind the podium cried out. "I didn't make no four times as much money last year as I did the year before! And I'm damn sick and tired of paying taxes so some drug dealer, who's making a million dollars every year selling tax-free crack cocaine on a ghetto street corner can collect his welfare check, too!''

The applause the speaker now got made the last round seem insignificant.

The racist behind the podium finished his speech, and another hooded man, shorter but with massively broad shoulders beneath his sheet, stepped up to take his place. This speaker's main complaint was illegal immigrants who were taking U.S. citizens' jobs away from them, and he ranted and raved for a good fifteen minutes before relinquishing the rostrum to a short fat man in a sheet and hood.

The speeches went on for another hour and a half, then the men began to tire of their own rhetoric. Tables with cold cuts, bread, cheese and other food, and ice chests full of beer were set up. The party began.

Some of the men, finding it difficult to eat and drink through the mouth holes of their hoods, and evidently not afraid to let their identities be known, pulled the white cloth masks from their faces and dropped them on the ground.

Able Team moved in with the crowd, standing in line and waiting as it moved toward the table. They left their own hoods on, knowing that it was possible that their unfamiliar faces might stir up a commotion. As the line moved forward, they listened to boasts, brags, threats and predictions of the evils that would befall the nation if the races mixed even further than they already had.

When they reached the buffet that had been spread out across the table, Lyons made a turkey-and-cheese sandwich as he moved along the line. Tossing a few potato chips on the plate next to it, he grabbed a beer from one of the ice chests, then moved on to follow his teammates toward a group of men sitting beneath the spreading boughs of a tall elm at the edge of the clearing.

Lyons dropped to a squatting position, resting his paper plate on one knee. Drinking his beer was difficult through the hood, eating even harder. But he managed.

The Able Team leader had learned many things about criminal groups during his years as an L.A. cop and then a Stony Man operative. One of them was that it didn't matter if they were Mafia, street criminals, terrorist groups or bigots, they were all based on the leader-follower mentality. The over-all organization always had a man—and some-times a woman—at the top who was smart and filled with charisma. But even when they broke into subgroups, someone took over the role of minicommandant.

The dozen or so men beneath the tree were no different. The listener-followers sat eating and drinking, occasionally grunting their agreement with the nonstop sermon prattling from the mouth of the talker-leader.

As the night wore on, fifth, quart and pint bottles of bourbon were broken out to be mixed with soft drinks, or swigged straight from the bottle to augment the beer. As the men got drunker, they got louder and braver but finally the alcohol began to have the reverse effect.

One by one or two by two, they began staggering off toward the pickups and other four-wheel-drive vehicles parked on the other side of the clearing.

Blancanales elbowed Lyons in the ribs. "Some Alabama highway patrolman could fill a month's quota of DUIs tonight if he was parked on the highway into town," he whispered.

Lyons nodded. "If he's not a member of this master race himself," he answered. "Okay, Pol. As soon as he leaves, I want you to follow the tall guy who spoke first. Tell Gadgets to zero in on Mr. Potato Salad here."

Blancanales turned to his other side and whispered to Schwarz.

Lyons watched the tall man—still hooded—finally end his oration and start toward them, weaving slightly from drink. He passed the group under the elm, nodded good-night and disappeared into the trees.

A moment later Blancanales followed.

The small-time potentate in Able Team's group finished his potato salad, stood and donned his hood once more. He bid several of the men goodnight by name, smiled at Lyons and started down one of the paths away from the clearing.

Ten seconds later Schwarz was on his heels.

Besides Lyons, only two men remained under the elm now, both passed out from their overdoses of alcohol. Lyons continued to sip his beer as he watched the man with the mammoth shoulders still talking to a group of eager extremists seated cross-legged by the tables. The man had removed his hood to display short-cropped, curly auburn hair and a tree-trunk neck to go with his shoulders.

As the assembly began to break up, Lyons watched the man with the big shoulders put his hood back on and start toward a path to the side of the clearing. Two other men, both wearing pistol belts, followed.

The Able Team leader let out a breath of disgust. Schwarz and Blancanales had gotten off easy—their targets had both left alone. But the thick-set man either had bodyguards or the three had come to the meeting in the same vehicle.

Which meant Lyons would have to neutralize them first.

The Able Team leader rose to his feet, then walked along the line of trees toward the path. He feigned a slight imbalance as he walked, making it look like he had imbibed more than his share like the rest of the Klansmen.

The last of the duo behind the muscle man was still visible along the path as Lyons left the clearing. The former LAPD detective accelerated his pace, quickly—but not obviously—catching up to the man in the sheet. When he was two steps behind the Klansman, he looked past to see the broad-shouldered speaker and the other man round a bend in the trees. He stepped on a twig, and the man in the sheet turned.

"Hey, Bubba," he slurred drunkenly, "one hell of a party, huh?"

"Yep," Lyons said. He fell in stride with the other man, reached under his sheet and produced the Colt Python.

A split second later the revolver came down on the Klansman's head.

Lyons jerked an Eliminator Government Model out of the Klansman's holster and tossed it out of sight into the trees. He replaced the Python beneath his sheet and hurried on, rounding the bend in the trees himself to spot the other two men ten yards ahead. They heard him behind them and glanced over their shoulders.

The Able Team leader waited for them to turn away again before the Colt jumped back into his hand. He gripped it by the barrel, then sprinted forward and brought the grip frame down on the hood of the man next to the speaker.

The broad-shouldered man turned in time to see his friend bite the dust. "What do—?" he started to say.

"Shut up," Lyons ordered, twirling the Python. He knelt and drew a Smith & Wesson .44 Magnum revolver from the holster of the man on the ground, then stood up and shoved both revolvers into the mouth hole of the other man's hood. "Drag your buddy into the trees."

"But—"

"Now." The sound of two revolver hammers clicking back to a cocked position echoed through the woods.

Lyons pulled the revolvers out of the hood and stepped back as the broad-shouldered man stooped and grasped his companion by the wrists, dragging him off the path behind a row of bushes. The Able Team leader stepped forward again as the Klansman dropped his friend's arms. With his free hand he reached up and jerked the hood from the other man's head, then patted him down for other weapons. Finding nothing, he said, "Okay, Curly, I want to know where you got the Eliminators."

None of the cockiness and bravado the Klansman had exhibited while speaking was detectable now. His face had turned the color of fresh milk, and his lower lip trembled as he spoke. "I...I don't know..." he managed to get out. "I don't procure the arms."

"Then who does?" Lyons demanded.

He never got the answer to his question.

Before the broad-shouldered Klansman could respond, a burst of automatic rifle fire broke the stillness of the night.

It was answered with a long stream of fire from a 9 mm Calico subgun.

CHAPTER THIRTEEN

Northern Ireland

David McCarter and Gary Manning sprinted out of the Millennium Malt room and across the lobby. They slowed as they reached the peat fire just inside the back door, then cautiously stepped outside. Somewhere on the other side of the centuries-old building they could hear the helicopter blades whirling in the air.

McCarter led the way to the corner of the building just as the chopper set down fifty yards from the stage. He raised the walkie-talkie to his lips and thumbed the button on the side. "Phoenix One, Phoenix Five," he whispered into the hand-held instrument. "You copy, T.J.?"

"That's affirmative."

"What's the situation at the towers?" McCarter asked. In the distance, he watched two men in conservative business suits step down from the chopper.

"Oh, nothing much. Just a couple a good ol' boys setting up to shoot someone."

McCarter paused, then said. "Affirmative. Manning and I are on our way." He released the button for a second, cleared his throat and said, "Felix, are you still by the trees?"

"Affirmative."

"You're the one with the credentials the royal's bodyguards will pay attention to. Start toward the chopper and see if you can keep them off the stage."

"On my way," O'Prunty replied, "but I'm a fair piece off. It'll be tight."

"Do your best," McCarter said. Static filled the airwaves for a moment. As soon as it had cleared, he thumbed the mike again. "Phoenix One to Two and Three. Come in, Two and Three."

"Three here," James said quickly.

He was followed by Encizo. "Two."

"Cal," McCarter said, "move into the crowd. The bomb inside the distillery was a hoax. They've got backup snipers in the towers. If they've gone to that much trouble, they may have scattered men in with the people over there. Be ready."

"Affirmative," both Phoenix Force warriors said into their radios.

The royal was still on board the chopper when

McCarter nodded at Manning, then led him along the rear wall of the distillery toward the other corner of the building, facing the Pagoda Towers. Even though they were out of sight of the crowd, they kept their weapons holstered and hidden beneath their tweed jackets.

Now was no time to take the chance of panicking people.

The two Phoenix Force commandos were almost to the corner before they drew their guns. As luck would have it, a jogging late-comer suddenly appeared from the trees, hurrying toward where the speaker would be. He saw the pistols and opened his mouth to scream.

McCarter turned his Browning Hi-Power toward the man and said, "Make one sound and it'll be your last, bloke."

The man froze in place, his arms shooting into the air as if he expected to be robbed.

Manning didn't have to be told what to do. The Canadian knew they didn't have time to explain the situation to the man or even bind and gag him. He was probably just an innocent party.

But probably wasn't good enough. There was always the chance that he was one of the IRA terrorists.

Phoenix Force's explosives expert reached the late-comer in three fast steps and brought down his Beretta 92 on the crown of the man's balding head. "Sorry, old chap," he said in a phony British accent as the man hit the ground. "Life's a bitch, isn't it?"

McCarter moved on to the corner of the distillery, dropped to one knee and peered around the stone. Barely visible in the twin towers were the tops of two heads, one in each tower. The heads moved up and down slightly, indicating that the snipers were probably making last-minute adjustments to their equipment.

The Phoenix Force leader pulled back. He had seen what he needed to see, and every additional second he looked was a second he risked being spotted. He raised the walkie-talkie to his lips again. "One to Five," he whispered. "Your location, T.J.?"

"I'm behind the shed just to your left. I can see you."

McCarter turned toward the shed and saw a hand move briefly into the open, wave, then disappear again. He keyed his mike. "There are two of them, T.J.," he said. "One in each tower."

"Affirmative," Hawkins said.

"Can they see you?" McCarter asked.

"Don't think so. At least they aren't showing any signs that they have yet."

"Affirmative, Five. Stand by."

The Phoenix Force leader stole another peek at the towers, wishing for a moment that he had a long gun and a scope. Well, he told himself, wishing wouldn't make it magically materialize. There had been no way to hide rifles in this crowd, and as always, he and the other men from Stony Man Farm would have to make do with what they did have.

On the other side of the building, the brass band positioned in front of the stage suddenly struck up a rousing rendition of "Rule Britannia." Many in the crowd began to cheer.

There was also a good deal of hissing and derision.

McCarter couldn't see anyone, but he knew that the royal had to be just now stepping down out of the chopper.

Raising the radio to his mouth yet again, McCarter said, "Phoenix One to MI-6. Come in, Felix."

The Irishman was desperately out of breath, and McCarter could hear his pounding feet, the applause of the crowd and the music over the airwaves as O'Prunty keyed his own unit. "MI-6 to One," he said, panting. "I'm trying to get to her, lad, but I shan't be makin' it in time." He took a deep, painful gulp of air. "Too far away."

McCarter turned to Manning, who now stood directly behind him, his back to the stone of the distillery. "Gary," he said, "this is going to be thin. The snipers will have to rise up to take their shots, and we've got to pick them off then. We'll have a couple of seconds. Maybe five. No more." He keyed his mike again. "Phoenix Five, Manning and I will take out the subjects as soon as they rise. Repeat. We shoot the moment they show their heads." He paused. "You still have visual?"

"Affirmative. I'll let you know as soon as their heads peek over the rail."

The Phoenix Force leader nodded. He pulled the slide slightly back on the Hi-Power and saw the gleam of the brass casing in the chamber. Then, turning to Manning, he said, "Just as soon as T.J. gives us the word, I'll lean around the corner. You stand over me. Take the tower on the right. I'll get the left." He took a deep, nerve-easing breath. "And remember the famous words of Wyatt Earp about gunfights."

Manning frowned.

"Take your time...in a hurry," McCarter said.

Manning smiled and nodded. Then his face changed to an expression of concentration and anticipation.

McCarter, still on one knee, set the walkie-talkie on the ground between him and Manning, and edged as close to the corner of the building as he dared. He thumbed down the Browning's manual safety and rested his index finger on the side of the trigger guard. Then he waited.

From the other side of the building came the sound of a man's voice over the speaker system. McCarter tuned the words out of his ears, riveting his attention to the task ahead. The man droned on, his voice heard but his words uncomprehended by the Phoenix Force leader.

After several minutes, the man's voice stopped and loud applause came over the sound system. As it began to die down, the voice of the royal said, "Good morning, ladies and gentlemen."

Polite applause—punctuated by a catcall or two—greeted the opening words.

Hawkins's voice sounded over the noise from the walkie-talkie on the ground. "Phoenix Five to One. I'm seeing movement."

McCarter didn't answer. He waited.

"Right tower," Hawkins said. "Head just popped up, took a look, then down again. Wait...okay...left tower, same thing. They're getting ready to make their move."

The Briton took another deep breath. He and Manning would get one chance, and one chance only. They had to shoot simultaneously to avoid alerting the snipers, and if either of the Phoenix Force warriors missed his target, the man would drop down behind the stone again. Then there'd be hell to pay trying to get the sniper out of the tower.

The royal went into the speech. Again Mc-

Carter listened to the voice but ignored the words. Perhaps thirty seconds later, Hawkins said, "Right tower, head up. He's raising his rifle."

McCarter prepared to lean around the corner and fire. Behind and above him, he could sense Gary Manning doing the same thing. The Phoenix Force leader took a deep breath, let half of it out and held it.

"Left tower up," Hawkins said quickly. "Rifle up. Go for it, guys."

McCarter and Manning leaned around the corner, looked up at the snipers in the Pagoda Towers and fired.

Kingston, Jamaica

JAMAICA HAD ONLY RATED one paragraph in Fielding's *The World's Most Dangerous Places* guidebook, but it deserved a volume of its own. *Dangerous Places* advised the visitor to exercise prudence, not walk around at night and use only licensed taxis or hotel-recommended transportation. Special care, the guidebook stressed, should be taken in the isolated villas and small establishments in the northern-coast tourist areas.

That warning wasn't even the tip of the iceberg, the Executioner knew as he strolled along the sidewalk separating the wharf from the stores, shops and saloons of Kingston. It said nothing about the organized crime that openly sold drugs, weapons and prostitutes of both sexes and all ages. It didn't mention that the tourist who violated the warnings stood roughly a fifty-fifty chance of waking up in some alley with his throat cut, or floating back to shore in whatever pieces the sharks had missed.

But other guidebooks said even less. They stressed the beaches, scuba diving, golf and tennis clubs, and the scenic beauty of the Blue Mountains that rose keenly up from Kingston.

The Blue Mountains had long ago become only dark, shadowy mounds in the night as Bolan strolled on along the sidewalk. Loud reggae music blasted from every open doorway. Men, women and children crowded the walkway. The odors of fish, alcoholic beverages, human sweat and curry assaulted the sinuses.

The Executioner passed a Rastafarian boutique featuring posters and framed photos of reggae bands, ganja-smoking paraphernalia and religious fetishes in the window. He continued on past an outdoor squash court where men played the game under bright overhead lights. Reaching into his pocket, he pulled out the slip of paper Grimaldi had handed him just before he'd deplaned.

"Keating and Gryphon Streets," it read. "Corner."

Bolan moved through the bright lights, finally

leaving the nightlife area and venturing into a commercial zone. The pedestrian traffic fell off somewhat but the streets were hardly deserted. The Executioner followed his memory of the Kingston city map he had studied during the flight, turning down a dark, narrow street and away from the population. He followed Keating, then made a sharp turn and found himself looking at a street sign that announced Gryphon.

Island Produce Distributors stood on the corner where the slip of paper said it would be. Delivery trucks were parked in a lot next to an open-air, bazaarlike market. A small office area that appeared to have once been a service station stood directly behind the marketplace.

Bolan saw native women dressed in baggy pastel shorts and blouses, their hair in curlers, filling paper sacks with fruit and vegetables. Several men worked the cash registers, giving out advice and ringing up sales.

The Executioner walked past the market, noting a separate, corrugated-steel storage building just to the rear of the office. Set on a concrete slab, it was a large structure, windowless and without doors save the entrance facing the market. The lone opening was secured with a heavy padlock.

The Executioner studied the lock as he passed, wondering idly just which fruit or vegetable it might be that warranted such tight security.

Circling the block, Bolan passed the open market once more, noting that the men selling the various items glanced now and then at the tin building. He moved under the roof that shielded the fresh fruits and vegetables from both sun and rain, and made a show of inspecting some small red potatoes. What he was really looking for— and what he saw—was a sign in the office window that advised the public the market would close for the day in less than thirty minutes.

He could wait.

Circling the block once more, the Executioner cut down an unlit alley in an effort to get a better look at the rear of the tin building. He heard a dog bark, a cat hiss, then the dog yelped in pain. Ahead Bolan saw the shiny silver reflection of a freshly painted fifty-five-gallon drum pressed into service as a trash can. As he neared the can, the shadow of a large rat scurried from the other side of the alley and behind the drum. The rat returned from hiding immediately, disappearing into the shadows from whence he'd come.

The yellow caution light in Bolan's head—the light that he lived with constantly—changed to orange. He wasn't sure why. He just knew he sensed danger somewhere in the alley.

Bolan walked on, his only light the slight illumination of the Caribbean moon that filtered down into the narrow path of the alley. He was abreast of the trash can when he saw a flash in his peripheral vision. He turned.

At first the long curved blade that swept toward him looked like part of the silver garbage can that had broken off and taken on a life of its own; he could see nothing else. His arm rose instinctively, his fingers and thumb separating to form a Y that snagged the wrist just beyond the hand wielding the blade. He felt the soft cotton of a long-sleeved T-shirt beneath his fingers and tried to catch hold of the wrist. But the hand holding the knife was too fast. Before he could grip down, it was gone again.

Bolan caught a quick glimpse of white around the dark brown eyes filled with the predator's lust for the kill as his attacker moved back into the shadows and out of reach. The Executioner reached for the Glock 21 on his hip. But before he could draw, the blade appeared again, this time launching straight forward in a thrust. Whoever it was employing the blade was dressed completely in black, and in the dim light, the weapon still almost appeared to move of its own accord.

Bolan stepped to one side, letting the knife pass by, and helping it do so with the palm of one hand. Again he tried to clamp his fingers on the wrist behind the knife. Again the blade was gone as fast as it had come.

The Executioner took a step backward, hoping

to gain time to draw a weapon, as well as lure his opponent away from the shadows and into what little light there was in the center of the alley. He achieved only the latter, but he caught another quick look at his assailant as the knife slashed through the air in a back slash.

Besides the long-sleeved black T-shirt and thin black leather gloves, the man wore black jeans and dark moccasins. His face had been streaked with black night-camo makeup, and his long black hair was tied behind him in twin braids.

Backpedaling away from the slash, Bolan stepped out of the way of a downward cut that threatened to halve his skull. Now he got a glimpse of the silhouette of the knife itself—an Al Mar Warrior, one of the most wicked-looking fighting blades ever produced. The primary cutting edge was factory sharpened to that of a razor's, as was an inch or so on the back. The rest of the recurved edge of the blade was made up of a series of huge, gaping sawteeth that grinned at the Executioner like some diabolic jack-o'-lantern.

Bolan tried for the Beretta this time but a reverse thrust forced him to move and block. Again and again the knife sliced the air. Again and again Bolan dodged, ducked, slapped and parried, always trying to grab the wrist that brandished the blade, always failing. He made a quick move for the Applegate-Fairbairn folding knife but the dark shadow saw it coming and shot the Al Mar forward in a short jab to the face.

The Executioner was forced to abandon his own weapon to keep from taking the ragged curved blade hilt-deep in the brain.

This man with the knife—the Executioner had now caught glimpses of high cheekbones and a large Roman nose under the camo makeup— wasn't just an expert with his blade. He was also one of the quickest combatants the Executioner had ever faced.

Bolan ducked under a shadowy thrust that missed his scalp by a quarter of an inch. His foot shot out, catching his assailant in the shin. He heard a spontaneous but muffled grunt, and the shadowy form backed away.

The Executioner threw his light jacket back away from his hip and ripped the Glock 21 from the Helweg speed rig. The web of his hand automatically hit the laser-activation button, and the red dot appeared on the ground in front of him as the Glock's muzzle cleared leather. Bolan walked the dot upward as he continued to raise the weapon from the draw.

But when it hit chest level, the specterlike form was gone.

Bolan used the red splash light of the laser as

a flashlight, searching the alley. He checked behind the trash can.

It was no use. His attacker had vanished like a wisp of smoke in a strong wind.

The Executioner kept the Glock in hand until he reached the end of the alley. Who had the man been? A mugger? The streets of Kingston were full of them, and many weren't only skilled but experienced at their work.

But not like this man. The man in the black jeans, moccasins and T-shirt was a professional. The blade dexterity he had demonstrated went beyond that of a mere street mugger. Oh, he knew the street tricks, all right. But during the course of the encounter the Executioner had fended off techniques that he recognized from the American military style of knife-fighting, the Japanese art of *tanto-jitsu,* and Filipino *kali.* And the man in black had picked the perfect blade for his peculiar mixture of forms—the Al Mar Warrior could be used well in all three.

Bolan waited at the edge of the alley until he heard the market close on the other side. Then, giving it five more minutes, he crept through the shadows to the front of the corrugated-steel building.

The Executioner didn't know for sure what he'd find inside the storage building, but he suspected it would be Eliminators. And he had every confidence that they'd be stored in unmarked wooden crates manufactured in Japan at the Takahata Box, Crate and Container Company.

Glancing up and down the street to make sure it was now deserted, Bolan rounded the corner and slid along the corrugated steel to the oversize padlock bolting the door. The lock itself was the size of his fist, and it was new, showing no signs of rust or deterioration.

Bolan reached into the side pocket of his jacket for the leather case that contained his picks, then cursed softly under his breath. They had fallen out somewhere in the alley sometime during the fight with the man in black.

But the Executioner could search for them later if there was time, and if not, Grimaldi would have a backup set on the Learjet.

For now, the game was beginning to draw to a close. He could feel it, touch it, taste and smell it. It made no difference if the men at Island Produce returned the next morning to find that the storage building had been entered.

Under the circumstances, the sound-suppressed Beretta 93-R would be the only key he needed.

Slowly the Executioner drew the weapon from the shoulder harness beneath his jacket. He held it close to his body as he looked up and down the street one last time to make certain no curious pedestrians were watching. Satisfied that the streets were deserted, he turned back to the padlock and pressed the muzzle against the steel.

Alabama

LYONS LOOKED at the Klansman who stood before him. His wild eyes and gaping mouth told the Able Team leader that the man was as surprised by the gunfire as he was himself.

Another rapid-fire burst from a Calico sent Lyons into action. Raising the Klansman's .44 Magnum revolver over his head, he brought it down onto the man's scalp and watched the bigot collapse to the ground.

The big ex-cop turned, sprinting back along the path toward the clearing. The man he had just struck might regain consciousness before he returned to ask questions, but if that happened, so be it. The gunfire meant that either Schwarz's or Blancanales's cover had been blown, and helping them rated higher priority.

AK-47 rounds, fired semiauto, continued to pepper the air as Lyons ran. The distinctive 9 mm submachine gun sounded again, then a second Calico joined the battle. Every few seconds the sound of a 12-gauge shotgun exploded above the roars of the other weapons.

That answered the Able Team leader's question as to which one of his men needed help.

They both did.

The blasts of gunfire grew louder as Lyons drew closer to the clearing. He slowed his pace as he neared the edge of the trees, then came to a complete halt behind the trunk of a thick elm. Dropping to his knees, he squinted into the open area of woods.

Only a fool rushed into battle without first stopping to see what awaited him, and Carl Lyons was far from being a fool. Peering around the sturdy tree trunk, he would take time to evaluate the situation before he blitzed blindly from cover and chanced taking a volley of 7.62 mm rounds himself. He'd be little good to Schwarz or Blancanales dead.

The only problem was, the clearing was deserted.

But the gunfire continued. From his new vantage point, Lyons could tell that the rounds were being fired on the other side of the open area, not far but far enough inside the trees on the other side that the shooters were all hidden from view.

Rising to his feet, the Able Team leader backtracked along the path, then began to make his way through the woods, circling the clearing. He stayed close enough to watch the free tract, keeping one eye on it, the other ahead of him in case he encountered any straggling Klansmen. Moving as quickly as he could without making unnecessary noise, he skirted the clearing, gradually getting closer to the ongoing firefight.

Finally nearing another small clearing perhaps two hundred feet from the main Klan meeting area, Lyons saw Schwarz and Blancanales pinned down inside a cluster of boulders. The stones were too small to provide real cover, and his men had been forced to the ground, contorting into strange-looking poses to take advantage of what little protection was available.

Taking fire from three sides, neither man could return the salvos, except for an occasional blind eruption around the edges of the rocks. What made things even worse was the positioning of those rocks—many rounds that struck one boulder ricocheted to strike others, rebounding back and forth within the stone fortress before their momentum was spent.

Sooner or later Lyons knew those bouncing rounds would find their marks.

The Able Team leader's first instinct was to charge forward to the aid of his teammates. But that would do no good—there wasn't enough refuge for two men, let alone three. No, he could better serve his men by staying away from the stone death trap and operating independently.

Lyons watched pebbles and white dust blow up into the air as a new burst of AK-47 rounds struck the rocks in front of Schwarz and Blancanales. He moved swiftly to his right, sidestepping tree trunks and thorn bushes and keeping his gaze focused ahead of him. He had gone less than twenty feet when he spotted a white sheet gripping one of the Russian rifles as it bucked in recoil.

Lyons drew the sound suppressed 1911 Government Model pistol and came to a halt next to one of the trees. Using the trunk as support, he lined the sights up on the sheet and fired.

The .45 coughed, its noise muffled by the suppressor. The man in the sheet toppled to the ground.

The Able Team leader moved on, ducking low-hanging limbs and stepping around other obstacles. A flicker of white showed ahead, and he checked his pace, studying it. It moved slightly, then the gleam of a rifle barrel glistened for a moment under the moonlight.

Lyons pulled the trigger of the .45 again. Another cough, another dead Klansman.

The next few feet revealed a trio of men, two bearing what looked like M-14s. Lyons squinted at them—there was something not quite right about the rifles. But he had no time to worry about that now.

The third Klansman fired a long-barreled, semi-auto, civilian-version Uzi. But someone had converted the weapon to full-auto, and Lyons watched the man pull back the trigger once and get a volley of five rounds to ignite.

The big ex–LAPD detective moved deeper into the forest as the onslaught at the rocks continued. He prayed silently that neither Schwarz nor Blancanales would take a direct round or ricochet before he could eliminate the shooters surrounding them.

Moving even with the three Klansmen, Lyons approached them from the rear. Again he steadied his muffled weapon along the side of a tree, the act bringing back memories of police firing ranges where wooden posts simulated the corners of buildings and other actual cover to aid training. Hooking out the thumb of his supporting hand, he pressed it against the bark, making sure the weapon itself was clear of the trunk and had plenty of room to allow the slide to cycle. Then, with a deep breath, he lined up the white three-dot sights on the back of the Klansman with the Uzi and squeezed the trigger.

The .45 hollowpoint round struck the gunman dead center in the back. His shoulder blades folded back as if trying to touch each other, bowing his chest outward. His head and neck shot forward, and Lyons saw blood and tissue shoot out from the front of the man.

All in all, Lyons thought as he swung his weapon toward one of the men with the M-14s, the man looked like a diver who had just sprung off the high board. But the Able Team leader wasted no time admiring his work, immediately pumping two more quiet rounds into the back of the Klansman to the fallen man's immediate right. This gunner fell as quickly as the first, but by that time the third man in white had figured out that a rear attack was taking place.

The Klansman whirled, aiming his M-14 into the trees.

Lyons wasn't concealed, but the trees and low light meant the Klansman had to take an extra second to locate his target before firing.

And an extra second was more time than the Able Team leader needed.

Lyons's .45 expelled another duo of hollow-point rounds, the first catching the white-clad gunner low in the left side. The man screamed as the force of the big slug spun him 180 degrees, back to face the rocks where Schwarz and Blancanales had taken refuge. The second bullet caught him in the nape and sent him flying forward into the trunk of a tree. He rebounded backward like a character in some slapstick skit, and fell on top of the man who had toted the Uzi.

The Able Team leader jumped back behind the tree, dropped the magazine containing one last round and started to reach for one of the fresh loads in the carrier under his right arm. As he did, he saw a flicker of white directly in front of him, then another rifle barrel being brought up into play.

With no time to reload, the former LAPD detective raised the Colt and fired. The round still in the chamber shot through a narrow passageway between several elms and a tall fern, clipping the leaves off the greenery before finding a home somewhere beneath the white sheet. The Colt's slide locked open empty.

Lyons drew the Python from his hip and let it hang at the ready with his left index finger in the trigger guard. He again reached for a new magazine. A rustling in the short grass caused him to flip up the revolver, his fingers closing around the rubber Pachmayer grips. Then a squirrel darted out of the grass and ran up a tree.

A hard smile covered his face as Lyons let the Python dangle again, blindly sliding a new magazine up the butt of the .45. A moment later he thumbed the slide release and jacked the top round into the chamber.

He had now worked his way halfway around the semicircle where the Klansmen were still firing into the rocks. Moving quietly again, Lyons left the tree and continued on, making his way toward the source of the remaining gunfire. He heard the shotgun detonate again with a loud boom, then a voice—it sounded like Schwarz—grunted behind the rocks.

Lyons felt the fires of hatred charge through his soul. Had Gadgets been hit? He didn't know. But he *had* known all along it was just a matter of time before the Klansmen got a lucky shot.

And time was running out.

Lyons quickened his pace, sacrificing silence for speed now as he cut between the trees. He had to get the surviving Klansmen.

The four white-clad men had taken sanctuary behind several large boulders and a dead tree that had fallen to the ground. They continued to fire, reloading their weapons when necessary.

With no good cover to use himself as he came to another break in the trees, Lyons dropped into a prone position. He might as well make himself as small a target as possible, he thought. He holstered the .45 under his arm. The time for silence was over. No shots could be heard coming from past the place where the Klansmen had barricaded themselves, and he rolled to his side, lifting his own sheet and swinging the Calico out on its sling.

Holding the rear grip with his right hand, the foregrip with his left, the Able Team leader dropped the safety next to the trigger guard to the full-auto mode. He aimed first at the nearest man, a Klansman who had stopped to reload the Russian rifle in his hands.

A burst of 9 mm Winchester Silver Tip bullets exploded from the Calico, the first two rounds hitting the AK-47 and sending it spinning from the Klansman's grip. Four more rounds stitched the man up the ribs, the final shiny silver bullet drilling into the side of the man's face.

The Able Team leader didn't wait to watch the results of his burst, instead raising the Calico's barrel slightly higher toward the Klansman with the shotgun. The man pulled the trigger a second before Lyons did, and another 12-gauge blast was drilled toward Schwarz and Blancanales.

Pulling back the trigger, Lyons sent another short burst into the man. The rounds crushed the sheet into the man's side, and tiny dots of crimson suddenly stained the white linen. The spots were already larger and were growing into blobs before the gunner hit the ground.

Lyons swung up his weapon again, the Calico leaping in recoil as his ensuing assault punched into the next man in line. The entire cluster of six 9 mm rounds fell inside a group the size of the Able Team leader's fist, and yet another sheet-clad bigot tumbled to the ground.

The final Klansman turned to face Lyons as the sights atop of the hexagonal magazine fell on his chest. The big ex-cop looked at the terror in a wrinkled, unhooded face, and wondered how much terror the man had implanted in the hearts of members of other races over the years.

Too much. Far too much for what Lyons was about to do to make up for it. But it was *all* he could do, and even though it wouldn't even the score, it would stop it from getting higher.

Lyons held the trigger back and let a full ten rounds penetrate the sheet.

The explosions died down, and for a moment the forest fell silent. Then a voice from behind the boulders inside the clearing said, "Well, Ironman, is that you or the Lone Ranger?"

There was a brief pause, then Blancanales continued. "I know it's not the cavalry riding in to save our butts. I didn't hear any bugles."

Lyons had no time to reply to the wisecrack. He felt something rip through his arm a microsecond before he heard its sound. His flesh felt on fire as a second rifle round echoed through the woods, missing him, but providing direction identification.

Before he even realized what he'd done, the Able Team leader swung the Calico toward the noise and fired.

Schwarz and Blancanales, frustrated for too long in their inability to shoot back, turned and joined the fray. All three Able Team warriors watched a man wearing three-color tiger-stripe cammies drop the scoped M-16 A-2 in his hands and jerk in a dance of death as several dozen 9 mm rounds from the Calicos riddled his body.

Caution screamed in Lyons's ear, and he called out "Cease fire!" As the explosions died down, he walked forward, knowing already it was too late. Whoever it was who now lay soaking in his own blood, he wasn't a Klansman. At least Carl Lyons didn't think the man was, considering how he was dressed.

He stopped over the body. The top of the man's camouflage BDU blouse had been left unbuttoned, and beneath it Lyons saw a matching camouflage T-shirt. The man wore a shoulder holster bearing a Smith & Wesson Model 629 .44 Magnum pistol, a Colt Gold Cup .45 on his belt and a custom made boot knife.

All three weapons bore stag handles, and the Able Team leader wondered if that had some significance.

CHAPTER FOURTEEN

Stony Man Farm

Kurtzman turned in his chair to face Dr. Glenn Barrister as the metallurgist walked up the ramp toward the bank of computers. Behind Barrister came John "Cowboy" Kissinger and a large man in blacksuit.

A temporary laboratory had been set up in one of the outer buildings as soon as Barrister had finished writing out the list of equipment and supplies he needed to isolate the steel in the Eliminators. Stony Man Farm airplanes, as well as land vehicles, had been departing for hours ever since, returning with the assorted equipment until the laboratory was complete.

Now, Kurtzman realized, the experiments themselves had to have ended. And at the same time the smile on Barrister's face suggested that they had been successful. "Roll up a chair, Glenn," the computer expert suggested.

The blacksuit following him—a DEA agent trainee who had been assigned as the metallurgist's personal guide during his stay—had already thought of it. He lifted a chair and carried it, rather than rolling it, after Dr. Barrister.

Kissinger moved in to stand next to the doctor as Barrister sat down. Kurtzman cleared the screen in front of him, switched disks and pressed several keys to link his computer to Akira Tokaido's. He glanced at the young man and nodded.

Tokaido nodded back.

"So, Glenn," the Stony Man Farm cybernetics expert said, "what have we got?"

Barrister opened a manila file and produced a bundle of pages. Placing them in his lap, he looked down and began to read off the data he had collected from his experiments with the various Eliminators in Stony Man Farm's possession. Kurtzman listened, typing the doctor's words at the same time. His flying fingers stopped momentarily as Barrister coughed and the tone of his voice changed.

"The first thing I did," Barrister said, "was to rework the tests Mr. Kissinger had performed. This is standard procedure when one takes over *anyone* else's experimentation. Please do not take any offense."

Kissinger shook his head. "None taken. But how'd I do?"

Barrister smiled. "Not bad. Not bad at all, particularly for someone working somewhat outside of his field. A general understanding of metallurgy is part of gunsmithing, I'm sure. But this was far more complex than what most armorers would have been able to understand, Cowboy."

Kissinger chuckled. "I think what you're trying to do is politely tell me I made some mistakes."

"Yes, but not many and not serious. At least not enough to keep our conclusions from being the same. You should actually be quite proud of yourself. We all have our individual fields of expertise." He glanced at the pistol on Kissinger's hip. "Don't ask me to fix that thing if it breaks. I wouldn't know where to start."

"Then we've been working along the right lines?" Kurtzman asked. "The steel going into the Eliminators *is* all coming from the same place?"

"Oh, yes." Barrister nodded. "By all means. In fact the vast majority of it even comes from the same batch, so to speak. The odds, I would say, are a hundred thousand to one that the steel was all smelted in the same furnace. But I'm at a loss as to how you're going to locate that furnace with all the different plants around the world."

Kurtzman held up a hand, tapped the keys on

his keyboard and sucked the Takahata Company files across the room from the hard drive in Tokaido's computer. Barrister squinted at the screen as Tokaido walked up the ramp.

Kurtzman introduced the two men. The computer man smiled as the gray-headed Barrister, wearing khaki slacks, brown wing-tip shoes and another of his short-sleeved white shirts, open at the collar, looked Tokaido up and down. Barrister's eyes paused first at the silver studded cutoff jean jacket, then at the tall black motorcycle boots that covered the young Japanese toe to knee.

Tokaido noticed the once-over and grinned. "Please relax, Dr. Barrister. I don't cook and eat small children, and am more efficient than I may appear to you."

Barrister chuckled and said, "Okay."

All heads now turned back to the screen as Kurtzman pulled up a roster of companies for which the Takahata Company made shipping crates. He typed in "steel manufacturers," hit the Return button and the vast majority of the list disappeared. Four company names remained, and he turned back to Barrister. "Want to make any guesses as to which one we should try first?"

Barrister shook his head in wonder. "I would ask you how you did that, Bear," he said, "but I get the feeling it's fairly complex and would take away valuable time from our project."

Kurtzman nodded. "A detailed explanation would. And I'd be glad to run it down after all this is over if you're still interested. For now could you live with this? I've developed my own program that cuts out all of the 'unlikelies' with a few typed words and the single press of a button."

Barrister nodded, squinting again at the screen. He silently read the names of the four steel companies. "Cowboy, didn't you say something about thinking this Eliminator person was located somewhere in the Caribbean? From other evidence, or something?"

Kissinger nodded. "We have a man checking out another lead in Jamaica right now."

"Then why don't we try the closest company to Jamaica?" Barrister said.

"That would have been my suggestion," Kurtzman replied, his fingers already moving over the keyboard. He moved the cursor on the screen down the four names to the bottom, then highlighted the words "Belcher, Belcher and Eby Steel, Birmingham, Alabama." A moment later he had linked into the files of the company.

Barrister leaned forward as Kurtzman divided the screen, the left side now exhibiting the results of the metallurgist's tests on the Eliminators, the right showing the formulas, processes and components that went into the company's steel. Kurtzman wheeled himself back and let Barrister scoot his chair even closer where he could work the cursor himself.

The screen's left half remained stationary as the right began to scroll upward. Barrister stopped periodically, studying the different formulas and comparing them to his own findings, then moved on.

Ten minutes later the metallurgist had exhausted the Belcher, Belcher and Eby Steel Company's files. "Well," he said, "that was a bust."

"Nothing?" Kurtzman asked.

"Oh, there are a lot of similarities," Barrister replied. "That's why I stopped and looked closer at several of the formulas. But that's to be expected. I mean, we're talking steel here and after all, the basics are going to be the same." He paused, took a deep breath, then added, "But I'd have to say that in my professional estimation, the steel that went into the Eliminators didn't come from here."

Kurtzman shrugged, feeling a mild disappointment.

"So what do we do now?" Barrister asked.

The computer expert cleared the screen and pulled up the other three company names again. "Keep trying," he said.

Northern Ireland

MCCARTER PULLED the trigger and saw the
.40-caliber S&W hollowpoint round find its target
in the sniper's left temple. A millisecond later, he
heard Gary Manning's Beretta 92 explode just
above his head.

Even before he saw the results of the shot, he
knew they had a problem. The sniper in the tower
to the right had flinched instinctively at Mc-
Carter's shot, and that flinch meant he'd moved.

Manning's 9 mm round caught the man in the
side of the neck as he tried to duck. Before
McCarter could swing his Browning that way, or
Manning could squeeze off a follow-up shot, the
head had disappeared below the stone barrier at
the top of the tower.

The Briton bit off a curse. He had started to
reach behind him for the walkie-talkie when the
second sniper's head suddenly reappeared.

The sniper had traded his rifle for a Sterling
submachine gun, and both McCarter and Manning
had no sooner ducked behind the corner than a
long burst of gunfire erupted, striking the stone
wall.

On the other side of the distillery, the Phoenix
Force leader heard what sounded like a riot break
out. Screams and the sounds of running feet met
his ears. McCarter found the walkie-talkie and
keyed the mike. "What's happening over there,
Felix?" he asked.

The MI-6 operative sounded even more out of breath than before. "To put it bluntly, mate," he said, "everyone's going ape-shit. The Yard boys are hustling the royal back to the chopper. The crowd doesn't know what's going on. They're running every which way."

The Phoenix Force leader tried to speak, but another volley from the wounded sniper drowned out his words. When the explosions died down, he said, "Felix, get to the Scotland Yard team and explain what's happening. Give them a description of all of us—a damn good description. I don't want them shooting at the wrong people."

"Affirmative, David," O'Prunty said. "What's the situation there?"

"One of the snipers is wounded. The other's down for the count." As he spoke, he saw Hawkins dart out from behind the shed where he'd been hiding and join him and Manning against the distillery wall. "We're going to have to try to get the man out of the tower without his shooting anyone else."

"And exactly how do you plan to do that?" O'Prunty asked.

"Felix, I haven't the foggiest idea right now. But get the crowd away from the scene and out of rifle range, then come join us."

He paused a moment, thinking, then said, "James, you and Encizo listening?"

"Affirmative," they both replied.

"Circle the tower," McCarter commanded. "Spread out and let's at least get into position where we can catch this man in a cross fire if the chance presents itself."

James and Encizo responded in the affirmative, and then the airwaves went dead.

McCarter turned to Manning, but the big Canadian spoke first.

"Sorry, David. I missed."

"You didn't miss," McCarter said. "And it couldn't be helped. The man jerked at my shot, and there was nothing we could have done to stop it. At least he's wounded." The Phoenix Force leader's eyebrows furrowed in thought. "What we need to know is how bad."

McCarter leaned around the corner again, presenting himself as a target. A moment later he saw the top of a head come up over the edge of the stone. Not enough to shoot at. The chances of success were maybe one in a hundred.

Then the sniper's Sten came over the edge, and another burst of fire drove McCarter back around the corner. But in the split second during which the IRA man's head and shoulders were visible, the Phoenix Force leader saw that he was bleeding profusely from the neck.

Risking another look, McCarter saw Encizo and James rushing from cover to cover on the other side of the tower. He had perhaps ten seconds before the IRA man, and the Sten, appeared again to drive him back behind the building. As the latest round of blasts died down in his ears, he heard the sound of running feet behind him and turned to see several men coming to join them.

A tall slender man with an aristocratic nose passed by Manning and Hawkins and stopped just behind the Phoenix Force leader. "I'm Captain Wise of the Yard," he said. "You'd be McCarter, I presume?"

"That I would be."

The man's eyes flickered at the British accent. "A fellow countryman, I see. Would you care to divulge under just whose authorization you are currently operating?"

"I don't think this is quite the time for a prolonged discussion of details," McCarter said, mildly irritated. "What did O'Prunty tell you?"

"Just that he'd been assigned to work with you and the Yanks," Wise said.

"I'm not a Yank," Manning protested. "I'm a Canuck."

"Yes, so I see."

"Any ideas you want to share with us as to how we're going to get this guy out of his tower?" McCarter said.

"Well, I don't know really."

"Good," McCarter said. "Then you won't mind me trying things my way." Before Wise could answer again, McCarter turned away. An idea had suddenly occurred to him.

During the entire mission, Phoenix Force had been developing informants with small pieces of the puzzle they were trying to put together, then losing them to enemy fire before they could be of much real value. Now there was a chance—however slim—of taking the sniper in the Pagoda Tower alive. And he wouldn't be some entry level flunky like McHiggins. To be given an assignment this important, he had to not only possess the skill to pull it off but also be a high-ranking member of the IRA.

Which meant he might very well know something about how the Irish terrorists procured their arms. And that meant, at least in part, the Eliminators.

"So, what are you planning?" Wise asked.

McCarter didn't answer. Instead, he leaned around the corner of the building. "You!" he shouted. "In the tower! Can you hear me?"

His words were answered by another burst of autofire.

But McCarter was smiling as he jerked back around the corner again, a split second before the 9 mm rounds hit the stone. He had caught another quick glance of the sniper from the shoulders up.

Now not just his neck but the entire top half of the man's body was soaked in blood.

The Phoenix Force leader didn't know exactly what damage Manning's round had done, but he suspected it had nicked an artery. In any case, the details didn't matter. The bottom line was that the man was bleeding to death. If he stayed up in the tower much longer without medical attention, he'd die.

And that might be used to Phoenix Force's advantage.

McCarter let the onslaught against the wall die down, then leaned around the corner again. "You're bleeding to death, mate," he shouted. "You know it, and I know it. I've seen you three times now, and each time you look worse." He paused, fully prepared to duck back behind cover when another burst of fire came over the stone.

But it didn't.

McCarter went on. "Okay, here's the situation. We can wait you out until hell freezes over. You're going to run out of ammo eventually—we aren't. But even before that, you're going to run out of blood."

For the first time the IRA man spoke. "Fuck off. It's a mere scrape I've got!"

The lack of strength in his voice betrayed his true condition.

"Look," McCarter said, "we both know better

than that, don't we? I know you believe in your cause and don't want to give up. But how much bloody good are you going to do the IRA when you're dead?''

The voice that answered now was even weaker than before. "You'll arrest me if I come out!" the sniper shouted.

"Of course we will," McCarter said. There was little sense in lying to the man; he'd never buy it. "You can't expect to try to kill a royal and not be arrested, can you? Look, mate, understand this. There are no other options but prison or death. There is no escape. You're completely surrounded."

He waited for a reply. When none came, he went on. "We haven't much time to play these games if we're going to save your life, mate. There's bound to be a doctor somewhere in the crowd on the other side of the building. I can call for him." He paused again, then said, "If there's not a doctor, any of my men are capable of stopping the blood flow while we get you to one."

A long silence fell over the yard, and McCarter knew the man was weakening emotionally, as well as physically. After thirty seconds or so, he called out, "So how about it? Life, or death. It's your decision. Take my advice. Cut your losses and come out now."

Another silence fell over the grounds. Then, finally, in a voice barely audible, the sniper said, "All right. I'll be comin' down."

"Throw your weapons over the side first," McCarter ordered. "First the rifle, then the Sten, and any pistols or other hideout weapons you're carrying."

The man did as ordered. First the rifle came sliding over the side of the tower to fall into the grass below, then the machine gun fell. They were followed by an Eliminator single-shot and a small boot knife.

"I'm comin' down," the steadily weakening voice called out again. "Don't be shootin'."

Soon the man appeared at the foot of the steps leading up to the a tower. McCarter studied him head to foot. As he leaned against the stone at the bottom of the stairs, his eyes blinked wildly, and he was soaked from head to toe now in his own blood.

The Phoenix Force leader wondered if they could keep him alive long enough to probe for information. The IRA sniper toppled forward to the grass.

Kingston, Jamaica

THE EXECUTIONER SWUNG out the metal door to the Island Produce storage shed, stepped inside and closed it behind him. He pulled the flashlight from his pocket and thumbed the switch to activate the laser light.

What he found hardly surprised him. Stacked along the walls and in the center of the building was crate after crate, wooden containers that looked identical to the ones he'd first seen in Australia, then later being manufactured at the Takahata factory in Tokyo.

He gripped the flashlight in his left hand as he moved forward to the nearest stack, drawing the Applegate-Fairbairn folding knife from the horizontal sheath on his belt. Flipping the blade open with his thumb, he dug it under the lid of one of the crates and pried upward. Working his way around the top, he dug out the industrial staples until the lid came off.

What he found inside was no more of a shock than the crates themselves. Wrapped in oil paper and still covered with packing grease were two dozen Eliminator Model 1911s.

Bolan dropped the lid back on the box and moved to another stack. These crates were of a different shape, and when he'd pried the lid off the one on top he found Eliminator grease guns. That was no surprise, either. But what was inside the longer wooden boxes stacked in the corner?

The boxes were roughly the shape and size of a cheap pine coffin, and Bolan frowned as he stepped up to the crates. The lids on these had been sealed with nails, and it took longer to work off the top. Holding the flashlight in his teeth, he finally uncovered the contents and shook his head.

The Eliminator, whoever he was, was branching out and upgrading production. What Bolan saw before him now were cheaply stamped and pressed reproductions of the U.S. M-14.

The Executioner lifted the rifle on the top, stripping away the paper. He examined it with the flashlight, noting that like the original M-14 manufactured by Harrington and Richardson Arms, it was capable of either full- or semiauto fire. The wood stock had been replaced with inexpensive plastic, and it looked like each box contained a dozen of the rifles. Bolan counted forty of the boxes.

That meant 480 7.62 mm caliber weapons heading somewhere into the hands of animal man. And this was only one storage site. The Eliminator might well have dozens or hundreds secreted around the world.

Bolan closed the lid, moving on to another stack. Inside these crates he found Eliminator versions of the M-14 A-1 squad rifle, complete with folding forward hand grip and a compensator fitted over the flash suppressor. Another collection of crates against the far wall yielded M-21s, the sniper version of the M-14. These weapons had even been fitted with variable-power scopes.

Bolan closed the final box and stepped back. He had seen all he needed to see, and it was time to contact Kurtzman with the new information and see if the computer wizard could add it to the intel he already had and make something of it.

Only one thing stood in Bolan's way—the men who suddenly burst into the storage building.

Bolan whirled as the sound of the metal door swinging open met his ears. The Applegate-Fairbairn knife still in his hand, he thrust it forward into the chest of a black man armed with an Eliminator .45 semiauto. Withdrawing the double-edged knife as the second man entered, Bolan saw the Eliminator grease gun in his fists.

The Executioner ducked under the volley of rounds that flew over his head, threatening to deafen him. At the same time he angled the flashlight's powerful laser beam into his attacker's eyes. Taking a fast shuffle-step forward, Bolan performed the same "heart surgery" he had a moment before on the first attacker, then killed the flashlight beam and dived behind a stack of crates as the third man came through the door.

Bolan crawled deeper behind the boxes as he heard the man's feet stop on the concrete floor. He had caught a quick glimpse of the assailant before switching off the flashlight: a tall, overweight Jamaican with a full black beard carried another of the Eliminator grease guns.

Now, as he drew the sound-suppressed Beretta 93-R and flipped the selector to semiauto, the Executioner listened. He could hear the man's labored breathing. Then the sounds of more men entering the shed—it sounded like two—met his ears. That meant three more attackers who would spread out to search the building.

Which they did. Bolan listened to them part ways. The nearest man came down the row of boxes toward him. It was too dark to see, but the Executioner could hear him tiptoeing down the aisle between the stacks of crates.

Bolan started to thumb the button on the flashlight, then stopped. The bright light would illuminate his target, but it would also act like a tracer round, pointing back to him. He would get the man he could hear; of that he had no doubt. But one, or even both, of the others might well be in place to shoot back at the flashlight before the Executioner could pinpoint their position.

The big American thought of the Glock on his hip. The laser would illuminate his mark and provide a much smaller target for the other men than the flashlight. But it would roar like an angry bull to give him away through sound. As it stood, he needed the 93-R's near silence. But he also needed the Glock for target acquisition.

What he *really* needed was the laser on the

quiet Beretta instead of the Glock, which he didn't have.

An idea suddenly hit the Executioner. Drawing the Glock, he shifted it to his left hand and gripped the Beretta with his right. Then, raising both pistols side by side toward the sound of shuffling feet, he pressed the laser-activation button with the web of his left hand.

The red dot immediately fell on the belt buckle of a man wearing a baggy African dashiki tucked into his frayed blue jeans. The splash light around the dot lit the rest of the man, groin to chest. Lifting both pistols slightly, the Executioner let the dot center on the man's chest as the splash light revealed a startled face above the dashiki. A split second later, Bolan squeezed the trigger of the Beretta, and the 9 mm weapon coughed quietly.

Bolan let up on the laser button immediately, rolling to his side as return fire came at him from one of the grease guns on the other side of the dark shed. But the man had fired at the spot where he'd seen the tiny red dot on the trigger guard a moment before, and the Executioner was no longer there.

Silently Bolan rose to his feet and moved forward. Two steps in front of him he came to where the man in the dashiki had fallen and felt the attacker's head against his shoe. He stepped over the man and moved back toward the center of the building.

Heavy breathing alerted him once more, and the Executioner knew it would be the big man with the beard. Turning toward the source of the sound, he raised his brace of pistols again.

The laser-equipped Glock provided the light and sighting system. The sound-suppressed Beretta next to it provided the bullet.

The fat man toppled forward to his face on the concrete, a pair of 9 mm hollowpoint rounds centered between his eyes.

Bolan stepped to the side as another swarm of angry .45-caliber rounds flew past him from the final man with the grease gun. He ducked behind another stack of crates, listening to the man try to move quietly across the room. The steps grew slightly louder, meaning he was headed forward.

The Executioner waited.

A moment later a nervous voice called out, "Listen, man, we don't want to kill each other. Let's just call it quits, what say?"

"No, thank you," Bolan said as he raised both guns again. The splash light exposed a man wearing a blue T-shirt. The red dot stopped in the middle, and the Beretta coughed.

Bolan jammed the Glock back into his holster and pulled the flashlight from his pocket. Holding the flashlight over his shoulder, he shone the beam on the fallen man and walked forward.

He was halfway there when an explosion went off behind shattering the flashlight in his hand.

The Executioner dropped to the floor as two more rounds sailed over his head. He rolled to his side, jackknifing back to face the door of the tin building. Cutting loose with the Beretta, he sent a 3-round burst at the shadow in the doorway.

But by the time the bullets reached the door, the dark figure was gone.

Bolan leaped to his feet and sprinted toward the door, the Beretta leading the way. He kicked the door open, holding the pistol in front of him and looking down the barrel.

A half block away the Executioner saw the dark figure racing away into the night. As the shadow sprinted under a streetlight, he saw the black T-shirt, jeans and a ponytail bobbing in the man's wake.

Before he could fire, the shadow had disappeared once more into the night.

CHAPTER FIFTEEN

Stony Man Farm

Harold Brognola, director of the Sensitive Operations Group, heard the whine of the engines and hurried to the window.

Outside he saw the first of the Learjets landing. A yellow Hummer, looking like an Army jeep on steroids, raced across the grounds from the vehicle storage barn.

Brognola watched Charlie Mott land the aircraft down on the tarmac. The plane taxied along as the Hummer stopped at the end of the runway and waited. Brognola, who doubled as a high-ranking official in the U.S. Department of Justice, had arrived himself only moments earlier from Washington, D.C.

Phoenix Force was here ahead of schedule, which was fine with the Justice man. As Sherlock Holmes would have said, the "game was afoot." Things were coming to a head. It was time for the warriors of Stony Man Farm to do what they did best.

Go to war.

The groan of more jet engines sounded in the sky above the main House as David McCarter, Calvin James, Rafael Encizo, Gary Manning and T. J. Hawkins left the Learjet and boarded the Hummer. Brognola looked up to see another jet circling the Farm. Although he couldn't hear the words, he knew that Price had been on the radio ordering the craft to wait while another plane landed.

A split second later his knowledge was confirmed as a plane appeared out of nowhere and taxied to a halt at the end of the runway. That meant that Able Team was now home, too.

Another Hummer picked up Lyons, Schwarz and Blancanales as Brognola turned away from the window. He saw no need to stay and watch the third plane, still circling, land. He had watched it happen hundreds, if not thousands, of times before. He knew what plane it would be— the Learjet 60—and knew that Jack Grimaldi would be bringing in Mack Bolan, the Executioner, the very heart of Stony Man Farm.

Brognola left the bedroom he used when he was at the Farm and hurried down the hall to the stairs. Descending to the first floor, he made a slight jog around the corner and tapped in the access code to the computer room. Hurrying up the ramp to where Kurtzman and Dr. Glenn Barrister sat, he said, "Let's go, gentlemen," then turned to face the glass dividing wall that separated Kurtzman's area from the communications room.

On the other side of the glass, Barbara Price had wheeled her chair around to face him. Brognola waved her toward them as he followed Kurtzman and Barrister down the ramp and headed for the elevator door in the corner of the room.

Kurtzman reached up from his wheelchair and tapped the Down button on the wall. Price had joined them by the time the car reached the first floor, and the door rolled open.

"You switch the phones, Barb?" Brognola asked.

"Of course. But I don't know why I bothered. Everyone who might call in is already here. Unless the President himself decides to phone."

Brognola nodded as the car descended to the basement.

By the time the door opened again, the men of Phoenix Force were already seated around the long conference table in the War Room. Brognola pointed Barrister to a chair between his and the spot Kurtzman would wheel to, and along with Price they hurried to their seats. The door buzzed, and Lyons, Schwarz and Blancanales walked in.

The Stony Man Farm director sat down and the lock sounded again. A moment later Bolan took his seat at the other end of the table.

"I'll begin with a quick summary, then we'll get down to the nitty-gritty," Brognola stated, taking a partially chewed cigar from his mouth and dropping it on the table in front of him. "The pieces have finally come together." He paused to draw in a deep breath, then went on. "Dr. Barrister here—I'm sorry we don't have time for introductions—with Aaron's help, has positively traced the steel in the Eliminators to the Goodman and Fine Steel Company in Pittsburgh. Isn't that right, Doctor?"

Barrister's wide eyes showed awe at both the new part of the Stony Man main house he was now viewing and the whirlwind events that were taking place. "Well," he said slowly, "nothing is ever positive. There's perhaps a one in one hundred thousand chance that the steel came from somewhere else."

"One in a hundred thousand is good enough for me," Carl Lyons said.

Brognola noticed for the first time that the Able Team leader's arm was bandaged. But whatever wound he'd suffered couldn't be bad. Lyons had said nothing about it when he'd called in a few hours earlier to report what he and his teammates had learned at the Klan meeting.

"Tell the others what happened after the battle with the Klansmen," Brognola said.

"Guy dressed in cammies instead of sheets shows up right at the end, like he's not really part of the Klan, and takes his shots." He lifted his arm. "We took him out, then I walk over and find that every weapon he carries has stag handles on them. I found out why when I lifted his billfold. The man's name was Staggs, Randolph Staggs."

Brognola nodded and took up the story from there. "With the info Ironman gathered from Randolph Staggs's ID, Carmen learned he was an ex–Green Beret cowboy who'd pretty much disappeared the past few years. But his military records showed he'd served under a man we'll be discussing in a few minutes." The Justice man turned to David McCarter. "Not many men get to save a member of the royal family," he said. "And I understand the sniper only said one word before he died—'Pen.'"

McCarter nodded. "I think he wanted to write something down. He had lost too much blood and was too weak to talk. I suppose he was so delirious the fact that if he couldn't talk he wasn't likely to able to write didn't occur to him."

"I've got another explanation but we'll wait a moment for that, too." Brognola looked down the table to the big man at the end. "Striker tracked a shipment of Eliminators to Jamaica through the crates manufactured in Tokyo. They were stored in a building belonging to the Island Produce Distributors. He found some surprising new developments...and was attacked twice during his search. Want to tell everyone about it?''

"There's not a lot to tell," he said. "Three of the men who tried to kill me inside the building were obviously local talent. The fourth took me on in an alley before I even got there, then showed up again at the end of the fight inside. He's a pro." He gave a brief description of the man, then said, "If any of you come across him—watch yourselves. He's as good as anybody I've encountered in a long time."

"How about what you found in the crates?" Brognola prompted.

"The Eliminator is expanding his business," the Executioner replied. "Besides the weapons we've come across so far, I found close to five hundred M-14 clones, some M-21s, and some other variations of the basic M-1 Garand."

A few of the men around the table drew in breaths. Single-shots could kill. Semiautos could kill even better, and the grease guns the Eliminator had started to manufacture would spray .45s as well as a Thompson subgun. But the M-14s could do serious, long-range damage. The Eliminator was getting serious. He was increasing the items in his underground catalog, and there was no guarantee he'd stop with the new rifles.

Gadgets Schwarz voiced everyone's concerns. "What's next? BARs? M-16s? Uzis?"

"Maybe explosives," Manning said. "Grenades, the like."

"Hell," Hawkins said. "It isn't that hard to build nukes if you can get the right stuff."

"And he's proved he can get the right stuff," Brognola said. "At least for firearms. But let's get back to the matter at hand." He waited until the last few comments died down, then said, "Hunt Wethers hacked into the Goodman and Fine Company's records and IDed the chief of their sales department. He's clean, but his second-in-command proved curious."

"Criminal record?" Encizo asked.

"No," Brognola said, "but he's a U.S. Special Forces grunt, too, and he served in the same unit as Randolph Staggs."

"Ah," Blancanales said. "The plot thickens."

"Yes, and it gets even thicker," Brognola told the men around the table. "Akira ran down the owner of Island Produce and it goes through several other dummy corporations. But eventually it leads back to one major stock holder. The man's name is Harold James Maddox."

Hawkins's ears perked up. The former Army

Delta Force soldier frowned. "Mad Dog Maddox?" he asked.

Brognola nodded. "For those of you who've been out of regular service a little longer than T.J.," he said, "Mad Dog Maddox is a recently retired U.S. Army colonel who owns an offshore farm-implement manufacturing company in the Caribbean—Mad Dog Farm Implements. It's located on a small private island he's named Mad Dog Island."

"Sounds like this guy has as many self-identity problems as Randolph Staggs," Blancanales offered.

McCarter suddenly leaned forward and spoke up. "Pen," he said. "The IRA sniper didn't mean he wanted to write. He was saying 'Penn'—with two *n*'s. Trying to say 'Pennsylvania,' as in Goodman and Fine in Pittsburgh, Pennsylvania!"

Brognola nodded his agreement.

"Is Maddox's farm-equipment gig on the level?" James asked.

"It appears to be," Brognola replied. "But we've checked the sales records, and they're far too meager to warrant the size of operation the man's got going."

Kurtzman reworded Brognola's statement. "It's obviously a cover for the guns."

Brognola nodded. "The President sent some USAF planes over earlier this morning to do a little recon for us." He opened a file lying on the table and pulled out several dozen aerial photos. "From these," he said, holding them up, "we've put together what we feel is a fairly accurate map of the grounds." Reaching for a stack of pages that had been beneath the photos in the file, he passed the maps around the room. "We estimate that Maddox has at least a hundred armed guards on the island, not to mention the workers who may or may not be part of all this."

The warriors of Stony Man Farm each took a copy of the map. When the stack had circled the table, Brognola stuffed the extras back in the file. "Unless there's something else someone wants to say, we go airborne immediately. And when we're done, I don't want anything left of Mad Dog Island but a grease spot."

Kurtzman started to speak, but Dr. Glenn Barrister got his words out first. Up until now, Barrister had remained quiet, knowing his part in the operation was over and that he was out of his field of expertise. But now the humanitarianism in the man forced him to speak. "Excuse me," he said in a hushed voice.

All heads around the table turned toward him.

"I've listened to everything everyone has said, and I agree the preponderance of evidence points to this man, Maddox. But is anything positive? I mean, the salesman at the steel company serving in the Army with the man with the stag-handled guns? And both of them having served under Maddox? I know I told you it was practically impossible that the steel came from anywhere but Goodman and Fine, but what if the one-in-a-hundred long shot comes through?'' He stopped talking, looked down at the table, and said, ''If it's all just coincidence, you'll be killing innocent men.''

Dr. Barrister was a fine man, and an expert in his field. He had been of great assistance to the Stony Man crew, and Hal Brognola admired his concern. ''I'm glad you brought that up, Doctor,'' he said. ''Because there's something I forgot to mention.'' He looked at Kurtzman.

''Thought you'd never ask,'' the computer expert said. He reached forward to a control panel on the table in front of him and tapped a button. A white screen came rolling down out of the ceiling against the wall. Another button lit it with light. Kurtzman stopped as Brognola spoke.

''You were all aware, I know, of the Eliminator's letter to the newspapers that he signed with a thumbprint. He threatened to begin killing journalists if he didn't start making the front pages again.'' Brognola stuck the chewed cigar back in his teeth and spoke around it. ''We've assumed that was to stimulate sales, and we have no reason to change that assumption at this point. But one thing *has* changed—my opinion of the Eliminator. He's smart, all right, but not as smart as he thinks. He thought a small misdemeanor arrest for drunk driving in Walla Walla, Washington, wouldn't be entered into the FBI's National Crime Information Center files. He was right about that. What he wasn't up-to-date on was the new AFIS computer fingerprint system.'' He pulled the cigar from his mouth and nodded to Kurtzman, who tapped another button and two fingerprints appeared side by side on the screen, the whirls, loops, arches and other specifics enlarged a hundred times.

''The print on the left is the one from the Walla Walla PD files,'' Brognola said. ''The one on the right is the one that appeared on the Eliminator's letter. By patiently linking into all the different AFIS systems currently operating in the U.S., the Bear was able to match them up.'' He looked down at Dr. Barrister. ''Want to guess who they both belong to?''

Barrister's face was a mask of relief. ''Colonel Harold J. Maddox, U.S. Army,'' the doctor said. ''Retired.''

The man from Justice nodded. ''And we're about to shut down his operation.''

In the Air above Mad Dog Island

THE FIRST NINE MEN to jump from the troop-transport plane were Mack Bolan and the warriors of Phoenix Force and Able Team. Then came forty handpicked blacksuits, all armed with M-16 A-2s, smoke and fragmentation grenades, and side arms of their choice.

Bolan glanced overhead as he free-fell through the first part of the HALO—High Altitude Low Opening—dive. Carl Lyons was second, right behind him, with David McCarter running a close third. The rest of the men of both teams were scattered just above their leaders, with the blacksuits tiny dots against the blue afternoon sky.

Bolan looked down, surveying Mad Dog Island. As it grew closer, the various buildings began to take shape, looking like the aerial photos he and the other men had studied during the flight from Stony Man Farm to the Caribbean. Tiny forms—looking like ants from this distance—moved about the premises.

But he knew those tiny ants carried a sting—a sting in the form of Eliminator-made weapons. The Executioner breathed a sigh of relief as he watched. The geography below matched the map folded and stuffed into one of the pockets of his own blacksuit. Aerial surveillance could be tricky sometimes, and tiny details were sometimes missed. But if anything had been this time, he couldn't see it yet, and he hoped that if it had, it wouldn't be important.

He glanced at his altimeter, then jerked the chute's rip cord. The eggshell blue canopy shot out above him, blending into the nearly identically hued sky. He looked up again, seeing the other blue chutes blossom.

A hard smile crossed his face as he readied the Heckler & Koch MP-5 slung over his shoulder. The men of Stony Man Farm would have a few more seconds of invisibility.

Then the guards of Mad Dog Island would look up, and the action would begin.

The Executioner used those last few seconds to go over the plan of attack again. The blacksuits had been assigned the manufacturing areas and workmen's barracks, and would proceed immediately that way upon landing. Their job was to determine which of the men were the enemy and which were merely workers, ignorant of the true purpose of Mad Dog Island. They would then eliminate the bad guys and do their best to sequester the good—separate the wheat from the chaff, so to speak.

Phoenix Force had drawn a circuitous route around the perimeter of the tiny speck of land, their responsibility to eliminate Maddox's outer guard. Gary Manning, equipped with enough C-4 and other explosive gear to blow the island completely off the map if he so chose, would make sure no one escaped on the cargo ships in the harbor.

Able Team would proceed first to the tiny shack that had yet to be identified. Then they would join Bolan as he cut a swath toward what appeared in the aerial photos to be Maddox's office building. The Executioner planned to confront the renegade colonel himself and, with any luck, the man with the Al Mar Warrior knife who had attacked him both in the alley, then again in the storage building of the Island Produce Distributors.

Bolan looked down again. The tiny specks he had seen before moving around the island now appeared as men—*armed* men, Maddox's guards. As he continued to descend, the Executioner saw one of the men look up, and knew that his few seconds' grace period was now over.

The man below raised what Bolan recognized as an Eliminator M-14 to his shoulder and pointed it skyward.

The Executioner opened the ceremonies with a burst from his MP-5, taking the man out of the play.

The chatter of the MP-5 caused guards all over the island to look up.

Bolan let his submachine gun fall to the end of its sling, drew the Applegate-Fairbairn fixed blade from the Kydex sheath on his belt and raised it over his head as his feet hit the ground ten feet from the first casualty. He sliced through the lines, and a moment later the canopy was sailing off in the Caribbean wind.

The Executioner resheathed his blade and slid the folding stock out of the MP-5. He slammed it against his shoulder as more of the guards awakened to the fact that an army of men was coming in from the sky, and cut loose with a long stream of autofire.

Four men fell, but the others began to shoot skyward.

Still in the air, the other men from Stony Man Farm opened up with return fire, and more of Maddox's henchmen fell to the ground. Bolan took out a guard wearing OD green with a quick 3-round burst, then swung his weapon toward a man in blue jeans and a BDU blouse as McCarter and Lyons touched down. The Sterling subgun in the Phoenix Force leader's hands began to jump with recoil, as did the Calico 950 carried by the head of Able Team.

The shrill sound of an overhead alarm suddenly erupted. Looking overhead, Bolan saw metal speakers mounted on poles around the island, a good example of the details aerial photos missed.

As the deafening noise continued, and the rest of Able Team, Phoenix Force and the blacksuits continued to land across the island, Bolan saw more men clad in OD green emerging from the various buildings. Bullets whipped past his head from the rear, and he turned to see a bearded black man firing one of the Eliminator grease guns.

Bolan swung the MP-5 a full 180 degrees and shot from the hip, feeling the subgun climb slightly as the 9 mm rounds blasted from the barrel and into the guard's belly and chest. He felt a presence next to him and saw Lyons in his peripheral vision. The ex-cop had switched the usual 50-round hexagonal drum magazine on top of his Calico for one of the 100-shot variety. And the way Lyons was using up ammo, it looked like he'd need every single round.

The Executioner finished off his own 30-round magazine on two men charging him with Eliminator M-14s, dropped it from the receiver and jammed a fresh stick into the weapon. Half of the fresh magazine went to a trio of guards who suddenly jumped from behind the shack where Able Team was headed. Four more green-clad gunners emptied the H&K once again, and Bolan found himself jerking yet another magazine from his carrier.

Lyons had left the Executioner's side to lead Able Team toward the shack, and Bolan watched the Stony Man commandos fire their Calicos as they went. Five more of Maddox's guards bit the dust.

In the corner of his eye, Bolan saw Phoenix Force sprinting down the beach, leaving yet more of the enemy bleeding in their wake. Across the island, the blacksuits had divided into two teams with roughly half headed toward the barracks while the other men raced toward the manufacturing buildings.

Bolan dropped two more men in green with short, 3-round bursts as Carl Lyons kicked in the door to the shack. Able Team hurried inside, with Schwarz sticking his head back out a second later.

"No one but an unarmed woman," he yelled.

The Executioner fired another stream of rounds into two men with grease guns. "Tell her to keep her head down and come on!" he yelled back.

The Executioner swung the MP-5 toward a quartet of guards who had dropped to the ground fifty feet away. They all fired Eliminator M-14 copies, and Bolan felt the air pressure as the rounds whizzed past his ears. Flipping the MP-5's selector to semiauto, he started on the right, putting a lone round into the spine of the first man in the prone position. A second later he'd taken out the two in the middle, and another second after that the last man lay dead with a severed spinal cord and bleeding heart.

Firing broke out on the other side of the island,

and Bolan recognized the roars of the blacksuits' M-16s. A momentary lull in the battle nearby gave him pause, and he turned his eyes toward Maddox's office.

"Let's go!" the Executioner called out as Able Team fell in behind him. He sprinted to the sidewalk, then followed it toward the office building. Six men appeared from behind various cover as he and the other Stony Man warriors ran past, firing their weapons at the moving targets.

Those six men died quickly, if not painlessly.

The MP-5 now empty again, the Executioner dropped it and drew the Glock .45 with the Aro-Tek laser sight. The siren overhead continued to wail. From the direction of the harbor came the roar of Gary Manning's first explosion.

Bolan eyed the office as he neared, seeing no guards outside the building. A second before he reached the front door, he lowered his right shoulder.

The door flew off its hinges as if struck by the winds of a Caribbean hurricane.

The Executioner burst into a deserted reception area, the laser's red dot looking like an angry firefly as it made a lightning-fast sweep of the room. He raced on to a closed door in the opposite wall and lowered his shoulder once again.

Bursting into the room, the Executioner saw a man in khakis standing behind the desk. A huge cigar was in Colonel Harold J. Maddox's teeth, and he gripped an S&W 645 pistol in both hands and aimed it toward the Executioner.

Bolan hit the ground, rolling into the desk and sliding it backward into Maddox. The pistol fell from the colonel's hands and toppled to the floor next to the Executioner.

The Executioner was reaching for the pistol when he saw the flicker of stainless steel descending. The sight brought a quick memory of the dark Jamaican alley, and he abandoned his quest for the colonel's S&W, rolling to one side a split second before the Al Mar Warrior knife whizzed past him and embedded itself in the wood floor.

Bolan rolled again, moving away as the attacker he remembered from Jamaica pried the knife out of the floor. But the man—a Native American—no longer wore his black T-shirt or jeans. He was dressed in a checkered Western shirt, faded denims, and wore a medicine bag around his neck.

The only things the same were the black moccasins on his feet.

Lyons burst into the office, followed by Schwarz and Blancanales. Able Team saw the knife wielder and raised their Calicos. A quick burst ended the threat to the Executioner.

Silence descended, making the sudden cackle from behind the desk sound even more eerie. All heads turned toward Maddox. The man had risen to his feet.

"Okay, let us in on it," Blancanales said.

Maddox leaned forward, resting both hands on the desk in front of him. "I don't know who you guys are," he said, "maybe FBI, maybe ATF...hell, you might even be Company." He shook his head, still smiling. "But it makes no difference. We aren't in the United States. You've got no jurisdiction here, and when I'm through suing your asses I'll be richer than I'd have been making the Eliminators."

The men of Phoenix Force had arrived just in time to overhear Maddox's arrogant comment. "Oh, we've got all the jurisdiction we need," T. J. Hawkins said.

"Really?" Maddox asked. "Okay, let me see some badges."

Rosario Blancanales of Able Team looked across the room at Rafael Encizo. Both men were of latino decent, and both men saw the opening.

"You want to say it Rafe," Blancanales asked, "or you want me to?"

"As much as I'd like to," he said, "it's more up your alley."

"Good," Blancanales said. "I've waited a long time to work this one in somewhere." He turned back to Maddox and cleared his throat. Then, in a perfect Mexican-bandit accent straight out the

Humphrey Bogart film *Treasure of the Sierra Madre,* he said, "Badges? We don't need no stinkin' badges!"

Slowly Maddox's smile began to fade as he obviously realized that Blancanales's statement was meant to be taken literally.

These intruders didn't have any badges, and they didn't intend to read him the Miranda warning or pay attention to any other distorted constitutional rights the operatives of police agencies would have been forced to observe.

"So you're the one they call the Eliminator," David McCarter said, stepping forward.

Maddox nodded.

"Well, Eliminator," McCarter stated, "meet the Executioner." He hooked a thumb toward Bolan.

In one last, desperate play, Maddox scrambled to open the top drawer of his desk, hoping to beat the odds and retrieve the single-shot Eliminator sequestered there.

Bolan raised the Glock and let the red dot center on Maddox's chest.

The explosion sounded louder than all the others still going off around Mad Dog Island.

**A violent struggle for survival
in a post-holocaust world**

JAMES AXLER

DEATH LANDS®

Freedom Lost

Following up rumors of trouble on his old home ground, Ryan and his band seek shelter inside the walls of what was once the largest shopping mall in the Carolinas. The baron of the fortress gives them no choice but to join his security detail. As outside invaders step up their raids on the mall, Ryan must battle both sides for a chance to save their lives.

**Bolan severs a mob-Chinese alliance
exporting terror...**

DON PENDLETON's

MACK BOLAN®

Rage
FOR JUSTICE

Bootleg electronic goods are manufactured by slave labor in a remote part of China, then imported by a Houston-based mob family and sold below market prices. This unholy alliance is making huge profits off U.S. consumers and the misery of the oppressed Chinese. A CIA probe goes sour, killing one agent and forcing another on the run, calling on Mack Bolan in the name of old friendship.

But even as Bolan revs into high gear, angered by ruthless greed, he knows that the stakes are high and the odds increasingly tough to call.

Available in January 1998 at your favorite retail outlet.

Desperate times call for desperate measures. Don't miss out on the action in these titles!